Pucker Up

Pucker Up

by

Michael Kalesniko

Strategic Book Group
Durham, Connecticut

Strategic Book Group
P. O. Box 333
Durham, CT 06422
http://www.strategicbookclub.com

ISBN: 978-1-60911-456-5

Book Design by Julius Kiskis

19 18 17 16 15 14 13 12 11 1 2 3 4 5

Part I

"Two roads diverged in the woods and I—
I took the one less traveled by . . .
which goes a long way in explaining
why you found my body way out here."

—Alfred Botchelko

Chapter 1

I was filling up my tank when I let loose the most jaw-dropping fart, and the guy on the other side of the pumps gave me what could only be called the stink eye.

"Hey it's a fucking gas station, isn't it?" I said.

That morning I had just Googled myself.

I realize that sounds like admitting to masturbation and in a sense it's equally onanistic, but the truth is it's entirely different and you know that if you've ever been caught masturbating by your wife. To this day Robin thinks I was exfoliating.

Furiously.

So I can admit to Googling myself without embarrassment. In fact, I do nothing else on the Internet but Google myself. Sure I buy shirts and shit from Territory Ahead and books and DVDs from Amazon and I just got rid of a bunch of worthless MGM stock on Schwab.com that I bought as an IPO at $21 that was now worth $12 and I could strangle Randy for that tip. And lately I've come to understand that just about everybody but me E-bays—E-Baying being the female equivalent of the masturbation euphemism, the way HGTV is my wife's porn channel. Other than that, the only thing Google is good for is Googling yourself.

So there I was, up early, sipping half a cup of coffee, the other half soy with a little French Vanilla Coffee-mate creamer—actually, technically, it was a quarter of a cup since the beans were mixed with decaf beans and then the soy because I'm gluten intolerant which means, for whatever reason, milk makes me sick as a rabid monkey.

Anyway.

Because of the new diet I didn't have the urge to shit and hadn't had it in three days and I was starting to think I had a massive lump of coal up my ass the size and consistency of a loaf of pumpernickel. I was looking for some sort of distraction before giving up on my anal retention and simply getting dressed for work when I quickly typed in my name. My real name. Not the one I go by. But the one on my birth certificate.

"Alfred Botchelko." In quotes.

One hundred and fifty-seven thousand three hundred matches. Accompanied by a boastful announcement that it took only 1.3 seconds to find them all.

In the past, when Googling myself—furiously—I'd only gotten twelve matches. And I was very proud of those twelve. Bear in mind, my closest brush with anything close to fame was once lighting Gwyneth Paltrow's cigarette on a street corner in Tribeca.

Oh, there was one other encounter with fame. I almost ran over Donnie Osmond on Wilshire. I think it was Donnie Osmond. When I tell that story, people invariably say, "Too bad you missed him." For whatever reason, I never have the guts to say, "I kinda like Donnie Osmond."

Either way, my twelve matches on Google broke down like this: five mentions at Kinko's training seminars, two of which I facilitated; three mentions of me in photos in the company-wide newsletter; an article about me, again in the company-wide newsletter, front page, in which I must now quickly add, "below the fold," before you and everyone else in your neighborhood and your dog points it out because people just can't seem to restrain themselves from clarifying this massive slight when I can't help but notice that their picture is nowhere to be seen either on the front page, "below the fold," or any-fucking-where else in the company-wide newspaper, or newsletter (pardon me), even though it's an international publication.

There's also a quote from me on a mountain biking site because the kid at Montrose Cycle was rude to me in front of my wife and I went home and drank half a bottle of merlot and then got even by finding the Montrose Cycling website and handing the little twat his ass on a plate.

Albeit in writing.

Finally, there's the fishing photo. But that's not me in the photo with all those salmon, that's my brother Dale. I was taking a leak at the time and they simply misidentified him. He didn't care about the mistake but it still annoys the hell out of me. They should have waited. This was the Queen Charlotte Islands for God's sake, where did they have to go in such a hurry? And two of those ten salmon were mine including the second-biggest one so I really should have been in that shot. I thought my fish was the biggest until the dock master weighed them and Randy's turned out to be bigger by half an ounce. Which is fine. They still tasted the same. Though Randy canned his. Big mistake. I filleted mine and grilled them in the backyard and they were lovely even though Maddy refused to eat any because she was afraid of getting "salmonella poisoning." I explained to her that you don't get salmonella poisoning from salmon and she said, "Then why is it called that?" And I couldn't answer.

That kid's so much like her freaking mother.

The very last mention of me on Google was in the Glendale City Council minutes when I stood up to complain about the fence law. In Glendale, backyard fences can be no higher than six feet and we're not allowed a front yard fence at all unless you live in the equestrian neighborhood. Then you can have a front yard fence as high as a drive-in movie screen apparently. So I asked them what the difference was between a cat and a horse and they replied, if you don't know the difference between a cat and horse buddy, we can't help you. That got a big laugh. I stayed calm and I said, that's not the point and you know it. And it sort of went back and forth like that for a long time until I forgot my point and they asked me to sit down. The Anti-fence Law Initiative Committee stopped inviting me to their meetings after that which was fine because it was my turn to hold the next meeting and I get squirrelly when there are a lot of people in my house. But what drives me really crazy is, I can still see right into my neighbor's back yard. Worse yet, they put in French doors recently, so now I can see into their bedroom as well. I don't want to see into their goddamn bedroom. And that's another thing. The mayor chewed me out for cursing at the city council meeting. I swear to you, until that day I never knew goddamn was a curse and damn was just an emphatic way of making a point.

So there you have it—all my Googles in total. And then this morning, 157,300.

I thought I'd mistyped it and I suppose, in a sense, I had. Because I go by "William Botchelko." I never liked the name Alfred. It was my grandfather's name and my grandfather once drunkenly declared over Christmas dinner when I was still just a boy that he never liked me and he thought that I thought I was better than everyone. Or, as he put it, "your shit doesn't stink." Then, visiting him at the hospital where he was recovering from one of a series of small strokes that eventually saw him to the grave, he turned to me in the visiting room the moment my mother stepped away and tried to butt a cigarette out in my forearm. I never went by the name after that.

I went by William.

Which is my middle name. Which means the staff at Kinko's thinks my name is Will. Everyone at college thought my name was Will. Everyone in high school thought my name was Will. And "William Botchelko" gets only twelve matches. But "Alfred Botchelko" gets 157,300. Add "Botch" in parentheses and it jumps to twice that. Botch? Now there's a nickname I could do without.

Alfred Botchelko, it turns out, is a poet.

An infamous poet. An infamous reclusive poet. According to Google. I'd never heard of him. Then again, I don't read poetry. It was getting late though and I didn't have time to read any more of the matches. And I needed gas in my car too. Which is why I was standing at the gas station filling up my car, my rectal cavity channeling Lucifer's breath, and I was pondering this other Botchelko when suddenly the urge to shit returned with a vengeance. So I raced to work and took someone else's parking space because someone took mine and then I jaywalked because I just couldn't wait for the light and I entered in back and dropped my briefcase and found a clean stall in the staff bathroom though I still wiped the seat down with toilet paper and water first and finally I sat down. And nothing. Absolutely nothing. Robbed.

Shitting can really piss me off.

I called Robin at work.

"Parts department," she said. I could tell it was her because she answered the phone with unmasked vitriol.

"You ever heard of Alfred Botchelko?" I asked.

"Is this a trick question?" she said. "'Cause I really don't have time."

Robin used to work for First Interstate. I don't recall her liking that job much either but she claims she did. She quit to stay home with Maddy. Then Maddy turned fourteen last April, or May, or whatever, so Robin went back to work. But the only job she could find was in the parts department of Star Ford all the way down Brand Boulevard. I'm not sure what her job entailed but it seemed a large part of it demanded she let me know daily how much she hated it. But hey, was I shouting Hosannas every morning because I was blessed with managing a Kinko's? I mean Christ, woman.

"I'm not talking about me," I told her. "I'm talking about another Alfred Botchelko."

"Oh God help us. You mean there's two of you? Does he want to build the Great Wall of Glendale around his property as well?"

"No, no. He's a poet or something. He's really famous."

"Are we accidentally getting his checks by any chance?"

"I've never heard of a wealthy poet in my life, have you? You think Maddy might know who he is?"

"No. And don't call her."

"How would I call her? She's in school."

Robin hesitated. "That's right. You can't call her."

"Wait. You didn't get her that cell phone, did you?"

"What cell phone?"

"I thought we agreed."

"Gotta go." She hung up.

The gall. Those two were in collusion. What the hell does a fourteen-year-old girl need with a cell phone anyway? Yes, dumb question. But still, the principle of the thing, and behind my back on top of it all.

Chapter 2

"Carlos, you ever heard of a poet named Alfred Botchelko?"

Carlos had his arms deep inside a color copier. The good one. The one that never broke down. Now it was screwing up too. Thank God Carlos could fix them. Carlos wasn't a certified photocopier repairman but damn could he fix a copier. Which saved my branch a ton of money. Which meant Carlos showed up late every single morning and took ten minutes extra for lunch every day because he had me over a barrel and he knew it.

"I don't read poetry," he said.

"Did I ask you if you read poetry?" I said.

People used to do that back when I smoked. I'd ask someone if they had a light and they'd invariably answer, I don't smoke. Look, if I asked you where the nearest liquor store was, would you tell me you didn't drink? Well, yeah, you probably would.

I suck at these examples.

"I just found out about this guy this morning," I told him. "But don't you think it's weird?"

"All poetry's weird. I like limericks."

"Don't you think the name's weird?"

"What's his name?"

"Alfred Botchelko."

No reaction.

"Same name as mine."

"Your name's Will."

"My last name's Botchelko."

"He your brother?" Carlos asked.

"If he was my brother, don't you think I'd know if he was my brother?"

"Not in *mi familia*, dude."

"Beatriz, you read poetry?"

Asking Beatriz was a long shot. She was a very dark, very round, and very illegal immigrant from El Salvador. But she never missed a day of work, worked OT without complaint—in fact never complained, period—never screwed up on orders, and was even relatively polite to customers. So I ticked "landed immigrant status" on her employment form and made up a Social Security Number.

Come and get me.

"Are you writing poems?" she asked.

"No," I said. "I don't even like poetry."

"Thas kinda weird, no?" she said. "'Cause yer brudder's a poet." She said that just as she ducked into the woman's restroom.

"What?" I said. I knocked on the door. "What?"

"Jes a minute," she said.

"You know about this guy?" I called through the door.

"Jes a minnuutte," she sang out.

I waited. There wasn't one sound coming from inside that washroom. What do women do in bathrooms? I get in there and it sounds like a flock of trumpeter swans invading a small lagoon.

"Could you stan' somewhere ells, pleez?" she said.

We weren't allowed to use the staff computers for private use. They claimed to monitor us and I didn't doubt it. These guys could pinch a penny till Lincoln moaned. But what was to stop me from using one of the Internet access computers we had in back for customers?

I logged on. The computer was huge, big enough to crush a grown man's skull. The monitor magnified the lettering like a book for geriatrics. The keyboard was sticky. The mouse was sticky too. Did the janitorial staff clean these things with Slurpees or something?

Once again, I Googled my name. My birth name. The name I didn't use. The name he made something of.

Alfred Botchelko.

What I expected to find when I opened that first site was the slow unfolding of an intellectual. A college professor. A man in tweed, hoity-toity, a pipe and an academic wife and a Yale degree. Your standard issue poet, right?

Instead, Alfred Botchelko looked like a murderer. I found one picture of him. Thick gray hair, unshaven, cigarette smoke curling around his face, red eyes glaring into the camera as he took a slug straight from a bottle of Jack. He was fifty-four. I was forty-two, forty-three in February. (Funny how when you're a kid you'll proudly say you're five-and–a-half, but when you're in your forties you never mention that half bit).

Botchelko published his first book when he was nineteen. *As God Plucks My Boiled Eye Balls*. What in Christ could that be about? Thirty-seven books in all, five novels and three short story collections. At least I could read those. He used to give rather infamous readings in the nineties, got drunk on stage, then chucked empty beer bottles at the audience. He'd been arrested eleven times. He did six months in jail in his twenties. It didn't say for what. He once lived in London, England, and Sydney, Australia. He wrote a lot of poems about gambling. He loved the track. What could you possibly write about the track? He hated sports but loved boxing. Boxing was okay, I guess.

"Why you interest in heem?" Beatriz asked. She was standing right behind me.

"I just want to know if we're related," I said. I think that's what I wanted to know. I didn't really know what I wanted to know.

"My boyfren' likes heem. He writes songs to his poems. He stole his address from an old man in a book store and wrote him letters."

"Did he write back?"

"No."

"Does he still write him?"

“Sometimes. But thees Botchelko, hees a bad man. I don’ like heem. He drinks and he fights and he spits.”

“He does?”

“Si. And he’s ugly.”

“I don’t think he’s ugly.”

“His eyes are ugly. He writes about sex and the girls and he says, ‘These are my poems’ but they no poems to me, and my Donovan smokes and drinks and he pretend to be heem.”

Beatriz made her way back behind the front counter. “They made a movie about heem,” she added. Then she turned to the tall scowling woman in front of her and said, “How can I hep you?”

Chapter 3

"They made a movie about him," I told Robin.

"About who?"

"Alfred Botchelko."

"I never heard of a movie called that," said Maddy.

We were eating rice pasta with Newman's Own sauce to which I added onions and garlic and mushrooms and some chopped shallots. In fact, I would have made the sauce from scratch but I work late Mondays which means I don't even start cooking until past seven and it was Robin who made up the schedule anyway. She said Mondays were too depressing for her to work near a gas oven because she might stick her head in it. So Paul Newman to the rescue. We were both drinking wine—Charles Shaw, a frickin' bargain, I might add. Two bucks a bottle, tasted okay and got you drunk. Why the winos didn't shop at Trader Joe's, I'll never know.

Maddy, on the other hand, was eating a salad. No dressing. She hated rice pasta and wanted to know why the whole family had to suffer because I was gluten intolerant. But I knew the real reason she wouldn't eat it. She thought she was fat. Fourteen and she thought she was fat. I caught her staring at herself in the full-length mirror in our bedroom once. She was wearing a pair of Lycra shorts and she was measuring the gap between her inner thighs. It struck me as terribly sad and a bit confusing too and I never let her know I saw her doing that. Then I made the mistake of trying to reassure her about her looks by telling her not to worry since DNA pretty much guaranteed she'd grow up to look just like her mother. And Maddy ran out of the room screaming, "I don't want a fat ass!" Robin didn't speak to me for three days. Maddy said it but Robin wouldn't speak to me. You try living in a house full of women. Even Nora, our cat, is neurotic.

"I don't think the movie's called that," I said.

"What's it called?" asked Robin. She slurred the "s" on that one. I heard it. She got drunk so easily these days.

"I don't know yet. I'll Google it tonight."

"I need the laptop tonight, Dad," said Maddy.

"Why?"

"Homework."

"I've never seen you do homework."

"Can I help it if I'm smart?" she said.

"Every night you talk on the phone and watch TV, you don't do homework," I said.

"I like the TV on while I'm doing my homework," she said.

"And the phone?"

"Fine," she said. "You want me to fail and drop out and turn out like Auntie Cheryl, then fine."

"What's wrong with Auntie Cheryl?" said Robin.

"No one's turning out like Auntie Cheryl," I said.

"What's wrong with my sister?" said Robin.

"Mom," said Maddy—and no one can say "Mom" with the derision of a fourteen-year-old girl. "You said when Grandma dies you'll never speak to Auntie Cheryl again."

"I never did," she gasped.

"Yes you did. You called Auntie Cheryl fat and stupid and you said her house was filthy and she was a Republican and she stole Grandpa's pocket watch when he died and"—she emphasized this one—"she-drank-too-much."

"I never called her stupid."

"Yes you did. Just this morning you threw down the paper and said, 'All Republicans are stupid.'"

"Well, I didn't mean your Auntie Cheryl."

"And you said she makes a fool out of herself . . . *when she-drinks-too-much.*"

Robin didn't say a word now and Maddy got up and left the table, taking her bowl of rabbit food with her.

"I never called her fat either," Robin said.

Chapter 4

I was up early again the next morning. And had to shit. I had only so much free time in a day and I was using it up shitting. Why couldn't I shit at work where at least I'd get paid to do it? So I simply took the laptop into the bathroom with me. I have to admit, setting up on the throne wasn't such a bad way to surf the Internet.

"Dad! You don't have the laptop in there! That's disgusting!"

Why didn't that kid just fuck off? She's the one who gave me irritable bowel syndrome in the first place. Hadn't had a peaceful moment in the can since the day she was born.

"You'll have to buy me my own laptop now. I'm never touching that one again!"

I ignored her. It was Botchelko time. The movie was called *How to Kill Your Neighbor's Dog*. I remember that on Starz but I never watched it because I don't like . . . what's-his-name? That English guy? With no lips? But Robin Wright Penn was in it and I knew Robin would like that because she liked Robin Wright Penn—mostly because of the name, I think. Robin also claimed people told her she looked like Robin Wright Penn. Yeah, and I look like George Clooney. Only twenty pounds heavier, less hair, a bigger nose and a receding chin. Otherwise, spitting image.

I read the description: "Peter McGowen (Kenneth Branagh)"—that's the guy. *Frankenstein*. Good movie—"is a playwright suffering from writer's block"—playwright? What the hell? "His wife (Robin

Wright Penn) is desperate to have a baby. When a handicapped girl moves in next door (Suzi Hofrichter), their lives are changed forever." Jesus fuck me—did that sound nauseating.

"Mom! Dad is shitting on the laptop!"

"I am not!"

"There's going to be shit all over it and then he'll wipe his ass with it!"

"Stop saying 'shit!'" Robin shouted back.

There was pounding on the door. I wish to God those two assholes would leave me alone. *How to Kill Your Neighbor's Dog.* I'd check the listing first but I'd probably just go and rent it from Blockbuster tonight.

"Are you in there with the laptop, Will?"

I didn't answer.

"Answer me, William?"

"I'll be out in a minute."

"What did I tell you," said Maddy and then she screamed like she was being stabbed in the eye socket.

"Disconnecting," popped up on screen. Someone had turned off the router. Fine—I was done anyway. I opened the door a crack, handed it out to Robin.

"I'm not touching that!" screeched Maddy. "I'm never touching that shit-smeared thing again!"

I climbed in the shower.

Chapter 5

I rented *How to Kill Your Neighbor's Dog* from Netflix. The DVD wasn't widescreen though. Which bugged the hell out of me. Why own a widescreen TV only to watch a movie on TV aspect ratio? And there were no extras. None. No director's commentary. No making-of featurette. And no mention anywhere of Botchelko's name. Where did Beatriz get the idea this was about Alfred Botchelko?

Robin and I settled in. Robin poured herself a glass of wine first. She recently bought herself a tankard-size wine glass from Crate and Barrel. I think it was a trick of semantics. Because now she could say she only had one glass of wine even though that one glass held half a liter. Maddy didn't join us. Any entertainment about adults and she wasn't the least bit interested. Funny, but I remember watching *The Mary Tyler Moore Show* and *All in the Family*, and even *Barnaby Jones* when I was a kid. Shows about adults. Even geriatric adults. And enjoying them. But not today's kids.

"Look, there's a little girl in it," I pointed out to her.

"She's a gimp," Maddy said and went to her room.

The description of the movie was accurate in a sense but it also wasn't. There was a lot going on this film. Yeah there was a little handicapped girl next door and yeah he had writer's block and yeah his wife wanted a baby. But they also had an Alzheimer's-stricken mother living with them (that was Lynn Redgrave who I think I like but don't know what I've seen her in). There's a lot of stuff in the theater and the janitor was pretty funny. But there's also a storyline where Branagh is being stalked by a fan who claims to be him. So Branagh ends up hanging out with this guy every night because he has insomnia. Which is the point of the title. He's being kept awake by his neighbor's dog and he jokes about killing it. Instead, the guy who's been stalking him ends up killing the dog, thinking he's doing him a big favor. I didn't hate Branagh in this, which is a first. He was pretty funny actually. But there wasn't one poet in the entire thing.

"She's playing me in this movie," said Robin.

"Who's playing you?"

"Robin Wright Penn. That's me. That's my life up there."

Robin Wright Penn played a dance instructor who worked with kids and smiled all the time and any man would die to be married to her and let me tell you for the record, she bore no resemblance to the woman slouching next to me with the world's biggest wine glass resting on her belly.

"You're drunk, honey. Go to bed."

"I'm not drunk," she said. "I had one glass."

See? I knew it.

That night, as Robin snored the racket of a caged and frightened wildebeest, I lay awake just like Branagh did in the movie and tried to figure out what exactly Beatriz was talking about. Her boyfriend was a big fan of Alfred Botchelko so he must know. But the fact is, Branagh was playing a playwright, he had a British accent, he was well off, he had a big house and a pool and he was being stalked by another Brit. So was it the personality then? The one-liners? The cynicism? How was that supposed to be Botchelko?

"Thas heem," said Beatriz.

"But it's about a playwright."

"Jes. I know. But it's Alfred Botchelko he is playing. Donovan read this."

"You know," I said, a little coy, "that's actually my real name."

"What is?"

I pulled out my driver's license and showed her.

"Hay-soos creest," she said. She looked at it, looked at me. "Are you heem?"

"No, I'm not him."

"It says you are heem."

I tried to take the license back. She wouldn't let go. "I'm not," I said. I tugged it out of her grip.

Beatriz wasn't convinced. Every time I caught her eye she was frowning at me, her little Salvadoran mind grinding away. To her, America was a mysterious place. Maybe poets went undercover for material. I shouldn't have said anything.

I called Robin.

"Parts fucking department."

"Oh my Christ!" I said. "Is that the way you answer the phone now?"

"Lay off me. I slept the shits last night."

"No you didn't. You slept like a baby. I slept the shits."

"Then why do I feel awful?"

"It's called a hangover," I said.

"Okay, you better back off with this crap. If you've become a born again or something, I'm just not going to take it. All that damnation and burn-in-hell garbage, you're driving me crazy."

"Have you lost your mind? When have I ever talked about damnation and burning in hell?"

"That one Thanksgiving. Remember? You and Dale. And you said hellfire was too good for Bush."

"Actually, I said Bush's nuts should roast on a testicle hibachi in hell for all eternity."

"There. That's born again talk."

"But you hated Bush more than I did."

"I know. But I just wanted him to get ass cancer or something. I never said anything about barbecued testicles in hell. Oh, and you say Jesus Christ a lot too." She suddenly dropped her voice. "Oh shit, here comes Buckethead. He thinks I'm stealing. Gotta go." And she hung up.

What in God's name was that about? Dave Buchanan was her

boss. Why did he think Robin was stealing? And stealing what? We didn't need car parts.

Chapter 6

I packed my own lunches these days. Unless it was the rare occasion where Randy and I went to Milano's or Don Cuco's or California Pizza Kitchen for lunch, then I had to pack my own. I couldn't eat ordinary sandwiches anymore, couldn't even eat a muffin for breakfast. In fact, breakfasts are the worst meal of the day. Everything's oats and wheat and grains and for years I skipped breakfast entirely, fearing shitting myself in public—which I've done more than once, by the way. But that meant by the time lunch hour rolled around—especially one o'clock lunch break—then my stomach was screaming for food and I was irritable and bitchy. Now Robin buys gluten-free muffins from Whole Foods. I like those. And then I usually make a sandwich of rice bread, chicken slices, rice mozzarella cheese singles and Nayonaise. Throw in a little mustard or sometimes pesto spread. Not bad.

I took my lunch and walked all the way down to Borders to find an Alfred Botchelko book. Thirty-seven books he's written. Think I could find even one? A chubby Asian girl at the customer service counter lit up when I asked about him.

"I love Botchelko!" she said.

"I've never read him," I said.

She tugged a card off a corkboard and held it up for me, smiling.

It read: "If it looks like shit, smells like shit and tastes like shit, it ain't chocolate no matter what they tell you."

"That's a Botchelko quote," she said. She pinned it back up. "I can order him for you if you like. Which books are you interested in?"

"Which would you recommend?"

"*Heliotropism* is great," she said. "But that's a novel. *Irascible Roses* is his best book of poems. *Various Indignities* actually made me horny." I wish she hadn't told me that. "Actually, that's not true," she said. Great, now she's going to clarify for me precisely what stimulation gripped her sex organs while reading. She tugged at her silver eyebrow stud and gave it some thought. "I like 'em all," she concluded. Then she stood poised with her fingers on the keyboard, smiling, ready to take my order.

"You know, I'll just order from Amazon," I said. You'd think I just said, "Your breath stinks and you're fat." She glared at me. She nodded once, then turned her back—actually turned her back to me.

That fat, smelly Nip.

I went across the street to La Cocchia, bought a soy latte, found a table out front and ate my rice bread sammy—and suddenly realized I was dying for a cigarette. I hadn't smoked since Maddy was born. But coffee triggered that urge sometimes. Coffee and cigarettes combined, on the other hand, triggered something else entirely. Talk about Liquid Plumber.

A dark, wiry kid was leaning across the front counter and talking to Beatriz when I got back to work. The moment I walked in, the two shut up and stared at me.

"Meester Botchelko?" she said. Beatriz had never called me Mr. Botchelko in her life. "Thees is my boyfren', Donovan."

I shook Donovan's hand. "That's not him," was all he said, staring straight into my eyes.

"It's heem. Show him the driver license."

So I pulled out my ID and showed Donovan. He stared at it the longest time. Then he held it up to the light. Then he laid it on the counter and started rubbing at the print with the back of a Bic pen.

"Can I have that back, please?" I said.

"One minute," he said and kept rubbing.

I glared at Beatriz.
“Donovan, geev it back.”
He sighed. He handed it back. “You’re not him.”
“Fine. I’m not him.”

Chapter 7

I ordered two of the three books she mentioned from Amazon. Almost all his books were out of print. I figured I'd start with those, ingest some poetry, but I was really interested in the novels and short stories. I used to read so much before I was married. I don't know if marriage killed it or if work did or just one too many Tom Clancy and Stephen King novels.

But while I was online, I kept hearing an odd electronic beep down the hall. It beeped once, a few minutes went by, then it beeped again. At first I thought it was outside. Even Nora sat up and listened, then curled up and went back to sleep, only to sit up with the next beep. I signed off, then went down the hall to investigate.

Maddy's room, of course. I knocked. "What?" she said. I opened the door. "Did I say come in?" She was lying on her bed, iPod ear buds poked in her head.

"What's all that beeping?" I asked.

"Nothing."

"I hear beeping."

"Shit. I know there's a silent setting for this thing." And there, in her hand, was a brand new cell phone.

"You're using that damn thing when you have a perfectly good phone right there?" I asked. "Do you know how expensive that thing is?"

"Text messaging," she held it up. "Texting's cheap."

"I should make you get a job flipping rat burgers to pay for that luxury."

"Every kid I know has had a cell since they were two, Dad. And I need this thing. What if some freak at school goes Kliebold, huh? You thought of that? You want me to just crouch under a desk and wait to get popped? This is no luxury. This is a matter of personal safety."

"By that reasoning, your mother should have bought you a gun."

"They don't allow guns in school."

Her phone beeped again. She stopped to read it. I turned to leave.

"Wait a sec." She held it up, aimed it at me. "Don't smile. Whatever you do." And she took my picture. Then her thumb danced all over the keypad. And she laughed to herself.

Chapter 8

Donovan started work at Kinko's. Randy hired him. Randy was the split-shift manager. I was store manager. I spotted Donovan in a Kinko's shirt helping carry in the paper delivery as I sprinted past. Once again I had to shit and shit badly and this time I was determined to get paid while doing it. But somewhere around the fourth red light on Glenoaks it started to look like a bad idea. I was within minutes of disaster. I could feel my guts bubbling, my pucker starting to lose its pinch. I'd been here before. This was bad.

Randy was just leaving as I passed him in the hall. I had no time to talk but I guess Randy merely thought I was eager to start work. He chased right after me. "You meet Donovan?" he asked.

I burst into the bathroom, spots dancing before my eyes, the room growing brighter like the lights were on an eye-razing dimmer. I didn't bother wiping the seat. I just yanked my pants down and let her rip.

"Holy fuck!" howled Randy. "Oh my fucking God! That's not normal, dude. You're dying inside!"

"Would you leave me alone please!"

Why didn't it feel better to let it go? Instead, the agony shot through my body with renewed intensity like a python was writhing about in my runny guts.

Randy grabbed the Lysol from under the sink and was spraying up a fog of fake pine stench. That didn't help matters.

"You should see a doctor," he said. "What are you eating?"

He's right. Dinner. I used normal bread crumbs on the chops instead of baking up some of my rice bread. What was I thinking? Now an anal hell ride was in the making.

"Why did you hire Donovan?" I moaned.

"You told me to."

"No I didn't."

"Yeah you did. You said we need someone to replace Psycho Boy, the guy who mumbled all the time."

"I didn't mean it was up to you to do it."

"Oh. Sorry. Donovan was just so enthusiastic. He said he was dying to work with you."

"He said that?"

"Yeah." Randy was quiet a minute. "I gotta get outta here. I'm feeling sick."

When I found Randy out back he was pale.

"You need your guts scrubbed or something," he said. "A hydrogen peroxide enema. Or maybe fire some Massengil Spring Time Fresh up there."

"I told you to leave me alone, didn't I?"

"I should have listened." He walked in circles, forcing out the bad air until his lungs wheezed, then sucking in great gulps of good air.

Beatriz was already taking Donovan through the paces at the front desk when I went back inside.

"Good morning!" he said to me and smiled and Beatriz did the same. He beamed at me the rest of the day.

Chapter 9

I*rascible Roses* was the first book of poems I ever read that I could understand. There was nothing cotton candy about the thing, or angel cake as Botchelko puts it. He never tried to be dainty or pick words with tweezers. They were stories really, just structured oddly on the page. There was dialogue in his poems and sadness but underneath it all was the strangest tenderness and joy.

I think.

I'm not sure why but I thought about them all day. He wrote about a jockey at the track, he wrote about a near riot at Hollywood Park and about meeting another writer he couldn't stand. I got the feeling he couldn't stand any other writers. He wrote about his daughter and I was pleased we had that in common. Though his daughter sounded quiet and thoughtful and gentle and not a five-foot, one-inch, one hundred-pound snarling badger like mine.

He wrote a lot about women. He knew a lot of women. I mean that both biblically and otherwise. We certainly didn't have that in common. Like Randy says about me, "I love a good fuck story. And I've heard both of yours." Botch knew young women and rich women and women screwed up on drugs or booze or simply screwed up on life and screaming in front of his apartment or passed out on his bathroom floor. He wrote about a woman he loved in London who was much older than him but she clearly never loved him back.

And then he wrote a poem about a cat. I copied that poem at work.

I swear the poem's about Nora though he only calls the cat "Kitty" and he didn't own the cat. It was already living in a house he rented at Big Bear. It was a huge cat and grumpy but all he had to do was keep its food dish, a dish big as a pie plate, filled to the brim with crunchies. If Kitty ever saw the bottom of the pie plate, Kitty got angry. And Botch, for the life of him, could never keep it full. Time and again, Kitty would attack him. In his sleep. While he wrote. Even walking by. Kitty would pounce on his ass and bite a cheek. He said Kitty was just like him. That's why, when the summer was over, he left Kitty right where he found him.

And always, always, he wrote about liquor. He loved alcohol. "These are the bricks that make up my life," he wrote. "I regret much less than I should."

Then he wrote, "Me and Churchill, we've taken more from alcohol than alcohol will ever take from us."

I liked that.

I sat up till two in the morning, Robin snoring her nasal symphony next to me, and read *Heliotropism*. There's no plot. It's Botch writing about himself once more, this time in his twenties and living in London, working as a bartender in a pub, a job he hated so much he drank all the time. When he's not at work he's pursuing a woman old enough to be his mother. I suspect this is also the same woman in many of his poems. He fist fights a lot in the book and then an Australian army Lieutenant, a guy who's gone AWOL just to follow Botch around, eventually beats Botch up so badly he leaves him for dead on a tug adrift on the Thames.

When I finally turned out the light, I dreamt all night that I was Botch in London and I was sharing a flat with seven roommates and sleeping on a mattress on the floor and I was drinking and fighting and obsessed with a slim classy older woman.

I awoke with the horrible realization that I've done nothing with my life worth writing about.

Chapter 10

I was half way to Vanni's when it struck me. Don't get a haircut. Vanni worked with his dad, Alfonse, an ex-boxer so deaf he shouted in your ear and spit on your neck while cutting your hair. Basically everyone preferred Vanni but nobody wanted to be so rude as to walk into Alfonse's and demand his son. But on Mondays, Vanni worked alone. Which meant on Mondays, his schedule was packed solid. I was booked for twenty after two and I was just rounding the corner down Lexington when I stopped.

I called and cancelled.

The next morning I didn't shave.

On the backs of both books were the same pictures of Botch. Not the one on the Internet, a different one. He has a smoke pinched in his lips, squinting into the camera, hair not really long, but not cut for awhile either, and a short scruffy beard. He didn't even shave his neck. I don't know how he could stand that.

Right now, let's get something clear. I don't think I consciously said to myself, "I'm going to look like Alfred Botchelko." It just started.

But Robin didn't like it.

One week later, with her mutant glass of wine almost drained, she started crying at the dinner table. Maddy rolled her eyes. "Just like Auntie Cheryl," she said as she got up from the table.

"It's because we never have sex anymore, isn't it?" Robin said and Maddy bolted out of the kitchen like her ears were aflame, screeching,

"Ack! Wait till I'm in my room!"

"What's because we never have sex anymore?" I asked.

"The reason you're having an affair."

"Robin, you're blitzed. Look at you. Screws are coming loose like crazy."

"Is she pretty?"

"Is who pretty?"

"The woman you're having the affair with."

"You've had your Big Gulp of liquor and now you're not making any sense."

"Does she shave her pubic hairs?"

"Oh for God sakes." I started gathering up the dishes. Not only was I cooking all the meals now, I was doing all the washing up too. Robin just broke too many plates. At this rate we'd soon be eating off ice cream bucket lids.

"They all shave their pubic hairs now," she said. "Shave your arm pits, shave your legs, and now you're supposed to shave your beaver on top of it all. It's just too much. Where do they find the time? Brenda gets Brazilians. That'll be the day I let some South American pussy-plucker tweezer my crotch."

Robin plunked down at a counter stool and watched me scrub. "Does your girlfriend paint her toenails? Because if she paints her toenails too, she doesn't work for a living, I'll tell you that."

"I'm going out," I said.

"I knew it!" she yelled.

"I'm going to Dutton's. I'm getting more Botchelko books."

"Likely story!"

I pulled on my jacket. "I'll be back in an hour."

"Does she have tattoos? I hate tattoos. I'll never get a tattoo, so don't even ask."

I grabbed the keys, hit the garage-door opener, and headed out.

As Charlton Heston once said, "It's a madhouse." But then again he also said, "You'll only take this gun from my cold, dead fingers," so maybe I should stop quoting the idiot.

Chapter 11

On a good day I can't find a book in an orderly bookstore. Thus, Dutton's was hell's basement. I hate asking for help. Trying to get a clerk's attention makes you look like a contortionist in Cirque du Soleil. Since no one wore uniforms or anything resembling a uniform, unless soul patches and piercings are considered uniforms, there was simply no way to tell who actually worked here.

So screw it. I'd help myself.

The store was too crowded to crouch in the aisles so that meant bending at the waist. Women can drop at the waist like a Slinky. Men cannot. So I stuck with the tall shelves. Found the entertainment section with ease. I'll remember that if I ever feel the need for three scripts by Ed Burns. Found the biographies. There was a Pollack biography so big you could beat a German Shepherd unconscious with it. Found the New Age stuff and then the parenting section. A woman was standing there suckling her baby while flipping through a book about breast feeding. You'd think she would have thought to research that subject a bit earlier. I tried to sneak a quick look at her boob but the baby was hogging the view. Probably for the best. I remember how Robin's breasts looked when she was finished feeding Maddy, shiny with milk and infant spit. If I think about it while kissing them to this day my gag reflex kicks in.

And then, to my shock, right there next to the front door, an entire shelf - Botchelko. I didn't see it because people were standing in front of it. Two kids in their twenties and a guy around my age were thumbing through the books. I squeezed up beside them, craned to get a look. These were pretty pricey. Twenty-six bucks for one skinny book, *The Winner in the Circle Jerk is the Loser in Love*. I liked the title. Everything was out of print. Several looked used too. I hate used books. I didn't want to reach through everyone so I waited until they moved on. When I finally had it to myself, I stood front and center with my feet wide apart and made it as difficult as possible for anyone else. *Even Cookies Give You Cancer* was the cheapest. I set it back.

A woman stepped up next to me, blonde like Robin—or I should say bottle-blonde like Robin, maybe ten years younger. I stepped back so I could count my cash. Fifteen bucks. I had my charge cards though so I could get at least one. When I looked up again our eyes met.

And she smiled.

Women in LA never smile at me. In fact, my attractiveness varies little from one end of this planet to the other.

"That's my name," I blurted out and pointed at the cover. I don't know why. I couldn't help it. She was smiling at me, damn it, and that makes a man do things.

"It is not," she said. So I shrugged, playing coy. "Let's see your driver's license." I knew she was going to say that. I had it ready. And she stared at it in stunned amazement. Then she stared at me.

"You look younger than I imagined."

"I'm off the gargle."

"The what?"

"The booze. I've cleaned up a bit."

"Can I have your autograph?" And she held the book out to me while digging for a pen.

Now why didn't I anticipate this? How could I ruin her book? I was just showing off. She had her pen now and was holding that out too.

"My name's Donna," she said.

She kept holding them out to me, smiling. And then her smile started to fade as she realized I wasn't going to do it. Christ, now what? I grabbed the book.

"Ellen, is it?"

"Donna," and she was smiling again and rising up on her toes.

So I wrote. "To Donna, the best cellmate ever." I spent an hour in line once to get Anthony Bourdain's signature in my copy of *Kitchen Confidential*, and that's what he wrote. I just ripped him off. Then I signed it, "Botch."

She took it back, read it, then actually clutched it to her chest, rising up on her toes again.

"Can I call you Botch?" she asked.

"Sure," I said.

"Can I buy you a drink?" Then she corrected herself. "A coffee?"

"Umm . . ."

"I know you're probably busy," she added.

"I am," I said.

"A quick coffee?"

"I have to go," I said. There was no way I could buy a Botchelko book now. She'd be on to me. I had to extricate myself from this one. I gave her an apologetic grin then stepped out the door. She followed me outside.

"You haven't paid for that," I said, and kept walking.

"Can I have your number?" she said. She was right on my heels.

"You have to go back in there and pay for that, or you'll get in trouble."

"Here's my number," she said, scribbling it down on a bit of paper and thrusting it at me.

"Call me anytime. If a man answers, just hang up and try again later."

"Thanks. I will." I crossed the street to my car, glanced back.

She was still standing there, still smiling.

"I'm being so pushy," she said proudly. "I'm never pushy."

I climbed into the Accord and drove away.

Robin was standing in the middle of the living room in her bathrobe when I got home.

"I knew it," she said. "No books."

Chapter 12

"You're looking pretty scruffy."

Randy and I were having lunch at Milano's. We were sitting in a booth by the window. I used to get the fusilli chicken because it came in this great vinaigrette sauce. But now that I couldn't eat pasta, it was either the chicken piccata, which was too salty because of the artichoke hearts, or the pork chops, which were fine but they were half a pound each so it was precisely the right portion for a pro-wrestler or a linebacker but a little much for me. I hated wasting an entire pork chop but all it took was one big lunch and I was so drowsy at work I wanted to curl up on a warm copier. Which meant taking the pork chop home. Where it would sit in the fridge until it grew a beard of fine blue hair.

My beard, on the other hand, was black with flecks of gray.

"They're probably going to make you shave that," Randy said.

"Who's going to tell Provo?" I said.

Provo was Kinko's corporate center. That's the way we referred to it at work. If the phone rang and someone said, "It's Provo," you knew who was calling.

"They'll see it at the conference," he said. "Two weeks."

Shit, that's right. I forgot about the conference. Topeka. Since they didn't ask me to prepare anything, it totally slipped my mind. Though now that I think of it, they didn't even ask me to be group leader either. What did I do to piss them off? My branch was rolling in it. We just moved down the street to the new building three years ago. My staff turnover was high, but not above average. So they could kiss my ass. I liked my beard. It was staying.

"How's Robin liking Star Ford?" Randy asked.

I pulled out my phone, dialed, and held it up to his ear. Robin answered, "Shit eating department."

I hung up.

"She's trying to get fired," he said.

"Exactly."

"Why haven't they done it yet?"

"That I don't know."

My cell rang. "Are you checking up on me?" It was Robin.

"I just called to hear your voice."

"You just called to make sure I was here so you could slip off and see your girlfriend."

"Get help," I said and hung up. "I think she's developing a pretty interesting drinking habit too."

"Does it make her wittier?"

"Weepier," I said.

My cell rang again.

"You're in a restaurant, I can tell. Are you with her?"

"I'm with Randy."

"Oh, so that's your cover."

"Say hi Randy." I held the phone out to him.

"Hi Randy," he said.

"Satisfied?" I asked.

"Not if it's Randy you're having the affair with."

"Gotta go." I hung up, then handed my dish to a passing waitress. I don't like looking at a meal when I'm done with it. It always looks a bit like a carcass.

Randy was still picking at his margherita pizza. "How's Maddy doing these days?"

"She has a new cell phone."

"Yeah? You bought her a new cell phone?"

"No. Robin did."

"Why?"

"Because she's terrified of her. I think Robin feels like she's abandoned Maddy at a vulnerable age. And Maddy, on the other hand, feels like Robin's abandoned her at a vulnerable age. So at least they see eye to eye on something."

"Thus Robin's trying to get fired."

The phone rang again.

"And making a good effort at divorce too," I added. "Hello?"

"I bought Maddy a laptop."

I hung up.

"Things are changing."

"Change is good," said Randy.

Chapter 13

Robin was drinking from a new eight-ounce martini glass when I got home. "Where'd you get that?"

"Crate and Barrel."

"Just one?"

"Why? Did you want one?"

"Where did you learn to make martinis."

"Gin, vermouth, ice, drink. What's to learn?"

"Where's dinner?

"Aren't you making dinner?"

"It's your turn."

"We'll order in."

"Where's Maddy?"

"On her new laptop."

"We can't afford a new laptop."

"You're the one who shit on the old one."

"I'm going out."

"Give her my love." And she drained her glass.

Donovan said he bought all his Botchelkos—or as he put it, "All your books," down at Baroque Bookstore in Hollywood.

"They're not my books," I corrected him.

"How many guys live in Los Angeles named Alfred Botchelko?"

"I'm still not him."

He counted off on his fingers. "Born in Trail, British Columbia."

"I was born in Omaha."

Second finger. "Raised by single mother who then marries a mean drunk."

"I was raised by two psychotic bohunks."

Third finger. "Now lives in . . . well, it don't say where."

"Glendale?"

"Botchelko don like Glendale."

"Yet here I am just the same."

"Maybe you move."

Donovan smiled at me so much I was growing convinced he was gay. Twice he brought friends over to stare at me. They wouldn't come inside the store. They just stood out on the sidewalk and peered through the windows. Donovan would yell, "That's heem!" every time I walked by.

I'll give you this for Donovan—I never had to tell him to load the machines, never asked him to store paper or unload the truck or take out the recycling, never once gave him a lesson in copying and collating. Beatriz did all that I guess. He was the happiest, hardest working employee I ever had. Next to his girlfriend, that is. The only thing he ever said to me that sounded anything less than upbeat was when he pointed at Carlos and whispered, "He don't fix the copiers."

"Which one needs fixing?"

"None of them. He pulls the backs off and pretends to fix them so he don have to work." That was news to me. "Oh, and Randy is dry fucking your ass," he added.

And with that, he loaded a cart with bound presentations and off he went to deliver them to Napp, Peterson, Clark.

Chapter 14

Baroque was on Cherokee, just across the street and down one block from Musso and Frank. I always wanted to go in Musso and Frank. Hemingway used to drink there. So did F. Scott and Miller and Saroyan.

And so did, apparently, Botchelko.

That was according to the skinny old man who owned Baroque. When I went to pay for the four books, I handed him my American Airlines Visa.

He handed it back. "Is this some kind of joke?"

I looked at the card. "Don't you take Visa?"

"Of course I take Visa."

"Well I'm sure the card's good." I handed it back.

"You got ID?" he demanded.

So I handed him my license. He compared the two, flipped them over and compared signatures, then looked at the photo and looked at me.

"Don't you have copies of these books?"

"No."

"People keep stealing 'em, I bet."

"Excuse me?"

"Hang on a sec."

He went in back. I could see him sitting in the dark, the glow of a computer monitor lighting his face as he clicked away with a mouse. He reappeared. "Were you at Musso and Frank?"

"No."

"It's Thursday. That's right. You only drink there first Wednesday of every month."

"I'm not who you think I am," I said.

"That's right. That's what you always say, isn't it?" He stuck out a hand. "Red."

"Red," I repeated. And then I said, or I meant to say, William. Somehow it came out "Alfred" instead. And Red smiled his dog yellow teeth at me.

"Can I buy you a drink up the street?"

"Oh I don't know. I really should get home."

"It would mean a lot to me. Not that that's your responsibility or anything. I don't mean to impose. It's just a drink after all. I'll pay of course. You still drink Jack?"

"Actually, I might like a martini," I said.

"But . . ." And Red took a sudden step back. He frowned at me. "But you said in *Botch's Progeny* that you hated martinis and you called the look of anyone walking with a martini 'the liquor enforced elegance of a marionette.'"

"I said that?"

"That's right."

"You know what else I said?"

"What?"

"Things change."

"When did you say that?"

"Right this minute. You can quote me."

Chapter 15

Red poked away at his cell phone as we walked the block up to Musso and Frank. But he didn't put it up to his ear. He put it in his pocket. Text messaging. I guess I really should learn what that's all about. But my new technology debt was growing by the second. If they would just come up with computer software that would send me back to the eighties, I'd download that in a minute.

Red held the door for me. We stepped inside. The maitre d', a gray-haired man in glasses, turned to face us. No smile. And certainly no sign of recognition.

"Mr. Botchelko's usual table," said Red.

The Maitre d' had no expression. He didn't move.

"Please?" added Red.

So the man shrugged, walked maybe six steps into the dining room, and he pointed at the bar. "Any one of those stools." And he walked away.

"I usually sit at the bar," I told Red.

"Of course," he said. "That makes sense."

We grabbed stools on the end farthest from the front entrance. A short little bartender in a red jacket stepped up.

"Mr. Botchelko will have a martini," said Red and he laid his hand on my forearm.

"He will?" said the bartender and he scanned the room.

"And I'll have a scotch on the rocks."

"What kind of martini do you think Mr. Botchelko would like?" the bartender asked Red.

So Red turned and looked at me.

"Gin?" I said.

"A Gibson?"

"Any brand."

"Would he like olives or onions?" he said patiently.

"Onions are fine."

"A Gibson," he repeated, apparently for my edification. "Where will he be sitting?"

"Right here," said Red. "Where he's presently sitting."

The bartender shrugged, grabbed a shaker, and got to work.

"Odd how he kept referring to you in the third person," said Red.

"You know Red," I whispered and leaned in conspiratorially, "I don't like to announce who I am."

Red looked like a child expecting a pat on the head but catching a smack instead.

"I've read every book you've ever written. Maybe half a dozen times each. You'd think I'd know that by now," he said, flagellating himself on top of it all.

I felt bad but I was playing a potentially humiliating game here. And I still wasn't sure why. I just liked being Alfred Botchelko. When I said that name, my birth name, it suddenly felt like I'd written all those books. Like I'd lived in London and Sydney and did time and I was tough. I could fist fight. And I could hold my liquor too. I walked a bit taller, with more confidence, the way an uncompromised man walks. The way a man in full walks.

Before I even got my first martini to my lips Red said, "Here they are."

And there they were. Half a dozen men and women in their twenties and thirties, eagerly squeezing in around me and not so much as meeting Red's eyes, just smiling nervously at me.

"Guys," said Red, "meet . . . " and suddenly he remembered and dropped his voice to a whisper, "meet Alfred Botchelko."

They all nodded to me, six heads bobbing simultaneously and smiling. No one had blinked yet. I didn't nod back. The eager nodding slowed and eyes darted to Red.

"I hope you don't mind?" Red said to me. "We have a pact. If any of us should ever meet you, we're obligated to give the others a chance to meet you too."

Red was jumpy. Apparently, Botch has a rep for being a bit unpredictable. So how does Kinko's most predictable office manager act unpredictably?

"I hope you all plan on buying?" I said. That was the best I could do. And they weren't just relieved, they almost cheered, bellying up to the bar, elbowing one another aside to buy the next round.

A tall kid caught the bartender's eye. "Another martini?" he asked me.

"Oh no," I said.

"A round of beers," he told the bartender. "Harps or Bass." He sat down on a stool, confident he'd ordered exactly what I wanted. "You love the Brit stuff, I know," he said.

Beer. Hops. Barley. Christ. I'd be shitting myself dizzy half up the Cahuenga Pass. Now what? The kids squeezed around me, blocking everyone's path to the restrooms but they didn't care. The little brunette pressed her leg against mine. Which meant the girl in the long skirt had to act fast so she slipped in on the other side, pushing the tall kid away, and made like she needed a napkin. Once she got her napkin though she stayed right there, pressed up against me with her arm on the bar behind my back.

"Amit," said the East Indian kid and held out his hand. "I run your website."

"I have a website?" I said.

And the kid looked like I'd just speed-bagged his nut sack. "It's a good site," he added.

"It's a great site," the brunette said, and they all agreed.

"I don't have any pictures of you though," said Amit. "Only that same one from all the book jackets. Do you mind if I . . .?" and he reached into his breast pocket for a camera, glancing to Red as he did so. But Red gave a quick shake of the head. Thank goodness. Amit, crushed again, stared off and sucked on his beer.

Now finished with that hideous martini, a sweaty beer awaited me. The others were almost done with theirs already. They were waiting for me, eager to buy the next round. I picked it up. I once liked beer. But it never liked me and I couldn't figure out what was wrong. Nervous stomach was the college diagnosis, then peptic ulcer, chronic heartburn, and finally Irritable Bowel Syndrome. It took until I was forty for someone—and it wasn't my doctor, it was his nurse while taking my temperature and flipping through my medical file—to suggest celiac disease. No wheat. No grains. Oddly, no dairy, no eggs, and I have a little trouble with beef too. But the blood test proved it—a diagnosis at last. Which meant every swallow other than saliva was a potential intestinal landmine.

But I couldn't let these kids down. This was my pickle and I was in it. I lifted the beer, "L'chaimed" them and took a slug. The brunette immediately ordered another round.

I was boned.

"When's the next book . . . Botch?" asked the wild-eyed bearded giant named Max. Even though he was wearing a long sleeve shirt that looked like underwear, I could see the blue ink of his tattoos stretching right down to his knuckles and reaching all the way up his neck to his ear. Who in their right mind would hire a freak like that? I don't care how good Beatriz was, if her flesh was crawling in "art" too ugly to hang on a bathroom wall but apparently good enough to permanently etch into your skin, she would never have gotten the job at Kinko's. People like this guy scare people like me. And people like me are the populace.

"It's okay to call you Botch, isn't it?" he added.

"It's the only name I got." Funny, isn't it, that Alfred Botchelko becomes Botch but William Botchelko becomes Will. On the other hand, they say nicknames are a sign of affection. Will was the sign that the name William was too sophisticated for the likes of me.

"It's been six years since your last book," said the girl squeezed up against me.

"Yeah, well, there's no rushing these things," and they all nodded in agreement.

"Poetry or prose?" asked Red.

"Little of both," I said. That seemed to excite them.

"What's it called?" asked Amit.

Shit. What's it called?

"Drink up," said the tall kid. The beer in my hand was still full and now he was handing me another. I had to get to work in the morning. How was I going to do that hung over and shitting like a gopher? I downed that first one the best I could, then struggled not to belch it all back up in a great bubbling gusher. I moved on to the second one, but now they were already ordering the third. I tried to calculate it. Half an hour to get home—light traffic, that is—and the traffic this hour should be light. As long as I'm on the road at the first sign of a gut bubble, I should make it.

They were all still looking at me for some reason.

"Don't you have a title yet?"

"Oh yeah," I said and reached for the beer, mind scrambling now, and just before I puckered up to kiss the bottle's opening, I stopped. "It's called *Pucker Up*."

They liked that and nodded. I guess it sounded sufficiently Botchian.

Max was the first to pull out a book. I should have known, with all those shoulder bags and backpacks they were carrying that they'd all shown up with books.

"You mind? Botch?" he asked and I could feel Red cringe beside me. Clearly I was meant to be as volatile as Russell Crowe on amphetamines. But I was clueless as to how to be volatile. I took the book and the pen.

"To Max," I wrote. And I was already stuck. Obviously, they wouldn't know about that Donna girl from Dutton's. So I just wrote the same thing. "The best cellmate ever. Botch." I handed it back. They all leaned in to read it, smiling. Then Max's smile faded.

"That's the same thing Anthony Bourdain wrote in my book," he said.

Oh fuck. My brain scrambled.

"Well where do you think Bourdain got it?" I said and I took a big slug of beer like I was pissed off at having my genius robbed. That seemed to satisfy them. But now the rest of the books came out.

The brunette was named Grace.

"To Grace. Next round's on you . . . and the round after that." I signed them all "Botch."

"To Amit. Love the website. But you need more pictures. Botch."

"To Amanda. Sorry about your mother. Get therapy. Botch."

"To Paul. You're too tall. Love Dad (Botch)." I was clearly getting drunk.

"To William." Now I was stuck again. William. It was like making one out to myself. I could say something about an ambulance ride maybe. Or ducking bullets. That's when my cell rang. Saved. I checked the call display. Robin.

Maybe not so saved.

"Who's Donna?" she asked.

What the hell! Was she channeling me or something?

"I just found her name and number in your other pants. So I called her. I asked if I could speak to Mr. Botchelko. You know what she said? Not, who's Mr. Botchelko? She said 'He's not here.' So me and your girlfriend would like to know where you are."

"Musso and Frank."

"I don't imagine your daughter is with you."

"No. Why?"

"Because she hasn't come home yet."

"You try her phone?"

"Of course I tried her phone. That's why I got her a phone. So I could phone her."

"Do you know any of her friends' numbers?"

"I don't know any of her friends."

"Try the speed dial on the phone in her room. I'll be home soon." I hung up. "Sorry about that."

They were all looking at me, clearly waiting for some sort

of explanation.

"New girlfriend," I said. "She has a kid. She's worried."

That didn't seem to do it.

"I thought you hated cell phones," said Max.

Oh. The cell phone was the problem.

"You change with the times, Max," I said.

"But I don't own a cell phone because you don't own a cell phone."

"You're kidding me," I said. I looked to each of their faces. "None of you?"

They all shook their heads. I turned to Red. "But you texted them."

"E-mailed actually," he said. "Blackberry."

What a bunch of freaks. "Hey, if you want to do what I do," I said, "then don't do anything anyone else would do."

They didn't seem to understand that one. Maybe it didn't make sense but if I tried to explain it I would lose all authority.

I finished the autograph. "To William. Thank God it was an exit wound. Kisses. Botch."

I thought I was done. When Red sheepishly handed his over. This one was wrapped in transparent paper. He carefully unwrapped it. Clearly this was a special edition, 80-lb cardboard cover with a three-color print of an artist's pallet and a dog, serrated edge paper stock. Pricey. Believe me, I know. I work with paper. And now I was going to ruin it. He even had a special pen he wanted me to use. He unscrewed the top, screwed it back on the bottom, and handed it over. He'd thought long and hard about this moment. I wanted to sprint out of there. I had the sudden urge to confess but Max was pretty big and so was William for that matter and it would crush them and if not crush them then maybe send them into a mob rage.

"Red," I said. "Can I come back in later and sign this for you? I'm not thinking clearly and I'd like to write something good in here."

Red wasn't sure how to respond. "You promise you'll come back?" he asked.

"I promise," I said.

I'm not sure how much bad karma a person can gather in such

a short period of time but I'm certain they were already clearing a special spot in hell for me. Probably somewhere Red could piss down on me for all eternity.

"I have to go," I said and with that everyone was on their feet. We headed to the door en masse.

And as I passed the Maitre d', I heard him say, "Nighty-night Botchy-boy."

My car was parked in front of Baroque. As we walked back Red said, "I have to confess something. I've written several times to your address in San Pedro. You're probably wondering how I got it. But it was on a slip of paper inside a box of books I bought. From your ex-girlfriend. From Carmen."

I didn't respond.

"The one you write about?"

"I remember Carmen," I said.

"I understand why you never reply, I just wanted to know—do you read the letters you get?"

"Every one."

That seemed to satisfy him. We stopped at my Honda. I shook all their hands, thanked them for the drinks.

Then just as I was opening my car door, Max said, "Can I ask you one small favor?"

I felt a twinge of annoyance. Small wonder Botchelko had nothing to do with his fans. These fuckers could pick you apart like crows.

"What's that, Max?" I asked.

"Could you . . . ?" He couldn't say it and his eyes dropped shyly to his feet.

"Could I what?" I was getting impatient. I had to go. Robin was probably break dancing in drunken rage right about now.

"Could you punch me in the face?"

I didn't think I heard him correctly.

"Could I what?"

"Could you punch me in the face?"

Was he unhinged?

"It would be an honor to be punched in the face by you," he said.

"You really need to get back on your meds," I said.

"Leave him alone, Max," said Red.

"But he's been in a million fights," he said.

"You want to fight me?"

"No. I want to stand here while you punch me in the face."

"Well I'm not going to do it," I said and I turned and stuck my keys in the door.

"Oh, I get it," he said and he suddenly spun me around. He shoved me up against the car. "How 'bout now?" He shoved me again. "Huh? How 'bout now?"

"Max stop it!" they all shouted but I got the feeling they really wanted to see this fight. It was like seventh grade all over again.

"Punch me. Come on, punch me," he was saying and each time he shoved harder. I didn't know what to do. My adrenal gland was open wide and flooding my system and my face must have been contorting in terror. "How bout now!" he shouted. He looked insane. He looked like Charles Manson. "You gonna punch me now …!"

I swung. I curled up my fist and I drove it right into his mouth.

But it barely moved his head. His body didn't move at all, not a step back, not a shudder, nothing. It sounded more like a thuck than a smack or a whack. Then there was utter silence. He stared at me. They all stared at me. Then his face broke out in a wide, bloody-toothed smile.

"Thank you, sir," he said.

"You're welcome," I said.

I jumped in my car before they could see my hands trembling. And as I drove up Cahuenga, I felt a strangely powerful elation. I had just punched a man. A big man. Right in the face. I gave him a bloody lip. I drew blood. I'd never punched anyone before in my life. It felt amazing. I felt incredible. And my stomach felt good too.

The house was dark when I got home. Robin was in bed as I crept into the room. I started to undress.

"Talk to Maddy in the morning, would you?" was all she said.

Chapter 16

I woke to the sound first. I wasn't sure what it was. Then I heard it again. My stomach gurgled as loud as a salt water aquarium. I rushed into the bathroom. I turned the water on full blast and immediately flushed the toilet but there was no covering the racket from this one. It took all night for that damn beer time bomb to trigger. But now it had me good. I was in agony.

Then I heard meowing. Then scratching at the door. It was getting louder. We kept Nora's litter box in the corner of the bathroom. Goddamn it was I never going to get a chance to shit in peace?

"Dad, Nora needs to get in there." It was Maddy.

"She can wait."

"But she really needs to go."

I could hear that deep meow now, the desperate one she used when we took her to the vet's. This is what happens when you live with three females.

"Okay, stand back. I'll open the door a crack and let her in."

"Let me get the hell out of here first."

I opened the door. Nora rushed inside. She got about halfway to her litter box when she stopped, spun around and bolted right back out again.

"Even the cat can't take the stink Dad!"

"Did you talk to your father yet?"

It was Robin now.

"No," said Maddy.

"Then you talk to him right now."

"Mom, he's taking a dump!"

"You come here right now, young lady. Will, do you have something you'd like to say to your daughter?"

Jesus Christ Almighty I wish a hit man would take these people out.

"Can't this wait?" I said.

"It can't wait. She has to face her punishment now."

"Believe me Mom, standing outside this door is punishment enough."

"Will, talk to her."

"Maddy . . ." What the hell was I supposed to say? "Maddy, your mother's right . . . " and with that I let loose an elephant seal-bark of a fart.

"There's no need to yell, Dad," she said and laughed.

"Maddy, listen to me," I said but I was interrupted again as Robin screamed, "Nora's taking a shit on the carpet!"

Chapter 17

I was hung over. I could feel it. Cotton head. A touch dizzy. Guts at Defcon Four and ready to launch. But worse, like a married man cringing as he remembers his fat one-nighter—or worse yet, necking with his fat one-nighter in public first - the image of signing all those books, right at the bar, the bartender watching, knowing I was full of it, made me feel like I'd had alley sex with a hooker. I don't know why I did it.

Or maybe I did know why.

A married man goes to hookers, not so much for the sex, but for the excitement, the danger, sparking up his life a little, feeling momentarily like another man before he returns to his dreary old life where he's the undesirable nobody once again. That's all I was doing. It was a $20 lap dance. It was a drunken hookup. It was a call girl at the Radisson once the convention center shuts down.

I was Alfred Botchelko. For one night I was Alfred Botchelko.

And I felt cool.

Besides, they didn't know where I lived. Red thought I was down in San Pedro. I never hung around Hollywood. They'd never see me again. I made their night. And I never ruined Red's collector edition either. There wasn't much to regret, not really. So the bartender and the maitre d' were on to me—so what? Max got his punch in the face. He'll be dining out on that story till the day he dies. The others got drinks with their hero. Amit can add a story to his website. And the girls wanted me. That was a nice feeling. I was desirable. Tough, talented, sexy.

God, if women would just smile at men once a day, we'd go about our lives so much happier.

But if you want to keep something a secret, don't tell anybody. Simple, no? Well I just had to go tell somebody.

I told Randy.

He stopped in to get his check around three. I grabbed him and we went a couple doors down to Porto's. He had a turkey sandwich. I had coffee. That damn sandwich looked good though. With my guts in the shape they were in today, I could probably eat a bag of wheat and it wouldn't have made a bit of difference.

Randy listened politely. I told it the way a married man confesses to a one-nighter too, glancing up and down the street, whispering, dropping my face in my hands. Randy just chewed slowly and stared at me. I think he was disappointed. He was hoping for at least a third fuck story to add to my other two. Christ I was boring. Randy got laid all the time.

"I don't have a clue what you're talking about," he said.

"Were you not listening to me?"

"Oh I was listening dude. Apparently you got drunk and pretended to be a poet no one's ever heard of. You signed some old out of print books that these guys picked up for a quarter in a sidewalk bin. And they were happy to buy you drinks all night. Jesus man, how can you live with yourself?"

Yeah. He was right. He was exactly right. Minor offense. In the grand scheme of things—and eventually we all make comparisons to what we imagine the grand scheme to be—this was the most minor infraction on the tiniest of scales.

The karmic retribution would probably be no worse than, say, a pimple, a flat tire, or maybe the hangover I was wrestling with now.

Chapter 18

"I have a gift for you," Robin said.

"I can see that," I said.

Robin made dinner. Pork loin. And I love pork loin. But she baked it with the canned pineapples on top when personally I find it's better with the honey-mustard glaze and then, maybe fifteen or twenty minutes before it's done, remove the tin foil, add fried mushrooms sliced thin, onions minced, and let it bake that last twenty. Then a sprinkle of parsley before serving.

Though this was also good.

"Not the pork loin," she said. "I bought you something. As a peace offering." She handed it over. A book, wrapped.

I tore it open. A Botchelko. *Various Indignities*. I didn't have this one.

"I know how much you like him. Look inside."

I opened it. And there on the inside cover was inscribed, "To William. Thank God it was an exit wound. Kisses. Botch."

"Jesus Christ!" I shouted.

Robin was beaming. "It's like it's made out to you. Isn't that cool?"

"Where did you get this?"

"E-bay. Where else?"

"That little fucker sold it."

"And I bought it."

"What did you pay for this?" I asked.

"Well—it wasn't cheap. He never signs his books, you know."

"How much?"

Robin hesitated. "Five hundred and seventy dollars."

"Oh Jesus Fucking Christ!"

Robin threw her napkin down. "I thought you'd be happy," she said. She went to the kitchen, pulled out her wine tankard and a bottle.

"You know how rare that is? He held that book. In his own hands. The man you worship. That's his writing. And it's made out to you. Now to me, that's karma."

"Oh it's karma, baby."

Robin was struggling with the cork. You'd think after all the practice she'd be pretty good at it by now. "I don't know what you're so pissed about," she said.

This is what happens. This is how God gets even. He takes your money. He turns your wife into a drunk. He makes you gluten intolerant. He transforms your daughter from a sweet—though perhaps a bit ditzy—child into a growling nocturnal rodent.

Robin sat down with her half liter of cabernet. There were bits of cork floating in it.

"His handwriting's similar to yours," she said.

That's right, keep hammering the nails in, just keep hammering.

"I think we should have sex this weekend," she suddenly announced.

"Don't threaten me," I said.

"I'm not threatening you."

"It sounds like a threat."

Robin jumped up again. She dumped her entire wine in the sink.

"What are you doing?" I asked.

"I don't want wine," she said. And she began to gather her martini accoutrements. The silver shaker, the shot glass, a green liter-and-three-quarter bottle of Tanqueray, Martini and Rossi Dry Vermouth. She even chilled the glass first with ice and water. Maybe she had trouble with a wine cork, but she sure as shit knew how to make these, shaking it furiously like a maraca, straining it, two olives. Then she plopped back down in her seat.

It was a different martini glass. Bigger. Ten ounces.

"New glass?"

"Mm-hm," she said and sipped.

"Crate and Barrel?"

"Mm-hm."

"Only one?"

She shrugged.

I picked up that stupid book, opened it again. I should have punched William in the face. I knew he was a cagey one. Not sycophantic enough. Not a real fan like the others. He didn't gush over me. He wasn't nervous. Tall, cocky prick. He should have put this book on a stand and found a special place in his house and lit candles all around it and worshipped the fucking thing. A signed Botchelko.

To be perfectly honest, I thought it would have sold for more.

"You're not pissed off about that book," Robin suddenly blurted out.

"I'm not?"

She shook her head. "You're pissed off about the pork loin."

Dinner was officially over. I started cleaning up.

"I happen to like it with pineapple," she said.

I loaded the dishwasher.

"When did you become Jamie fucking Oliver?" she said.

I went in the living room and turned on the TV. *Blind Date* was on. A drunk girl was flashing her boobs at the camera. The boobs were blurred. Her date was grimacing. His face was not blurred.

"Long live pineapple!" Robin yelled.

Chapter 19

I was watching Carlos. I'd used the copier by the window only a minute ago, loaded and tested it. Usually that was Beatriz's job, but she was at the doctor's. Donovan took her. So it was me and Carlos. I told him I was calling Provo and when I got back down he was elbow deep in the back of that very same copier.

"Excuse me?"

A little balding man in glasses was standing right in front of me. I hadn't seen him. One look and you knew, without any conscious thought, that this was a man everyone ignored.

"Are you Alfred Botchelko?" he asked.

I gotta tell you, Botch's fan club seemed to be made up primarily from the lunatic fringe. "Yes I am."

He stuck out a hand. "Barry Abenathy."

I shook it. "What can I do for you, Mr. Abenathy?"

"You can start by paying me back the $70,000 you owe me." He pushed his glasses back up his nose with his forefinger and waited.

"I'm not that Alfred Botchelko."

"The debt you once owed several gentlemen has since been transferred to me. Make no mistake, Mr. Botchelko, this is a substantial gambling debt that you must pay back immediately."

Carlos was peeking above the top of the copier, listening.

"I said you've got the wrong guy."

"Are you or are you not Alfred Botchelko?"

"I am, but I'm not the poet."

"I don't care if you're a soothsayer, you're the Alfred Botchelko who's been negligent on his debt payments for a number of years now."

"The poet is the one you're looking for, not me."

"Then explain this to me. How is it a book of yours, a signed book, was suddenly being offered on E-bay?"

"I don't have to explain that. It has nothing to do with me."

"This book, an autographed book, very rare for a Botchelko, was suddenly available on E-bay. I believed this to be you, in need of money, selling anonymously."

"It wasn't."

"Correct. But I bid on it anyway. I lost the bid. Do you know who won the bid?"

"I have a pretty good idea."

"You're lovely wife. Who works at Star Ford. Parts department."

"I know where she works."

"Curious way of dealing with the public, that woman."

"She's trying to get fired."

"Interesting. When I drove over there not half an hour ago and introduced myself, I informed her about your serious gambling debt."

"Tell me you didn't."

"And her reply? 'That explains everything.' Curious, don't you think? She gave me this address to find you."

"The wrong Alfred Botchelko."

"You ever Google yourself, Mr. Botchelko?"

"Once or twice."

"There's a website. Devoted entirely to you. With an updated photo recently posted. If you're not the Alfred Botchelko who drives a red Honda Accord, then you have a twin with the exact same taste in motor vehicles."

Fuck. Amit. That little bastard must have snapped a shot of me. Probably during that dust-up with Max.

"Do you deny you're the Botchelko in that picture?"

Carlos was finished "fixing" the copier. He was behind the counter now, measuring and cutting cover board.

"Carlos? Could you do that over there please?"

"No worries." He moved off. Not far enough though.

"You researching a book or something, Mr. Botchelko?" asked Barry the little debt collector.

"Yeah. That's right. Fifteen years of research."

"Could you make out a check for me please?"

He pushed up his glasses again. He was such a skinny weasely little dink. Maybe 120 soaking wet. Carrying a brick. After a big meal. How did he ever manage to get a penny out of anyone?

"Get out of here before I call the cops."

"And tell them what?"

"That you're harassing me. Debt collectors are not allowed by law to harass people at their place of work."

"You sound well versed in debt avoidance, Mr. Botchelko. But these debts and the manner in which they're collected do not fall within the normal boundaries of the law. And I think you know that."

"You a mobster?"

"No sir."

"You connected?"

"No sir."

"You packing?"

"No I'm not, sir. And I appreciate your colorful use of underworld colloquialisms. Who says television isn't an educational tool?"

I had enough.

Enough Carlos's. Enough inebriated wives. Enough whiny daughters. Enough E-Bay, enough Google, enough Celiac, enough Alfred Botchelko.

Enough.

I grabbed Abenathy by the lapels and dragged him halfway up the counter. I jammed my face in his, nose to nose. "Fuck off. Now. Or I will kill you."

Then I shoved him and he stumbled backward to the door, barely regaining his balance. He looked a little startled. He hadn't expected that. Not from me. I didn't expect it either. He straightened his glasses, straightened his tie, smoothed his lapels. He moved his brief case from his left hand to his right. He took a breath, nodded once, then walked out the door.

There.

That's how men defend themselves. Don't fucking push me. I punched a guy in the face once, you know.

And it felt great.

Chapter 20

Robin didn't call me all day and I didn't call her. She was going to be waiting for me at home. I knew that. On the bright side, this should put an end to her silly affair accusations once and for all. Not that it will make her sheepish or contrite in any way. She had another juicy bone to bite.

And she bit.

"What kind of gambling?"

"I don't gamble."

"Cards?"

"Have you ever seen me play cards?"

"Sneaking out every night, sitting in some smoky gambling den, drinking and playing cards."

"Suddenly we live in Ho Chi Minh City?"

Robin had traded up once again. The twelve ounce martini glass. You could bathe a terrier in that thing. She was on her feet, standing triumphantly over me, drink perched thoughtfully up near her mouth as she ruminated my addiction. I was sitting on the couch, pretending to read the paper.

"Cock fighting?" she guessed.

"It's not Tijuana either."

"Are we going to play twenty questions all night or are you going to come clean?"

"I don't have a gambling problem, Robin. The guy's got me mixed up with somebody else. With the other Botchelko."

"Getting help is easy. But accepting that you need help is the hard part, William."

"What? Are you Dr. Drew Pinsky now?"

Suddenly, Nora bolted from the living room. Nora was terrified of visitors. She was our early warning system. Robin glanced out the front window.

A black-and-white unit was in the driveway and two cops were approaching the front door.

"The cops! Ha! Now look!"

She was happy. She was actually happy about this. Imagine what life must be like if you were married to a woman who *doesn't* love you. I've said this about her before and I'll say it again: maybe she loved me, but she sure didn't like me.

Robin pulled open the door before they even had a chance to knock.

"Hello. Come in, come in."

"Mrs. Botchelko?" I heard one of them ask.

"Yes, we've been expecting you. Come on in. Please."

The two cops stepped inside. A tall, dark Latino guy with his head shaved, and a short, dark Latina woman with wide hips that looked wider still with the holster and gun and baton and cuffs and you name it.

Robin led them to the center of the room then left them standing there facing me as she hurried round the coffee table to sit at my side. She took my hand, squeezed it earnestly and waited.

"Do you know why we're here?" he asked.

"We know exactly why you're here," said Robin.

"We'd like to ask you a few questions."

Robin turned to look at me. She squeezed my hand harder, shook it to make me respond.

"Yes, go ahead," I said.

"I was addressing your wife," said the cop.

And Robin's face slowly turned away from mine and she locked her worried eyes on the officer. "Me?"

"Mrs. Botchelko, your boss, a Mr. Buchanan at Star Ford, claims you've been stealing his stemware."

Stemware? What the fuck? And all eyes in the room drifted down to that martini glass monstrosity perched damningly in the middle of the coffee table.

"Oh God!" Robin shouted and she dropped her face in her hands. Then she jumped up and ran out of the room.

"What did she think we were here to talk about?" asked the female cop.

"I haven't the foggiest," I said.

"Can you get her back down here, sir?" the male cop asked.

"I'll do my best," I said.

It took almost half an hour to get Robin out of the bedroom. She was blubbering like I've never seen before. She didn't cry this much at her father's funeral. I finally had to give her one of the gift hankies I never use since she had already burned up an entire box of Kleenex. I coaxed her back down the hall and back on the couch.

Apparently Buchanan did a lot of on-line shopping. He was stocking a new bar and had all the boxes shipped to work. Where Robin signed for them. Then put them in his office. Then made a habit of helping herself to a glass. One glass. From each box.

Crate and Barrel, my ass.

"Mr. Buchanan asked us to have a word with you."

"Is he pressing charges?" I asked.

"Not yet."

Robin looked up, a glimmer of hope at last. "Is he firing me?"

"No. You'll work to pay him back. He wants to give you another chance, see if you'll straighten yourself up, change your attitude. And then he'll consider whether he's pressing charges or not."

Indentured servitude.

Robin slipped off to bed the moment they left, her posture bent under the weight of shame. She slowly brushed her teeth as the tears rolled down her cheeks, then she said goodnight, squeezed my hand and lay with her back to me, every once in a while letting go the smallest whimper.

Until she finally fell asleep. And started snoring the death rattle of a bull elephant.

Chapter 21

I was walking past the smokers in front of Jax when I spotted Abenathy cruising past in a blue Ford Taurus. Then, stepping out of B of A, there he was again, cruising by in the other direction but never meeting my eye.

I called Robin at work.

"Star Ford Parts department. Robin speaking. How may I help you?"

"Jesus, is that you?"

"Yes, Mr. Botchelko."

"You sound like a Stepford Wife."

"Have you tried calling home for messages today?"

"No," I said.

"Something's funky with the phone."

I called home.

"This number is no longer in service."

I called AT&T. They informed me that I had requested the service be terminated. When you think about the bewildering chronic ineptitude out there, it makes you wonder how a plane ever stays in the air. Let alone how the planet doesn't spin off its axis.

I got the number hooked up again, only cost me $80 dollars, struggled to remember my mother's maiden name—Wendell—then mixed up the last two digits on my social security number.

"Is that five nine or six nine?" I asked her.

"You tell me."

I guessed. "Six nine."

"Bingo," she said.

The next day it was shut off again. And the cable TV with it. I got a call at work from Washington Mutual informing me that I'd missed a mortgage payment. Which was impossible because we had automatic withdrawal. Then Robin got a call about the car. Even though I drove the Honda, it was in her name. No car payment either. Then I realized my cell phone had been suspiciously quiet too. Sure enough—no service.

Maddy was being her usual stoic self that night.

"How am I supposed to do homework? How I am supposed to watch TV? How am I supposed to call anyone? This is embarrassing. What do I tell my friends?"

Botch tells a story about the day his daughter was born. He looked out the hospital window on busy Sunset below and wondered how it was possible that the world hadn't stopped and stood still in acknowledgement of this wondrous event.

When Maddy was born, Robin had a cesarean. They lifted her entire uterus out of her body. Maddy looked like a pink hamster with greasy black hair on her head and the placenta made me vomit my El Pollo Loco burrito into a wastebasket.

The only miracle of that birth was that I ever managed to have sex with Robin again.

Chapter 22

Lunch time was crunch time at Kinko's. Mostly office staff running personal errands. The little jobs took up the most time and paid the worst. So there was a crowd at the counter when I glanced up and spotted Abenathy making copies near the door. I marched over to him.

"This would be a bad time to make a scene, don't you agree, Mr. Botchelko?"

"Stop harassing us."

"Harassing you?"

"You're ruining my life. You're ruining my credit rating."

"I'll take a page from your book—you have the wrong guy."

"I will get the police involved."

"Would you like to use my phone to call them?"

He walked past me and got in line to pay for his copies. I went back behind the counter and waved him past everyone.

"Hey, we were here first!"

I ignored them. If I wanted to hear from an asshole, I'd fart. Abenathy joined me in the corner.

"I'm not the Alfred Botchelko you think I am."

"Is it or is it not your picture on the website?"

I had checked out the website. It was my picture all right, leaning back against my car, looking like I had a mild case of retardation.

"It is, but I was . . ." I dropped my voice even lower. "I was just pretending to be him."

Abenathy shook his head. "How pathetic."

"I know. I'm a Kinko's manager, for God's sake. Put yourself in my shoes for a minute. Botchelko's life is exciting. Mine's pathetic."

"No. That lie's pathetic. Seventy thousand, Mr. Botchelko. Have the bank add it to your mortgage. Use your equity. While your credit rating's still good." And with that, he walked out.

Chapter 23

I was back at Musso and Frank.

If I heard Red correctly, Botchelko came in the first Wednesday of every month. I had Maddy's cell phone in my pocket. Hers still had service for some reason. Getting it out of her iron grip was another matter. Robin told me to bribe her. Maddy was begging for a pair of brown leather pants with a crotch that laced up like running shoes. But the things were so low I'm certain she'd be the first girl at school showing vaginal cleavage. So instead I folded up her new laptop and threatened to take it in the bathroom with me. Her cell was mine for one night only.

I stepped up to that same maitre d'. "Do you expect Alfred Botchelko tonight?"

"I'm sorry?"

"Alfred Botchelko, the writer? Is he coming in tonight? 'Cause I don't know exactly what he looks like, so maybe you could point him out to me."

"I thought you were Alfred Botchelko," he said and grinned. Okay prick, be that way. I'd figure it out for myself.

I sat at the bar. The bartender stepped up.

"What can I get you, sir?"

I didn't know how long a night this was going to be. I wasn't having beer, of course. And there was no way in hell I was having another martini.

“Do you have cider?” I asked.

“Don’t be fucking ridiculous,” he said, then he laughed the mad bray of a hyena.

Actually, he did no such thing. He just said, “No sir.” But it felt like it.

“Then I’ll have a glass of Chianti please.”

“Ruffino?”

“Fine.”

Maddy’s phone beeped. I pulled it out of my pocket. Text message. A number was displayed—818 area code. Read message? it asked. I hit select. “tittie luv. sw’t cheeks.”

That’s all. What the hell did that mean? Maddy had developed rather large breasts over the past year. That had better not be the reference I thought it was. I set the phone on the bar top.

“That’ll be seven dollars, Mr. Botchelko.” I reached into my back pocket, only to look up and find the bartender wasn’t addressing me. He was addressing the man standing next to me. And I felt a squirt of adrenalin zip through my chest. I froze. I needed to do this turn naturally. I needed to glance at him casually. I needed to . . . he walked away.

I watched his back as he crossed the restaurant. He was tall, around six foot, with the slight hunch of a man who spent too much time at a typewriter. His hair was graying and looked as though he grudgingly pushed a comb through it before going out. His pants were beige canvas, a bit wrinkled, and he wore a dark blue sweater. He was heavy. I could see the thickness of his waist. He was carrying a cocktail of some sort, rum or whiskey or something, I didn’t catch the order.

He approached a booth in the corner where two other men sat, both around his age, one wide in a black suit and one tall and heavy. Finally, he turned.

And I got my first look at Alfred Botchelko.

I’m certain to this day I could have picked him out of a police line up. He looked exactly the way I imagined him, a beard flecked with gray, more gray than dark in fact and it could use a trim, hair combed back but it still looked like it needed a wash. His eyes were a bit red, his face puffy and tired. Fifty-four. He looked older than that. And he didn't look so tough either.

Maddy's cell beeped again. I checked the message. "Hon'y box. Luv?" *What the fuck?* Honey box? I felt my scalp constrict. I checked the number. A different one this time. What the hell was going on here? Was my daughter the Heidi Fleiss of Glendale Junior High?

I sipped my wine, fuming. And I tried not to openly stare at Botch. He and his companions didn't order food. They didn't even have menus. The waiter didn't bother them either. He knew.

Now how was I going to do this? I couldn't approach the table. I'd look like a fan and besides, he's supposedly unpredictable. There was no way I could bring up a gambling debt in front of his friends either. Maybe when he came back for another drink I could introduce myself. That was the best plan. So every time someone stepped up to order, I placed my hand on the empty stool next to me. "Sorry. Taken," I said. The bar was crowded. That might help ensure he steps up beside me again.

The cell rang this time. I checked the number. Didn't recognize it. So I answered it in the angriest, giant father voice I could manufacture.

"Yes."

"Who's this?" Male. Teenage deep already. The hormones had him and he wanted my pure-as-driven-snow daughter as a sex toy.

"Who's this?" I said back.

"Can I speak to Maddy?" he asked.

"And who's calling?" I said again.

"Leonard," he said. "Now put Maddy Botchelko on."

Why that little asshole.

"You're talking to *Mister* Botchelko, you punk-ass fuck," I said and from my peripheral vision I saw the bartender snap a look at me. And the man standing next to me, the man I hadn't noticed a moment ago, turned completely to face me. I could feel them both staring. Leonard hung up. But I kept the phone to my ear. I didn't know what to do.

As Botch, very slowly, set an empty sweaty highball glass down on the bar top. He kept staring at me. Then he turned and walked away. I stole a quick glance at him. He heard me all right. And now he was heading to the back of the restaurant. This was my chance.

I hurried to catch up but he slipped with such ease through the bar crowd. People stepped aside for him. Apparently I had accidentally hit my Space Ghost button yet again because nobody stepped aside for me. I lost sight of him by the time I squeezed through. The men's room in Musso and Frank is in the very back, near the kitchen, and next to some old, folding-door phone booths. I glanced around the other dining room. Glanced around back. Even peeked out into the parking lot. No Botch. He had to be in the restroom.

I pushed open the door and was greeted with a warm gust of ancient urine stink. I cringed and stepped inside. There he was, back to me, standing at the urinals. I knew not to step up beside him. I'd get wee-wee freeze and besides, you don't want to shake hands with a man who was only recently shaking the last drops of urine from his penis. I waited by the sink. He didn't sneak a glance over his shoulder. He simply kept pissing. Then he zipped up, flushed, and turned toward me. He started to approach.

"Excuse me, Mr. Botch—"

Suddenly, I was upended and came crashing down on my hip. The fucker foot-swept me.

"Yeah cunt?" he growled and he grabbed me by the shirt and heaved me sprawling across the floor and I slid into a stall. He booted me in the ass—and I mean, he booted me. Not a foot on the cheek but at least three of his toes rammed straight up my asshole. Then he had me again, picking me up and forcing my head into the toilet.

"No stop! Stop!" I was screeching.

"Who's the punk-ass fuck now, huh?"

He kept his hand on the back my neck, forcing my head into the bowl and mere inches from the water, my chest squeezed against the filthy toilet rim. He pulled my wallet out of my pocket, shook the contents on the floor. He snapped up my license.

"Cute. Just like the movie," I heard him say. "You know how

many assholes have seen that movie? I didn't know Starz cable had so many subscribers."

"What movie?"

"*Neighbor's Dog*, pinhead. What other fucking movie? Fake ID obviously. Pa-fucking-thetic."

"It's not fake," I said. "That's my real name." My words were echoing so loudly in the bowl it hurt my ears. How could people not hear this? Why didn't anyone help me?

"I can spot a fake anywhere, Zippy," he said. "I'll just do us both a favor and keep this." And he pocketed my license.

"But I need that."

That's when he punched me. Right in the kidney. I'd never felt pain like that before. I thought I would shit myself. I almost started crying. "I see you again," he warned, "and you'll be lucky if they stretcher you into the emergency room instead of the morgue." Then he brought his mouth next to my ear and roared, "Got that!" And my eardrum thundered into my skull.

He released me. I heard the door squeak open. He was gone.

It took me a minute to get to my feet. My kidney was killing me. My asshole hurt worse. It was throbbing. My ear was ringing. I staggered to the door, pulled it open, only to be met by a phalanx of busboys in green jackets and one waiter in red.

"Leave now and we won't call the police," he said. He pointed like I was being banished from Eden. I left out the back. I never got validated. Parking cost me fifteen dollars.

Chapter 24

I flew American Airlines from LAX to Dallas. Why they couldn't book me on a direct flight to Kansas City, I don't know. The wait was an hour–and-a-half there, and though I've never set foot on Texas soil outside of the airport itself, I still didn't like the place. I saw cowboy hats. I saw big-haired women. I saw big-boned women. And I saw Republicans. Republicans ooze hate with a breezy ease.

On the flight to Kansas, I was still in steerage class. I had a Bloody Mary. Those are hard to screw up. Then I remembered Vodka was made out of grain. Not potatoes. This is America. But I drank it anyway. Kansas City International, an exhaustingly long thing, invites you to leave. I caught a small commuter plane to Topeka.

When I got to the Radisson, they told me I didn't have a room. Instead, I had a message. Go straight to the conference center. I caught a cab there. The conference was in yet another hotel, the Delta, which made no sense to me. I only had my wheeled carry-on but I was still annoyed. I wanted to check in, maybe have a glass of wine, maybe just lie on the bed and stare at the ceiling and summon up the courage to step out there once again and continue faking enthusiasm for my life.

There was another message for me at the sign-in table. "You're expected in Room 1804. Brenda Banishee, Walt Powell, Dave Badger."

I'd met Walt Powell before. He was the bushy-eyebrowed guy who wanted to go to a strip club called Bob's Jumbo Clown Room the last time he was in LA. I replied, like fuck I'm going there. So I don't think we really connected.

I saw Brenda Banishee once. She's one of those women who only has sex with men on a higher pay scale. She always wore short skirts, she talked fast, and she shook hands like a man.

I didn't know who Dave Badger was.

Standing outside Room 1804, I realized there was a stain on the lapel of my sport coat. It looked like bird shit. How does a bird shit on you on a plane? I was picking frantically at it when Brenda pulled open the door.

"Come on in, William," she said. Not a smile, nothing. Something was up. Until that very second I was still convinced they had finally realized their oversight about not having me facilitate a group exercise and they were going to beg me for forgiveness because they needed me to fill in. Clearly, that wasn't going to be the case.

Their suite had a separate meeting area and Brenda lead me in there. Walt and Dave were already sitting in hard-backed chairs facing the sofa. Walt stood and shook my hand. Dave looked like a redheaded Clint Howard. He didn't bother to stand or even make the effort to pretend to stand by at least uncrossing his legs. He shook my hand without a word. The peach colored sofa was all mine. I took a seat.

"We feel we have a rather serious problem," Brenda said. I knew she would be doing the talking. Her ass wasn't even in the chair yet and she already had the driver's seat.

"What would that be?" I asked.

"You don't know?" she asked back. This was the third-grade math-class moment when Mrs. Devitt knows you don't know the answer—maybe the fact that your hand isn't waving madly in the air like Connie Leith's is a big clue—and now she wants you to squirm. When I was eight, I squirmed. I'm forty-two now and I recently had my head shoved into a toilet William Faulkner once shat in. And they still hadn't cleaned it. I squirm no more. I sat back and crossed my legs.

"I haven't the foggiest," I said and I simply turned to Walt. "What's this about, Walt?"

"Um, well . . ." started Walt, but Brenda jumped back in.

"Is your real name Alfred?" she asked.

Shit. Again. But how bad could this be? "Yes, but I go by my middle name," I said.

"Is Alfred your nom de plume?"

"I know where this is going," I said. "You think I'm the writer, Alfred Botchelko, but—"

"Why do you suppose we'd think that?" she interrupted.

"Be*cause*," I emphasized, struggling to suppress the annoyance in my voice, "I decided recently to start going by my real first name and have unwittingly triggered a chain of events . . ."

"We have some Alfred Botchelko books here," said Brenda and she held them up. She had *Botch*. That was the most autobiographical. Also the hardest one to get.

"He's written a lot of them," I said.

"They're pornography," she said.

"They are literature, I beg to differ. He is recognized around the world as a great poet."

"In Provo, they're porn."

"Either way," I shrugged. "I didn't write them."

She flipped one open. "They're full of sex, drinking—lots of drinking," she amended. "Gambling." Then she held a page face out to me. "Here's a poem about masturbating while watching a twelve-year-old girl skateboard. Would you call that literature?"

"It's not my work, it's his. He's not even a relative. I don't have to defend him."

Brenda looked to Dave. That was his cue. He opened his book now. He showed me the inside cover. "Is that your hand writing?"

I fucking knew, Goddamn how I knew at the very second I put ink to paper I would pay for that one-night-stand impersonation for the rest of my days.

"See, okay—there's an explanation."

"Your picture is also on a web site. Got an explanation for that?"

They wanted me to overreact. They wanted me to storm out, to quit, to raise my voice, to threaten and shout. They were trying to corner me. So I sat back once more and I took a deep breath.

"Have I broken the law?" I asked.

"You've got a beard," said Dave. "Your hair's too long, you're walking around with—what is that—is that bird shit on your lapel?"

Walt finally spoke up. "And we've been informed you have substantial gambling debts."

"Quite simply," said Brenda, "this is not a suitable image for Kinko's management, and certainly not the type of image we would want our corporation to be associated with."

"I'll shave and cut my hair," I said. "Immediately. Once I get a room. Will there be anything else?"

Dave and Walt looked to Brenda. But Brenda was locked on me. She wanted to kill. But her plan to destroy the minion wasn't working. I'd like to think she was even getting a bit turned on by me at this point.

"Kinko's would not be comfortable having the author of these works in their employ," she said again.

"That would mean Kinko's is walking straight into a big first amendment issue here," I said. "You cannot fire me for being a 'respected' author. And I think the lawsuit and subsequent attention this would bring Kinko's is something the corporation could really do without."

Dave and Walt were buckling. I could feel it. They simply wanted to smile now and say, "Just kidding," and we'd all go downstairs and have Mojhitos and laugh and maybe make a couple lewd asides about ol' Brenda Ball Busting Banishee here. But Brenda was saving the best for last. She pulled out a stack of billing duplicates and laid them on the coffee table.

"These are copies for over ninety hours of repair work on the copiers at your branch. Yet not one repairman ever set foot in the place." She let that sink in a moment. I had no smart reply. "That's called pilfering. What would the Bill of Rights say about that . . . *Alfred*?"

"I can . . . explain—"

"Can you? And what about using the public computers for personal Internet use?"

"How did you know about that?"
"Ha!" she shouted. "I was just guessing!"

My flight back was delayed in Dallas. I called Robin at work.
"Star Pord Farts Department."
"Your attitude's coming back."
"Is it?" she said. "Hm. Can't feel a thing."
"Please do not get fired from that job," I said.
"Why?" she asked.
"Because I just got fired from mine."

Chapter 25

People seed their work spaces with little reminders of home. Sometimes there's pictures of wives or girlfriends. Somehow those always feel like they've been framed begrudgingly, maybe by the wife or girlfriend themselves, and set there just in case the "loved-one" pops in without warning. Children are most prevalent, no matter what age. Infants are big, but kids in soccer uniforms, scout uniforms, Halloween costumes, Santa costumes, school pictures, graduation—these are the starting line up. Then there's the drawings the kids make, no matter how blatantly empty of the slightest trace of talent, yet there they are, stick figures, crayon bugs, black ink sun and orange grass. Then the final line of defense, the royal guards—greeting cards. Homemade cards take precedent, mother's day far surpasses father's, birthdays are good. The last items, the wolverines, the resistance fighters of the domestic against the corporate, are the cute gifts. Pocket sized. A shiny brown rock with "Solvang Nov 01" written on it, a dice with "vodka, smoke, valium" on the sides instead of dots, a tiny figurine of Lucy, eyes closed, waiting to be bussed by Sherman undoubtedly.

My desk had nothing.

So there was no reason to go back. I didn't even like my stapler. And it was a gift from my grandmother when I left for college. I had no intention of setting foot in Kinko's ever again as long as I lived. My copying needs were just not that urgent.

But I had to find Abenathy.

I waited at Porto's, ordered a coffee, and jumped my way from one empty table to the next until I finally had one on the sidewalk. Then I finished my coffee. If I got up for a second cup, I'd lose the seat. I sat there a good forty minutes and finally gave in, crossed the street, and waited outside Hallmark, the source of the knickknack Nile. Finally, I took up the benches, waiting.

Just before noon, Abenathy found me. I was reading a discarded *LA Weekly*, pulled it out of the trash when no one was looking, and I glanced up to find him standing before me.

"You sent those books to my employer. Now I'm fired. How am I supposed to pay you back without a job?"

"So you admit the debts are yours?"

"No. They're not. It's your reasoning that makes no sense. It's like sending someone to debtor's prison. How can a debt be paid from prison? You've cut off everything I need to maintain a home and now you've gotten me fired. For what? To what end? Do you know of bums making seventy large a year? I mean, let me in on your secret!"

"You're right."

"I'm right? Of course I'm right. How am I right?"

"Getting you fired doesn't serve my purpose. Which is why I'd never do it."

"Then who did?"

"I don't know."

Abenathy took the concrete barrier next to my bench.

"Don't your books make any residuals?"

"They're not my books, Poindexter. When does that actually sink into your skull?"

"I'll give you three weeks to find a job."

"Give me two to find Botchelko."

"And I'll get your services turned back on."

"Why don't you just get out of my life?"

"I will. For three weeks exactly." And he got up and walked away. I think there was a bounce in his step.

Chapter 26

I followed Beatriz and Donovan to the Ralphs on Central. One day I'm going to run down somebody on that street. And not just for fun. There's something visually confusing about it and I become momentarily blinded, usually at the crosswalk. Beatriz grabbed a noisy cart and went inside and Donovan stayed in the car, put the seat back, closed his eyes, and put on some Tejano tunes. He didn't hear my approach. He didn't hear me crouch down next to his open window.

"Give me his address."

"Hay-soos Creest!" he shouted and bolted upright, smacking his rearview mirror off. "This is how a man gets killed," he said and fumbled under the seat for the mirror. I wasn't sure if he was referring to heart attacks or acts of revenge.

"I need Botchelko's address," I said again.

"I can't give this to you. It would not be right."

"Since when are you the moralist? You stole it off Red's desk."

"Yes. Which is why I have a responsibility not to give it out to fanatics."

"Fanatic? You're the one who came to work at Kinko's in Glendale just because you think I'm Botchelko."

"This I'm not so sure about anymore." He was trying to hang the mirror back up with chewing gum.

"Fine. Let's settle it once and for all. Give me his address and I'll get you a picture of him."

The mirror was barely holding. He flicked off his radio.

"Autographed," I added.

He thought about this a moment, finger pressed to his chin. There was something about Donovan that made you want to pull his hair.

"I won't give you his address. But—" and he held up that finger "—I will take you to his address."

With that, the rear view mirror clattered to the floor again. I am clueless as to how his suggestion was better.

Chapter 27

I'd never spent much time in San Pedro. Now I knew why. For a coastal spot, it didn't have that arrogant-slash-laid-back coastal feel. This felt more like East LA built on an ocean-size sewer. Or Compton with a shore line. Some streets and stores tried for that quaint Cannery Row décor, but it had the bet-hedging stink of Disney's California Adventure.

Donovan knew the way without a hesitant moment. We exited off the 110, made a right and a left into a hilly residential neighborhood, then straight up a steep street where he pulled over about halfway up the block and jerked on the e-brake.

He pointed to a house with a long driveway set back off the street. It had a high, thick hedge growing all the way around it, but you could still see the front door from here. It wasn't a bad place—bigger than mine, Spanish style, with a separate stairway that led to quarters above the garage. I wasn't sure what I expected, but I didn't expect this. It looked so . . . domestic.

Donovan pulled out a green thermos. He dug out a bag of Doritos and a can of sour cream Pringles. He put his seat back, flicked on the radio to a Spanish music station. Finally, he pulled out a pair of binoculars. And he settled in, sipping coffee, plucking chips and chewing each slowly and thoroughly, binoculars pressed to his eyes. Either he had seen a lot of cop shows. Or he had done this before.

Once again, I wanted a smoke. Also some wine would be nice.

Nothing kills time like drinking wine. Maybe because the mind starts to wander, maybe because anxiety slowly evaporates. Either way, if you're bored at four, crack a bottle of red and you won't be bored by five.

I remember one night when Maddy was only a baby, not even walking yet, maybe eight or nine months old, and Robin went out with her sister to the movies. I put Maddy to bed and I made a drink. I think it was Crown Royal with ice, but that was long before my wheat allergies hit. I put on the B-52's "Roam." And I turned the lights off. And I struggled to recapture that time in college, that dead zone on Friday or Saturday nights while getting ready to go out, maybe ironing a pair of pants or blow drying hair, when the music would come on the ghetto blaster. The Police or maybe Men at Work. And suddenly we'd all be drinking and dancing together. Six men slugging longneck Buds or Gala Keg wine and bouncing around a basement suite in socks and underwear. It was usually the best part of the evening.

So I tried to do that one last time. I tried to just drink and dance and wring that zeal, pry that exuberance, that anxious joy from my limbs and ears and mouth as though by going through the motions, the music, the dance, the drink, then that sleeping cell would somehow reawaken.

But it was clumsy and awkward and my limbs were heavy as sod and I wound up sitting on the floor in the dark. I hadn't cried in years and wouldn't cry that night either. I didn't cry again until my parents suddenly and explicably started threatening divorce, all their long-held resentments suddenly boiling to the surface, and I drove up to Lancaster and instead of refereeing a truce, I laid my head on their kitchen table. And wept. My mother stroked my hair. My father said nothing at all. But the fighting suddenly stopped as quickly as it had started.

I desperately wanted to cry in that living room that night. Here was yet another thing from my past I never realized I'd miss. That simmering youth, kindergartners with pubic hair and booze. I longed for that kid like a dead friend. When Robin's headlights swept the wall, I rushed down the hall and jumped into bed. So I wouldn't have to explain the bewildered emptiness in my eyes.

"Cheep?" Donovan said. He poked me with the Pringle can. I

shook my head. “Dorito?” he asked and shook the bag. I shook my head again. “Well, you can’t have any coffee ’cause I don’ have enough.” And he actually drew the cup back like I was going to snatch it out of his hand.

“Did I ask for fucking coffee?” I said.

“Well, you sit there like a hump on a dog. You don’ bring nothing. You think he’s going to invite us in and make us ranchos huevos?”

“Don’t worry about me. I’m fine.”

We were quiet again. There was no way to tell if anyone was home. The front light was still on. But the curtains were pulled. Robin and I must be pretty Dutch that way. I don’t remember ever pulling the curtains in any room, ever.

“Randy sent the books to Provo,” said Donovan suddenly.

“What books?”

“What books? Why are we here? His books is what books.”

“Why would Randy do that?” I asked.

Donovan shrugged.

“Why didn’t you tell me this before?”

“I warn you,” he said. “I warn you long ago ’bout heem. And what do you do? You tell this man more and more, you confide in heem. You shoot yourself in the foots. Both barrels.” Then Donovan acted out shooting himself in the temple. Clearly metaphors weren’t his strength.

“The billing orders too? And the website?”

But Donovan didn’t answer. Instead he pointed to Botchelko’s house and snapped up his binoculars. A mailman was approaching the front door. He had a bundle of letters bound by elastic. He rang the bell. My heart picked up a beat. I don’t know why. He rang the bell again. Then the door opened. The mailman smiled. A hand came out, took the bundle, signed something. And the mailman left. That was it. But now we knew someone was home.

“I’m going to knock on the door,” I said.

“Don be crazy!” said Donovan and he grabbed my arm. He had a damn strong grip for a little guy.

"Why is that crazy? It's just knocking."

"You know what he's like." Actually, I knew exactly what he was like. He shoved my head in a toilet. And punched my favorite kidney. What was I thinking? I had no plan. What did I actually think was going to happen just sitting outside this house? That he'd see me? That he'd recognize me? That he'd invite me in and make me rancho yo-yos or whatever the fuck they were called?

Donovan grabbed my arm again. Which made me fart a bit.

"Would you stop doing that!" I yelled. But Donovan was pointing like a Mexican retriever again. Another man was approaching Botchelko's front door. He had two big bags, heavy bags by the looks of it. He set them down on the steps and rang the bell. He rang again. He knocked. And then we saw him.

Botch.

He was creeping along the side of the house, wearing a tee-shirt and sweats, slipping up on the front door. He put his hand to his mouth and called out. I snapped off the radio, but we missed it. Botch was already scurrying away as the delivery guy stepped back from the door, frowning, and headed around the back of the house. And the very moment he did, the front door swung opened and someone grabbed both bags, pulled them inside, and shut the door again.

"That happened last time," said Donovan. "Thas his treek. You think they learn."

The delivery man returned, mumbling and shaking his head. Then he noticed the bags were gone. He banged on the door and shouted and banged some more and finally, futilely, he kicked the door once and headed back down the driveway. He climbed into a little pink Ford Fiesta, Velvet Rope Liquors written on the door. And then he just sat there, glaring at Botchelko's front door. Eventually he spotted us. Two cars, three men, all staring at Botchelko's house. So he hopped out and came marching over to us. He tapped on my window. I rolled it down.

"He reep you off too?"

"Sort of, yeah," I said.

"That fucker! I jes start this job. Two hunerd dollars booze he take from me. Is bullshit!"

"You should call the police," I said.

"No." He was an illegal immigrant. Illegal immigrants never call the cops. Thieves know this. "What you deliver?" he asked me.

"What did we deliver?" I repeated.

"Yeah. What he steal from you?"

I thought about it. "A fridge," I said.

"A freedge?" he repeated and his eyebrows popped up. He looked back to the house with new respect.

"And he pushed his head in a toilet," offered Donovan.

The delivery guy seemed a little less angry suddenly. "Maybe I go," he said and started walking away. "Hey, when you call police? Send them to Velveet Rope. Hokay? Ask for Victor."

"Your name's Victor?"

"No," he said. He jumped in his car and we watched as he drove away. When we looked back to the house, there he was again, Botchelko, standing in full view in his front window. The curtains were pulled back. He was openly glaring at us.

"Same as last time," said Donovan. "He stands there now and stares like this."

"What do we do?"

"Is stakeout. We do nothing. We watch."

"It's not a stakeout."

"What is it then?"

I hadn't really thought about it. "Okay, it's a stakeout." I looked back to Botchelko. He could really glare, I'll give him that. I was growing uncomfortable. Should I wave? Would he recognize me? What if he came out and approached the car? I'd have to be a man about this sometime. Maybe that would be for the best. Though the mere thought conjured up one heck of a gas bubble that burbled its way through a few dozen yards of my intestinal mass. I don't know what was in those gas bubbles, but they tended to dissolve fecal matter like Drano. Then Donovan grabbed my arm again. This time I almost had a full-blown brown trouser and I grabbed my asshole in panic.

"Stop fucking doing that! Christ man! Don't you know about my guts? I'm a fucking crap merchant here and you're not helping matters!"

But Donovan didn't say a word. He just pointed with his thumb out the back window. I turned to look. A cop car. And two cops stepping out.

"Same as last time," said Donovan.

Chapter 28

Randy sent me a copy of "Botch." Out of guilt, I'm sure. Or maybe just to goad me. I wonder where he got it, the piece of shit. Probably the same copy he lent to Brenda Berserk Banishee.

I started reading it immediately.

In it, Botchelko uses his real name. For the first and only time. His wife's name is Natalie. His daughter, only twelve, is Anne. Natalie leaves Botch because of his drinking. Botch takes his doctor's advice and rents a cabin up in Big Bear, right on the lake, and he attempts to straighten himself out. In the process, he starts dating a college girl. That doesn't work out. He meets a local guy in a bar. They fistfight and become best friends and it turns out the guy is struggling with his sexuality. He's closet gay. Botch also hangs around with a retired carpenter who lives in the cabin next door. They drink and even go fishing once and he tells Botch jokes and Botch accidentally kills his rabbit. The gay guy, Wally, eventually drowns himself in the lake. This tears Botch up and he goes on the wagon instead of a bender, and at the end he asks his wife and daughter to join him at the cabin. His wife tells him she'll send the daughter, but she's not sure if she'll come too. The last paragraph is Botch waiting, flowers in hand, as the bus doors hiss open. He leaves it at that.

How's that sound? Odd, right? For Botchelko. It had a bit of a plot. And a happy ending. Sort of. It was a different publisher too and instead of cardboard stock two-color cover, they used glossy with a five-color spread. You don't have to be in the paper business to know that's a gilded lily. Still no photo of Botchelko though. At least he stuck to his guns there. But I can't explain why the book unnerved me. It was readable and funny and acerbic. Vintage Botchelko. But it felt as though he wrote it—dare I say—sober? Going by that bag of booze he had delivered the other day, he Humpty Dumptied off that wagon long ago.

Bags of booze. Wife leaves him because of booze. Booze is his Achilles heel. In fact, in the book, the only reason he first endures his neighbor's company is because the old guy keeps showing up with beer. But I'm sure lots of fans have shown up on his doorstep bearing liquor and still got chased away. But how many showed up with two bags of liquor? Not fans, that's for sure. Only a liquor store order would work. Which means he'd have to place the order himself. I knew I couldn't intercept a call. But I could intercept an order.

I called Velvet Rope Liquor in San Pedro.

"Can I speak to Victor please?" I heard them shouting around the store. Victor! Victor!

Finally a different guy came on. "Who's calling?"

"This is Alfred Botchelko's accountant. I'm calling about his outstanding debt at your—"

"Speaking. This is Victor. You're his what? His accountant?"

"Yeah, accountant."

"Your client, that cockbitin' prick, has ripped me off twice. Once with a rubber check that went bouncin' around this shop like fuckin' Super Chicken. And the second time he pulls some trick on my new delivery guy, who's a bit thick, granted, but he steals the stuff from him, actually beats the guy up and steals all the fuckin' liquor."

"Um, I don't think that's the way—"

"And for that alone your fuckin' client deserves a kick right in the cum factory."

"Listen. Maybe I can collect what he owes you."

"Good. It's 400 and change. I'll get the exact figure. Hey, Vatos!

Yeah you, asesino. That Botchelko cunt, what's his outstanding? Yeah, I'm talkin to you, mama la ping, can't you fucking hear? Look it up you pinche tortuga!"

"I have an idea."

"You got employees?"

"Me? Uh, no."

"No employees? You a one-man show?"

"That's right."

"Lucky cunt. Ten years ago I couldn't speak Spanish. Now look at me, gibbering spic like a Matador. You got an idea, you say? Great, I love ideas. What's your idea?"

"The next time he places an order . . ."

"He ain't placin' anymore orders here brother. Hey, *cabron*! What the fuck? Numbers don't change when you wade across the Rio Grande, fanocchio. What's taking so long?"

"Just hear me out, please. The next time he places an order . . . wait! . . . just call me. I'll swing by, I'll pay for the order myself. Then I'll deliver it. And maybe I can get the rest of your money for you."

"What's with the fuckin' 'Spy Kids' routine? Why don't you just pay his tab yourself?"

"Because he owes me money too."

"Lovely. Reassuring to know you fuckin CPAs are as dumb as the rest of us. Okay, gimme your number, chucho. Oh shit, sorry. Didn't mean the name calling. Christ I'm gettin' bad. Can't even ask my fuckin' wife to get me a roll of shit paper without calling her a cocksucker. What's happened to me? I used to be nice. Okay baboso, what's your number?"

Chapter 29

I wore a tee-shirt and jeans and a dark blue Kinko's baseball cap. I figured that's what a delivery guy would wear. At Kinko's, of course, we had a uniform to go with the cap. Actually, it was just a shirt and we didn't call it a uniform, we called it "blues." As in, "Where's your blues?" You weren't supposed to ever work without it, but I was lenient on that. Me, I always wore a dress shirt and tie. But I was boss and that was a rule I made for myself. Carlos wore his blues only half the time. I never said anything because, as I recall, he was "fixing" copiers and saving my branch a ton of money. I don't remember what Randy wore. That bag of shit.

Botchelko ordered two bottles of Stoli, the one–and-a-half liter size, another big bottle of Seagrams, and two fifths of Myers. Three bottles of Aussie red, all Yellowtail Shiraz, two bottles of Oxford Landing Chardonnay—for the ladies, I assumed—and one can of Coke. Just one. Diet. No caffeine. That I didn't understand.

One hundred and seventy six dollars total. I paid cash to a tall, skinny Mexican kid wearing a doo-rag.

"You Victor?"

"Victor? No. Victor, he's in the hospital."

"What happened?"

The kid shrugged, slowly, closed his eyes, frowned. "Victor, he walks into a wall. Maybe the wall's name is Hiemy. Not asesino. Not fanocchio. Not mama la ping." He shrugged that same slow shrug again. "People walk into walls alla time."

Chapter 30

They let me use the Velvet Rope Fiesta. Here was a car that made a man appreciate walking. I parked right in Botchelko's driveway. I left both doors unlocked, pulled on the e-brake. I wanted to insure a quick escape if things got ugly. In other words, if he chased me. The house looked the same as last time, front light on, curtains pulled. I couldn't tell if anybody was watching my approach. There was no movement behind the curtains.

I stepped up to the front door. My heart instantly started pounding against my rib cage. I couldn't catch my breath. I could hear the bottles clattering as I struggled to suppress the shudders. This was madness. This wasn't worth it. Maybe I should just get another job and pay the seventy thou myself. That thought, of course, was true madness. I got myself into this. I had destroyed my own life, not Botchelko. And now I had to get myself out.

I rang the bell. I waited. Nothing. I rang it again. Still nothing. No movement, no sound. I was expecting him to call from the side of the house. At first I planned to take the bag with me. But then I thought, no. Leave the bag on the steps like he expects, then simply step aside and hide, make it look like I've gone around back, only to step front and center when he pulls the door open.

I rang again. Still no movement. Did he leave? Did I take too long? The guy at Velvet Rope said they told him to expect delivery at one. It was quarter after.

I called out. "Helloooo?" I knocked. "Helloooo?" Not a sound. I bent and pushed his mail flap in, tried to peer inside. “Anybody home?”

And then something poked my asshole.

I glanced back.

A dog had his nose jammed between the twins. Not just any dog. A black dog. A big black dog.

A Rottweiler.

My sphincter pinched tight so fast I could have bent rebar. My balls cinched instinctively up against my crotch.

And a deep phlegmy growl rumbled through the dog’s throat.

“Easy.”

I stood. Slowly. I raised my hands as though it was a stick-up. The growling grew deeper. His lips rippled back from his teeth.

Where did this thing come from? I never saw it yesterday. I reached slowly down for the bag. He barked. I threw my hands in the air again.

“Easy now.”

I was pressed flat against the door. I rang and rang the doorbell. But nobody. I was screwed. I had to get to the car. I took a step down. Then another. He turned like I was magnetic north, chest rumbling. He gulped and lapped at his own drool and a long string of thick saliva flipped right across his eye. And still he growled. I stepped around him. The car was behind me now. If I bolted, I was dead. I glanced back at it and he barked and I jumped and he barked again and feigned a lunge. I reached up, lifted my hat like I was saying howdy. Then I slowly, ever so carefully, held it out to him. He immediately snapped it out of my hand and shook it like a cat.

And I bolted.

I ran for the passenger side. I jerked open the door, leaped inside and slammed the door just as his body hammered against it. The thing went wild, pawing at the window, trying to bite it, his teeth clacking against it and slobber smearing across the glass. But fuck him. Fuck that animal. I was safe. And I laughed with the glorious relief of gorgeous life reprieved and I pointed at the dog, taunted it.

“How ’bout now, you piece of shit, huh? How ’bout now!”

I glanced to the door. The bag of booze was gone.

Motherfucker.

He got me. The bastard got me. He won again. I just got screwed and it was always the same guy doing the screwing. And then I saw him. Standing in his front window. This time he was doubled over with laughter. Then he reached into that bag, pulled out a bottle, cracked it, and took a big slug, the vodka dribbling down his cheeks, grinning madly.

That's it. No way. Not again. Not this time.

I looked around the car for a weapon. The only thing that could possibly take care of this dog was a Boss twelve-gauge. Even a monkey wrench wouldn't stop him. There was a frayed length of nylon rope. The cut off end of a hockey stick. A spool of wire. An old roll of duct tape. All right, this was my "Apollo 13." How to make that, fit into that, using only this?

I rolled the window down a bit, just enough to give the dog false hope. Of course he immediately tried to jam his face inside. Only the tip of his nose got in and he sprayed me with a blast of snot. Why would God create an animal like this? What was the reasoning behind it? I rolled the window down a bit more. He got his entire snout inside now. He tried to bark but couldn't get his mouth open wide enough. Good boy. I ripped off a long stretch of duct tape. I got it in position just under his jaw. I readied myself, took a breath, counted: one, two, three—and I wrapped it around his snout, slamming his jaw shut tight. The dumb thing didn't even react. I thought it would bolt, lunge backwards, howl. But it only had one thing on its mind. Eating me.

I grabbed the roll and wrapped tape around and around his snout. Finally he got the picture. He jerked his head out. I could actually see the confusion in his big, stupid brown eyes. He brought one paw up to his snout and rubbed. Then he just sat there and looked at me. He whined.

Chapter 31

"I know you're in there and I've got your dog!" I screamed through the mail slot. "I've got your fucking dog! He's not so tough now!"

Botchelko was hiding again.

"And I'm taking it to the pound!" I shouted. "I'm removing his collar. And I'm taking him to the pound. And I'm having him put down! Do you hear me? I'm having him—"

"Okay, shut the fuck up."

I saw his pant legs approach. Then the door swung open. And there he stood. Botchelko. Flesh gray, beard gray, greasy hair sticking up, eyes Tabasco red. And I stood defiantly before him with a big, sweet dog sitting at my feet, snout muzzled with shiny duct tape, and a yellow nylon rope tied to his collar.

"I'll give you this," said Botchelko. "You're the toughest delivery guy yet."

"I'm flattered."

"What do I owe ya?"

"Seventy thousand dollars," I said. "Seventy thousand fucking dollars, that's how much you owe me."

Botchelko didn't say a word. But he clearly recognized the dollar amount. "You appear to be out of your mind," he finally said.

"Stand aside. Stand aside, I'm coming in."

"That fucking dog's not coming in here."

"He's your dog."

"He's the neighbor's mutt. I just borrow it now and then."

"Your neighbor's going to be damned pissed off if his dog is put down."

"Her dog."

"Whatever."

We stood there in silence, Botchelko blocking the way. I was panting, red faced, neck steaming with sweat.

"Are you letting me in or what?"

He stepped aside. I led the dog in. I gave the living room a quick once over.

Tasteful. Shockingly. A big white sofa and loveseat. Cherry wood coffee table and end tables. A leather mission chair and matching stool.

"I'm a little short on cash," he said and he grabbed a checkbook and immediately started scribbling in it.

"I don't want one of those rubber chickens," I said. "I came here to talk. That's all."

And slowly Botchelko lowered the checkbook as it dawned on him. "I know you," he said. That was all he had to say. His eyes turned hard and his jaw set. I stopped myself from taking a step back. "Looking for your driver's license?" he asked.

"That happens to be my real name. I was born Alfred William Botchelko. I was named after my grandfather. But the man hated me and I hated him. So I started going by William. And that just became my name. It was only when I decided to go back to my real name that I got into all this trouble."

"I get the feeling you think your problems should interest me."

"Because they're your problems. I inherited them. I got fired from my job. Creditors are after me. I'm broke. All because the man that holds your gambling debts thinks I'm you."

Slowly, a smile crept across Botchelko's face. He plopped down in a chair. He grabbed a cigarette and lit up. "Let me see if I have this straight," he said. "My gambling debts are now your gambling debts?"

"Correct."

"I am no longer seventy large in the hole? I'm flush?"

"No. You're still seventy large in the hole."

"How you figure?"

"Because it's your debt. I don't gamble. Abenathy thinks I'm you and he's ruining me."

"I don't know any Abenathy."

"Wanna meet him?"

"No thank you."

Botchelko reached down and grabbed the vodka. He poured a couple fingers in a dirty wine glass. He was still grinning, eyes twinkling.

"So you can see the situation I'm in," I said.

"Oh, I feel for ya. I was there once myself."

"You're still there."

"Mm-mm," he said and shook his head.

"Mr. Botchelko . . ."

"My friends call me Botch."

"Okay—Botch . . ."

"You're not my fuckin' friend."

"Mister Botchelko . . ."

"How come they never called you Botch?"

"I don't know," I said. "I've wondered that myself."

"Seems like a natural sort of nickname, don't you think?"

"It does now."

"Nicknames are a term of endearment," he said. "Does no one find you endearing?"

"Can we—just discuss the debt, please?"

Botch smoked thoughtfully for a moment. He did a French inhale. Then he blew two perfect smoke rings. No one ever plays with their cigarette smoke anymore. Oddly, that dated him.

"Let me ask you a couple questions . . . Mr. Botchelko," he said and he chuckled with the absurdity of interviewing himself. "You were at Musso and Frank the other night. Correct?"

"Looking for you."

“That’s not how I understand it. As I understand it, you were claiming to be me.”

“I was using my own name.”

“Were those your books you were signing?”

Man, weren’t they a bunch of girls down there at Musso and Frank? Now how to answer this? It’s not like I didn’t know it was coming, but contrition seemed the only recourse.

“I made a mistake.”

“I’ll fucking say you did, Botchy-boy. Look at your hair, your fucking beard. Who you bullshittin’, standing there with a dog that almost nibbled yer prick off.”

“Your debt—”

“Who’s picture is that on my fuckin website?”

“You Google yourself?” I gasped.

“Everybody Googles themselves, Zippy,” he said and suddenly he whistled. Loud. And I jumped. And the dog bolted from my grip and ran straight to him. “Atta boy,” he said and he crouched on the floor to pet him. “Good dog.” Then Botchelko started to unwind the duct tape. Slowly. As he did so, he fixed his gaze on me. “If I was you—Alfred—I’d get my pink ass outta here while I still had one.”

Chapter 32

"That's his place right there."

But Abenathy sat in the passenger seat and stared at me instead.

"You're not even looking." I pointed.

He continued to stare at me.

"Do you have a job yet, Mr. Botchelko?"

"No."

"Have you been looking for a job, Mr. Botchelko?"

"No."

"Do you want me to turn up the heat again, Mr. Botchelko?"

"He admitted those are his gambling debts. I've done all the footwork. I found him for you."

"Soon I won't need to manipulate your other creditors. They'll be coming after you all on their own. You have a mortgage, you have a car payment, everyday bills, insurance, a daughter in school . . . and only one measly income."

"I'm collecting unemployment."

"They pay seventy grand now?"

I saw the curtains rustle across the street. He was watching. "I don't deserve this," I said.

"There's Gamblers Anonymous."

"I. Don't. Gamble."

"You're always a gambler. It's like alcoholism. The first step is admitting it."

"Listen to me. I don't play board games. I hate bingo. I wouldn't play solitaire if I was left alone on an island with a deck of cards for twenty years. I'm bored watching a horse in a parade, let alone one in a race. To me, a Seabiscuit is a salty fucking cracker. If you told me you spent the evening with a one-armed bandit, I'd be amazed to learn there's handicapped hold-up men. When I think of Vegas, I imagine tigers that eat gender-questionable performers. I've never even owned fuzzy dice. I don't flip coins. Heads or tails is hooker shop-talk to me. I've never bought a lottery ticket in my life. I don't know what rolling snake eyes means, let alone to be behind the eight ball. My brother had to explain the ending of *The Sting* to me. So what do I have to do to convince you those are not my gambling debts?"

Abenathy sat there a moment thinking. "I bet you twenty bucks I can prove you're a gambler," he said.

"You're on."

Chapter 33

I was lying in bed, listening to Robin snore like a Bonobo ape in heat, when the phone rang. We never used to have a phone in our room. Until Maddy turned thirteen. Suddenly, a phone in the bedroom seemed like a good idea. I'd been thinking about Maddy while lying there. She'd come in late again. I said nothing. She was starting to intimidate me. And I was sick to death of confrontation. If letting Maddy's behavior slide gave me momentary reprieve, I'd take it. I was also a little worried about Robin. She seemed to have curtailed her drinking, which was good. But she was developing an increasingly pronounced lisp. Or not a lisp. A sibilance. Like Holly Hunter.

That's when the phone rang. Which made me bolt upright like a punch to the belly. I hate the phone ringing after 8 p.m. It sounded like someone kicking at the door. Anybody who wants in that badly can only do you harm. But when it rings after ten, I find myself somewhere between terrified and enraged. I snapped it up, fumbled with it, hit the big, glowing talk button.

"Hello?"

"This Botchelko?"

"Yeah."

"It's Botchelko."

"I just said yes."

"No. It's Botchelko. Calling."

"Botch?"

"What did I tell you about calling me Botch?"

"Only your friends call you Botch."

"That's right."

"Then I guess nobody calls you Botch."

"Impersonates comedians and writers. What a fucking guy."

"How'd you get my number?"

"You still wanna resolve this thing or what?"

"How did you get my number?"

"I've got your driver's license, dick-lick. And you're in the book. Now you wanna resolve this thing or what?"

"Of course I do."

"Good. Maybe we can help each other out. You busy tomorrow?"

"I'm unemployed."

"Feels good, doesn't it? Now meet me at my place. You need the address? Or you have it memorized by now?"

"I think I can find it."

I hung up.

"Was that Maddy?" whispered Robin.

"Maddy's in bed," I said.

"Did you have a talk with her?"

"Yes."

"Good. Girls love their daddies." And she turned away and fell back asleep.

Chapter 34

He was waiting at the end of his driveway, smoking a thin cigarillo. He was wearing a buttoned white long-sleeve shirt, his belly straining against it, gray slacks, and what looked like Doc Martens. Which seemed odd. He'd run a comb through his hair but there was still a tuft sticking up in the back. His face and eyes were swollen with sleep or booze or both. I pulled up and he climbed in.

"Funny, but I don't like the name Alfred either," he said. "Everyone calls me Botch. Not just friends. I was fucking with ya. Mind if I smoke?"

"No."

We sat there.

"What are ya waitin' for?" he asked.

"Where are we going?" I asked back.

"Okay, here's the plan. I gotta climb out of this hole, right? I climb out, you climb out with me. We both get our lives back."

"It's what I've been saying all along."

"Let's start with Velvet Rope Liquor."

"I've got a debt collector destroying my life," I said. "I don't care about your liquor bill."

"We'll just start there. They've brought the cops in, see? So I need to get them off my back first. Okay?"

"Why am I here?"

"You know them. You can negotiate. Tell them I'll make payments if they call the cops off. Then we'll talk to your guy."

It was a start.

I parked in the Velvet Rope Liquor lot next to the pink Fiesta.

"Tell them a hundred bucks a month," said Botchelko.

"You're not coming in?"

"Cops. Have you forgotten? Christ, you upstanding fuckers think cops are your friends. I'll wait right here. If they agree, come out and get me. Does this cigarette lighter work?"

I went inside. Victor was behind the counter. I knew it was him because his eye was purple and swollen shut and his lip was stretched tight as though stung by bees and his right arm was in a cast strapped tight to his barrel chest.

"You Botchelko?" he asked.

"You Victor?"

"That's right."

"I heard about what happened to you."

"Dangerous city," he said.

"One of your own employees, too."

He frowned. "What the fuck are you talkin about? I was mugged. I was attacked from behind. Chickenshit motherfucker. My employees love me, puta. Don't start trash talkin. They owe me. I give them work, they rent from me. They'd give me their first born if I actually knew what to do with another fucking greaser."

"But I heard Hiemy attacked you."

"Hiemy? I sent that fucker back across the Rio weeks ago. If I say I'm deporting, I deport. You got my money?"

"No. He didn't give it to me."

"He? Who's he?"

"Botchelko."

"You're Botchelko."

"I'm the other Botchelko. The Botchelko with the liquor debt asked me to come in and negotiate for him."

Victor just stared at me. He slowly shook his head. "You got more scams than anyone I've ever met in ten years in this business. And that's sayin' something."

"No, no—"

He listed them off his fingers. "You do the back-of-the-house gag. The rubber check gag. The deliver-to-the-neighbors gag. The I'm Botchelko's accountant gag. The killer dog gag . . ."

"Wait a minute. That was done to me."

He called out to that same tall skinny kid. "Hey fanocchio, this the guy who came in before?"

The kid peeked over a shelf. He took a look at me. He nodded.

"His dog bite the seat out of your pants?"

The kid nodded.

"He almost lost a nut, you know? Tooth punctured his sack. Shoulda heard the poor fucker scream when I splashed the rubbing alcohol on his tool bag. And now you have the fucking hide to come waltzing in here, look me straight in the eyes . . ."

"Eye."

". . . and lie to my fucking face."

"The real Botchelko is right outside."

Then Victor held up my driver's license. "This you?"

"Where'd you get that?"

He banged on the wall. A door pushed open. And out stepped two cops. They quickly moved to either side of me. One of them took the license from Victor.

"If it isn't our little boy trouble," he said.

"No wait. The real Botchelko wants to clear this up."

The second cop flipped open his pad. "According to our records, you've done six months for assault in County, you've got three DUIs . . ."

"We can clear this up right now."

". . . nine domestic disturbance calls, five drunk and disorderlies . . ."

"None of these are mine."

". . . a loitering warning right here in San Pedro . . ."

"Oh, that one's mine."

". . . a theft report in Glendale involving your wife and stemware . . ."

". . . mine again."

"And now theft and assault with a deadly weapon. The weapon being a . . ." he checked his pad again. "Rottweiler." He closed it up. And the first cop pulled out the handcuffs.

"Okay wait! Wait!"

They waited.

"He's right outside," I said. "In my car. Let's just step out there. One second. And you'll have your man."

Victor joined us. The four of us marched out the door. But as we approached the lot, a sickening feeling washed down me. No way. There's no way he played me again.

There was my car. In the lot.

Empty.

"Shit," I said. They handcuffed me.

Chapter 35

Whenever I was lost in an airport, trying to find a gate, trying to find baggage return, trying to decipher the departure monitors while looking up at the arrivals, I would say aloud, "What do the stupid people do?" Then one day it struck me.

I was one of the stupid people.

Botch taught me a gambling expression: If you can't pick out the sucker at the table, the sucker's you.

I was once a Kinko's manager. Twice a year I went to employee business conferences. I was facilitator at some. Randy was my best friend and Carlos my best employee. I had a little girl who put on plays in the living room. And charged us a dollar apiece. She hated peas so much she'd dry-heave and she once marched out on a play date because she said her dad was the smartest dad in the world and her friend held an opposing opinion. My wife was a happy person. She used to trim her own hair because she was intimidated by her hair stylist. She went to the gym once every two or three months and she made all the dinners but Sunday's. She was assistant soccer coach, which meant she gathered all the balls and orange cones, and she made Maddy's Halloween costumes every October from birth till she was twelve. Once, when we drank too many margaritas at Don Cucos, we came home and had anal sex.

I think.

My biggest problem then was being diagnosed with Celiac.
Then Maddy got a bra. Robin got a job.
And I Googled myself.

Chapter 36

Robin drew an advance on our Visa and gave it to Victor. In exchange, he temporarily suspended the charges. Then we drove back down to San Pedro and picked up my Accord. I didn't swing by Botchelko's house. I didn't have to. Because Victor also looked up Botchelko's number off his call display. He gave it to me. I called when we got home.

"Leave a message," was all his curt little machine said.

"Here's my message, you shit-eating prick. I have, as of this very minute, officially become Alfred Botchelko, writer-slash-alcoholic-slash-con man. Tomorrow I'm giving an interview to *LA Weekly*. I'm announcing my return to public readings. That's right. Public readings. And I'm charging for those readings and I'm going to puke up some of your insipid drunken caterwauling. I think you call them poems. And then I'm going to throw in some of my own. One's called, 'I'm a Lonely Fat Motherfucker Who Doesn't Bathe.' They can sound like crap, it doesn't matter, because who can tell the difference between your crap and my crap? Then I'm announcing my new book. Yeah you heard me. I'm writing a book. It's going to be called *Pucker Up*. I don't know why *Pucker Up*. I just like the sound of it. It's about this guy who Googles his real name and discovers there's a famous underground writer with the same name—only to get stuck with the famous fucker's debts. How's that sound for a story, huh? Painfully fucking real, I'd say. Well write what you know. It's all in the details, you fat piece of shit. I'll be peddling that to the publishers. Oh, and one more thing. I'm posting your address on the Botchelko web page. Which means your lunatic fans—excuse me, I mean your adoring public—will be gathering on your front lawn before midnight."

Finally, I took a breath.

"Or . . . you meet me at Musso and Frank. Tonight."

And at that very moment he snapped up the phone.

"Farmer's Market. Tomorrow. Near the bar." And he hung up.

Part II

"Men don't make passes
at women with fat asses."
Conversely
"Women don't make passes
at men who pass gases."

—Alfred Botchelko

Chapter 37

"You surprise me."

"Thank you."

"That wasn't a compliment."

"What are you going to do, stick my head in a toilet again? I'll scream like a girl if you so much as raise a finger to me."

"Lower your fucking voice."

We were in the old Farmer's Market. If you're from LA, you only go to the old part. "The Grove" was for the rest. I even found parking in the old lot and not the behemoth. Botch was already at the 326 Bar. When you say, meet at the bar, that's the one you mean. Not the new one at the other end. But we moved anyway. It was too noisy. We found a table in between the Crepe Company and Loteria. I pulled up a chair. I sat there for an easy two minutes without uttering a sound. I was going to force him to speak first. He did.

"What are you drinking?"

"What do you recommend?"

"Doesn't matter. You're buying."

"I'm not buying. You're buying."

"I'm skint."

"So am I."

"Beer or wine?"

"No beer. I'm gluten intolerant."

"You're what?"

"Celiac disease. I can't eat grains."

"Did you think I was going to order you a sack of oats or something?"

"Red wine," I said. He got up. "A merlot," I added but I don't think he heard me.

He came back with a plastic glass of beer and a glass of red antifreeze.

We were silent again.

"You can sell your house," I suggested.

"Can't. It's in my wife's name."

"Where's your wife?"

"Gone."

I thought for a moment. "How about getting your books reprinted."

"Can't. My publisher retired."

"What about another publisher?"

"No way. You ever see *Botch*? Ugly fucking joke book. Who am I, Anne fucking Rice? Never again."

"Public readings?"

"Too dangerous."

"How?" I asked.

"People throw beer bottles at my head," he said.

"I heard it was the other way around."

"Well sometimes they throw them back."

"We had better come up with a solution here, Botch. Before we leave this table."

We were silent again.

"You got kids?" he asked.

"One. A girl."

"How old?"

"Fourteen."

"I'm so sorry. She and your wife get along?"

"Mortal enemies."

"Mothers and daughters, eh?" he said.

"How old's your daughter now?" I asked.

"Twenty-three. No four. Nope . . . three. I don't fucking know, gimme a break man."

I sipped my wine. He lit a smoke.

"In *Botch*, you wrote that when your daughter was born you momentarily expected the earth to stop spinning in acknowledgement of the great occasion."

"I did?"

"Yes."

"Hm." He held up his beer. "Amnesia in a glass."

"How did you get into this situation?" I asked.

"A fierce dedication to imbecility," he answered.

"If you let me, I can help you out of this."

"Who are you fuckin kiddin', Toodles? This is the hole I dug. You jumped in on your own. Uninvited, I might add."

"You'd rather be broke?" I said. "Is that what you're telling me? On the street? Penny-fucking-less? Stealing booze from liquor stores? That is pathetic."

"Yeah? How pathetic does that make you that you can look at my life and wish it was yours?"

"Not anymore."

"Well too late, darling. You're boned. You're desperate because you've got something to lose. When you got nothing, society has no hold on you." And he held his arms out to say, consider me.

"I know you want me to go away but I'm not going anywhere. Societal abstractions aside, I have a problem and I'm going to solve it. Now either you're going to solve it with me, or I'm solving it alone. But the threat I made on your machine last night, I fully intend to carry out. Make no mistake."

Botch slugged the rest of his beer back in one gulp. "Ready for another?"

I wasn't. He left. And then that uneasy feeling swept over me once more. He was tricking me. Again. I jumped up and hurried to the bar. He wasn't there. I rushed out into the parking lot. I craned my neck for a look around. That bastard gave me the slip. I rushed to the men's room. There was one old man standing before a urinal mumbling. Maybe a bum, maybe a concentration camp survivor. Couldn't tell. I did another pass by our table just in case, keys out, ready to race him back to his place. And there he was, smoking.

"Where'd you go?" he asked.

"Took a piss," I said.

"We almost lost this fucking table. I had to chase away a bunch of Nips with umbrellas. Don't you know Farmer's etiquette?"

"I know Farmer's etiquette," I said and sat down.

He grinned. "You thought I was making a break for it, didn't ya?" Then he pointed across the table at me and roared laughing and the boney old woman behind him jumped.

"Hey, once bitten . . ."

". . . twice clichéd," he answered. Then he held his empty glass up to his eye and peered through it. "Your shout."

"Pardon me?"

"Your buy, sweetheart. Make mine a wine too."

I didn't recognize any of the wines except the Fetzer. I got two glasses of that. The fat English girl behind the bar filled them to the very bulge of the meniscus skin. Only the Brits. I slowly waddled back to the table, trying not to spill. But when I looked up, there was a family of five at our table. Cameras, overloaded strollers and shorts no matter what the weather. Why do tourists insist on looking like tourists?

I looked around. Then I spotted him on the other side of the crepe place, seated with two women. All three were waving at me.

I made my way over. One woman was very dark, her teeth glistening white. The other was young with short brown hair and glasses. They were both beaming smiles.

"This is my brother, William Botchelko," Botch said.

"Are you really?" the younger one gasped.

"I'm not his brother," I said. "We just have the same name."

"Same debt load too," said Botch.

I set the wine down and he slid them over to the girls. I went back and got two more. Then I spent ten minutes looking for a free chair.

Farmers was more crowded than ever these days. I suppose they were right building that horrible Grove, strictly in terms of cash flow. Even though they kept the old Farmers intact, you could feel the looming presence of the Grove like an amassed enemy army.

The dark girl's name was Amelia. I realized now she was easily in her forties. She had a Puerto Rican accent.

"But I'm really Espanish," she said.

"Yeah, every Puerto Rican says that," said Botch. She laughed and swatted him. The other girl was Lucy. She was Amelia's new roommate.

"Do I have a sunburn?" Lucy asked me and she slid her strap off her shoulder and peered back at me. A sudden urge to kiss her shoulder blade gripped me.

"No," I said and looked away.

"But you're not looking," she said.

"I looked. No burn."

"Are you a writer too?" asked Amelia.

"No. He does impressions," said Botch.

"A debt collector thinks I'm him," I said.

Botch lit a cigarette. "I'm sitting here 'cause you guys said you were buyin'," he reminded them.

"That's right!" the girls said and they both jumped up and scurried off.

"This isn't why I came here," I hissed.

"Yeah? Well listen to me, Goober. We're not going to solve this debt business in one afternoon. Now strictly in practical terms, I've already found a way for us to get free drinks. Haven't I? Which means I'm on top of this. You should be flossin' your gums with my bum fuzz in gratitude."

"Seems to me you concentrate all your efforts on getting free liquor," I said.

"A searing indictment. Am I to whither under such barbed criticism? Where do you suggest I start in the debt-reduction effort, Hooner? Panhandling? Pimping? Flippin' dog burgers?" Then he pointed right at me. "No one's making you stay here, shit-skull. Now relax or fuck off."

I thought about calling Robin. After the third round. And after the fourth. And again somewhere during the fifth. Both Amelia and Lucy had cell phones but if I borrowed one I'd have to explain to Robin where I got it. Then I went to the men's and noticed there were payphones right next to the door. But I knew if I called she'd be on to me instantly, my guilt pouring through the phone line like electronic data. Robin knew I was meeting Botch. That should do. For the time being, it was simply better not to call.

Then, while washing my hands, I slipped my wedding ring into my pocket.

"What happened to your wedding ring?" asked Amelia when we were all squeezed into my Accord and heading west on Santa Monica to Barney's Beanery.

"Oh didn't you hear? His divorce just came through," said Botch. He was sitting in back with Lucy. "That wedding ring's like an electronic collar and the divorce courts just signaled it to pop off."

"Is that true?" said Lucy and Amelia reached back and swatted her arm and Lucy said, "I warned you about hitting me."

I hadn't been in Barney's since college. It had changed. Now it was open and light and the restrooms were in the back and there was an area out front for the smokers. The license plates were still tacked to the ceiling. I remember one of the plates was polar bear-shaped. I felt the gravitational pull increase by tenfold the moment I stepped through the swinging doors.

We sat at the bar. I stuck with the wine. The other three switched to beer and Cuerevo Gold shots. Then Lucy got up to find the ladies but the moment we looked away we heard a "plop," and there she was flat on her ass in the middle of the floor, the startled expression of a toddler on her face. Amelia let go a peal of laughter and I got up to help her.

At the very same instant another guy did.

"Are you all right?" I asked her but he grabbed my arm.

"It's okay. I'll handle it," he said.

"That's fine. I've got her." I reached under her arms to hoist her to her feet, but he grabbed me again.

"I said I'll handle it."

I jerked my arm out of his grip and Lucy's ass plopped on the floor again. "This is none of your business," I said and suddenly the man seemed much taller and younger and gym-fit and calm and I had to give in to a swallow, either that or drool, and that made me look cartoonishly frightened.

Lucy stood up right in between us, brushing her ass and swaying. "Guy, guys," she said and she placed a hand on both our chests which for some reason made me push back as though I really wanted to rumble now.

"Do you know this girl?" he asked me and he didn't blink or avert his eyes and I could feel the urge to wither, adrenal gland firing squirts of fecal-liquidating fluid through my guts.

"I'm his wife," Lucy said.

"Yeah?" the guy said, stunned. "Is that true?" he asked me.

"Who lies about being married?" I said.

But he didn't believe us and muttered, "Bullshit."

Then Lucy grabbed the back of my neck and she planted a big, gooey kiss over my lips, eyes closed and swaying, and her entire tongue plunged deep into my gaping maw. She pulled away and dragged the back of her hand across her mouth and blinked ever so slowly and said, "I gotta pee."

Off she went, bumping her way between the tables and chairs. And I was left still facing a man who I swear had just grown another three inches. "Good luck," he said and smiled one of those over-bred, over-confidant, car salesman-slash-frat boy smiles. He turned and walked away.

I went back to the bar and sat. Botch was hunched over his drink, staring straight ahead at the bottles lining the bar. But Amelia was staring at me and grinning excitedly.

"You are the white knight," she said. "So gallant." Then she poked her finger into the bulge of Botch's back fat. "Would you do this for me?"

"You mean this?" said Botch and he grabbed her face and kissed her and she kissed right back and I suddenly felt ridiculous sitting there but envious too as I stared at their slippery lips crushed together like fat wet worms and I looked up to the ceiling, then glanced around the bar, then finally just watched them in disgusted fascination. When they broke away, Botch grabbed his pint and his smokes and stepped outside.

Amelia wiped her mouth with a bar napkin. "He taste like cigarettes."

I joined Botch outside. "I have to get home. Robin will be wondering."

"We need a lift to my place," he said.

"All the way back to San Pedro?" I said. "I thought I just had to take you back to Farmers."

"Don't have a car," he said.

"But how'd you get to Farmers?"

"Neighbor."

I looked at my watch. Ten fifteen. It was after ten. "I'm grabbing my car, you get the girls and have them out front. Let's go."

I scurried off, got the car from where I left it up the street past IHOPs. The three were standing out front, but I had to wait for the light before I could pull a U-ey. When I finally lurched up, another guy was standing out there with them.

I got out of the car. He turned to face me as I approached. It was him. From inside. And he smiled that smile again. "I just wanted to apologize," he said. He held out a hand. "I didn't know this was your wife."

I took his hand and shook it.

"I'm not married," said Lucy. Then she suddenly remembered. "Oh yeah. I'm his wife." And Amelia let go that awful coyote laugh of hers and she swatted Lucy's arm. "What did I fucking say about hitting me?" said Lucy.

Botch pulled open the passenger door. "Everybody in the car," he said. The girls climbed in the back and I made a move for the driver's.

But that fucker wouldn't let go of my hand.

"I get the feeling you're lying to me," he said.

I've never been in a fight in my life. Not really. Once, in sixth grade, Derek Kranz shoved me and I turned around and start punching him in a fit of rage that I think stunned everyone. Including me. We were both sent to the principal's office and, to be frank, Derek didn't have so much as a scratch. Then in college my roommate Jason and I toed off in the middle of a party, fists up and shouting, "Come on! Come on!" But everyone pulled us back and not so much as a punch was thrown and we ended up drunkenly hugging each other for half the night. I'd never even been hit in anger until Botch punched me in the kidney. But things weren't going to end quite so simply with this guy. I felt geriatric old looking up at him and his granite chin. I don't think this guy was even in his thirties. And he held a finger up to me. "No no no no no," he said. "You lied to me. And I don't like people lying to me."

"I don't want any trouble," I mumbled and I knew I was dangerously close to begging. I looked to Botch for a suggestion. But he was just lighting up another smoke. "We done here?" he asked.

"Not until your friend starts telling me the truth," he said and suddenly he grabbed the front of my shirt and pulled me up on my tiptoes and I heard a squeal and caught the faces of the people standing out front smoking, all smiling and eager and loving my shame and thrilled that someone was about to be beaten before their very eyes. I picked out one moon-faced girl so excited she looked delirious. What did I ever do to them?

Botch was trying to get my attention. "We done here or what?" he asked again.

The guy turned on him now and stuck a finger in Botch's face. "Mind your own business old—" and that was all he got out because Botch chomped down on his finger. The guy screamed and let go of me but Botch was wrenching on that finger like a puppy on a pig's ear. The guy didn't punch Botch which surprised me but grabbed his face and tried to pull away and he was shrieking in panic and Botch was shaking furiously on the finger and I heard a scream from the spectators. The second Botch let go he charged the guy, shoving him backwards. The man crashed against the rails and dropped to his back and Botch charged up and started stomping him, ramming his heel down on his forehead and cheeks and roaring, absolutely roaring like a bull. Then he stepped back, chest heaving, sucking air through his open mouth, his teeth bloody and bared as the crowd hung over the rails for a better look. Botch collected himself, then he leaned over the man. And very gently, he spat a long string of shiny pink gob on the man's bloody face. He nodded once to the crowd. Then he got into the passenger seat.

I hurried behind the wheel. My hands were trembling and I suddenly couldn't remember how to drive. I was aware that someone was bending low and peering in the passenger window at Botch. I put the car in drive. I pulled away and a car laid on the horn. In the mirror I could make out the beaten man's legs jutting out across the sidewalk and someone was standing in the middle of the street with a pen and a napkin, scribbling down my license number.

We passed around a bottle of wine as we drove. Amelia ran into a 7-Eleven before we got on the freeway and bought a couple rosés. No one spoke during the ride. Except Lucy. She held up her forefinger as though she'd never seen it before and said, "I know this is ridiculous, but my finger actually hurts." I missed the exit to Botch's so we took the next one and doubled back until we approached his place from the other direction, facing down the steep street instead of up. Botch unlocked his front door and swung it open, stepped inside and held his arms out wide.

"Let's get this party started!" he said.

Chapter 38

Botch had nothing but vodka and rum and I can drink rum because it's made of sugar cane as I understand it. He had two-liter bottles of flat Coke everywhere and no ice. It was like being at my parents' place. "Why pay for ice when we can make it at home for free?" is the logic but then they only have one ice cube tray and it sits in the freezer so long the cubes taste like onion. It didn't matter though. I was getting weary and heavy instead of drunk and the adrenal charge from Barney's had wiped me out. I felt like I'd spent the day lugging bricks.

But I was afraid to drive home. Not just because I was drunk. I was also certain my car description and license number was on every cop's computer screen from here to Vegas by now. I didn't call Robin either. I'd do that later. Once I thought of what to say. All of this was running through my mind when Lucy slipped up behind me in the kitchen and covered my eyes and said, "It's your wife," and I suppressed a tiny scream.

Botch, on the other hand, was feeling good, pouring the drinks, the cable station on to a '70s hits channel and he was sort of dancing to "Taste of Honey." Amelia jumped up to dance with him and Amelia could really dance, like a stripper, sliding up and down Botch's leg and shaking her skinny bum. Lucy tried to pull me up but I just could not get the energy. So she danced with them for a while but Amelia kept getting between her and Botch. Finally, she joined me on the couch, pouting like a child, and she offered me a cigarette. I took it.

And I lit up.

I sucked back a deep drag on that Camel and I expected to double over hacking, my lungs pure and pink and untouched by cigarette smoke for thirteen years now (except for that one New Years at my brother's and a quick one at Jax before they banned smoking altogether and, okay, I smoked an entire pack of Virginia Slims Ultra Light Menthols by myself sitting in Verdugo Park but that was after Robin chewed me out for not rushing outside to help her bring in the groceries and I went into a fit of rage because the truth is I was shitting my brains out and the anxiety of knowing she'd be angry made me shit even more and the moment she finished letting me have it I suddenly started screaming back at her and not one word was a word, just screaming. I bought the pack down at the corner market and I smoked them all. It took five hours. I threw up in a barbecue pit and I knew I was done with smoking for good).

But apparently I wasn't. And the smoke felt strangely good. Bewilderingly so. Like suddenly discovering you can breathe under water. I took another drag and kicked back and watched Amelia dance, Botch finally exhausted and slouching low in a chair, the call of the booze stronger than the call of women. Amelia was putting on a pretty good show for Botch when suddenly Lucy jumped to her feet and began dancing too. I think Lucy was a bit better, only because she pulled her sweater off and threw it at Botch, which left her in nothing but a sheer bra. You could just make out her pink nipples through it. So Amelia grabbed it from behind and snapped it.

"Don't fucking hit me, bitch!" Lucy screeched and she slapped her open palm into Amelia's mouth.

"You beech!" Amelia screamed back and she grabbed Lucy's hair and Lucy grabbed Amelia's hair and they were both slapping and scratching and ripping out hair with such sudden ferocity that I went to jump to my feet when I caught Botch's eye. He wasn't reacting at all. His chin was resting on his hand, cigarette pinched in his lips, and he winked at me as the girls flipped over the hassock and rolled behind the couch.

"You're the only one who hasn't been in a fight tonight," he said and grinned and I saw Amelia pop up behind the couch and her top was ripped open exposing her black bra and I think she was giving Lucy the Botch treatment by stomping her skull.

"Shouldn't we break this up?" I asked.

"You ever stuck your hand in the middle of a cat fight?" he said. "You're lucky if you come back with a hand. Let 'em burn off some steam."

Suddenly, the phone started ringing and then Amelia stumbled, balancing on one foot like that, and over she went and Lucy sprang to her feet and she was completely topless now and it was both disturbing and erotic and I realized, outside of magazines and movies (and when Robin's sister Cheryl was breast feeding, but I don't count that), I hadn't seen another woman's bare breasts in over sixteen years. Lucy's were small but pert and her nipples were erect and coincidentally, so was my penis. Lucy could fight like a featherweight and she pounced on Amelia swinging furiously. A lamp went over, and then a vase, and that's when Botch got to his feet and maneuvered behind Lucy and scooped her up in his arms in one quick snatch.

He held them apart, Lucy's nipples peeking out over his arms as she kicked wildly, and he pointed at Amelia to back down and she did. He let Lucy go. They were both panting, chests heaving, hair hanging down in front of their faces and in their mouths. I couldn't stand or they'd see the juvenile thrill in my pants and when I reached for my smoke it was dancing between my fingertips and I barely got it to my lips.

Lucy charged up to me and pointed at Amelia. "I warned that bitch, didn't I? She's been hitting me all night, hasn't she?" But I just stared at her breasts as though they were telling me the secret of life.

"She's a beeg beech," said Amelia and Botch grabbed her hand and said, "Sit there," and he guided her to the couch and she plopped down. "And you sit over there," and he pointed Lucy to a chair and Lucy obediently sat. Now there was nothing but the sound of their panting.

"Did I hear your phone ringing?" asked Lucy.

"That was the two-ring warning," said Botch.

"Warning?" I asked.
"Yes. The cops are on their way," he said.

Chapter 39

We crouched in the dark in the corner of the living room. We smoked and waited. All the lights were out. And the cops were banging on the door. A flashlight was poked through the mail slot and we watched the beam dart around the room. But we were hidden out of sight from either the front or the back doors, all four squeezed into a corner between the book shelves. Clearly, Botch had done this many times before.

"Who called the cops?" I whispered.

"My neighbor," he said.

"Is this the same neighbor who drove you to Farmers?"

"The same," he said.

"The same neighbor with the dog?"

"Mm-hm," he said.

"I'm not sure if he likes you or hates you," I said.

"She," he corrected. "And I'm not sure either."

Lucy still didn't have her top on. It was dark but in my mind's eye I could see her breasts perfectly. Simply because I had burnt their image into the back of my retina like I had been staring into the sun. In fact, I could have described them in minute detail to a police sketch artist.

Amelia waved a bottle around. "This one is feenished," she said.

We were dry. There was a big plastic bottle of Stoli on the coffee table. A flashlight beam passed by the floor and we drew our feet in closer.

"I'll get it," said Botch.

"Don' do eet!" hissed Amelia and she tried to grab him but it was too late. He scurried across the floor on all fours. He squeezed into the corner of the sectional just as the flashlight beams passed by again. We started to giggle. He reached up and snatched the bottle off the table. He unscrewed the top, took a big slug, then screwed it back on, laid it on the floor and rolled it over to us. And it stopped about four feet short. A flashlight beam passed over it. Then it doubled back and stopped on it. We could hear mumbling outside. Another beam landed on it. The bottle had its own spotlight. Lucy was starting to snort with laughter and we shushed her. Then one beam moved away. Then the other. And the moment it did, I dashed out, grabbed the bottle, and lunged back just as a beam reappeared. Suddenly, three beams joined it. The talking outside grew louder. The banging started again.

Then the phone rang four times. We heard Botch's voice on the machine snap, "Leave a message or leave me alone."

"How rude," said Amelia.

We heard a man's voice. "Hello Mr. Botchko, this is . . ." He stopped. There was a mumbled correction in the background. "Hello Mr. Botchelko, this is the San Pedro police department. We received a disturbing the peace complaint regarding this address. We're outside your home at present, and if you are listening to this message, we ask that you please make yourself known and come to the door. Either that or pick up the phone Mr. Botch—Botcha . . ." Someone mumbled in the background again and the cop said, "Well it's a mouthful, okay? Sir, we'd appreciate your cooperation in this matter." And that was it. Silence again. The machine beeped off. We could see the message light blinking now in the dark.

Suddenly, Botch scurried back across the floor and squeezed in there with us again. Amelia hugged him and giggled and I could feel Lucy's breast pressed against my arm. It felt like we were kids at detention and we all struggled not to burst out laughing as we passed the bottle back and forth. Suddenly the phone started ringing again. That just made it more exciting. I couldn't restrain myself any longer.

I bent and kissed Lucy's nipple.

"I was wondering when you were going to do that," said Lucy and Botch's machine beeped and Amelia said, "Do what?" and Botch's voice snarled, "Leave a message or leave me alone," and Lucy replied, "He kissed my nipple," just as my wife said, "Yeah, this is Robin calling. William's wife? Or Alfred's? Or whatever he's going by these days. I was just wondering if he's there. It's kind of late. Could you call me when you get this message?" And she hung up.

"Whose wife is thees?" asked Amelia. "Which one of you?"

"His," said Botch.

"You probably shouldn't be kissing my tits then," said Lucy.

Chapter 40

When a woman asks you what you're thinking, she's not interested in hearing your thoughts. She wants you to be thinking what she's thinking. She wants to hear you say, "I was thinking of you." Even if it's a lie and she scoffs and swats your arm, that's what she wants you to say. So when she asks you a second time, don't correct yourself. Don't say, "Actually, I was thinking about getting the oil changed in the truck," or "I should really call my mother this afternoon," or "I was just laughing over something Dale said," which will lead to you having to explain what Dale said but since it was lewd, you have now armed her with a further reason to hate you. When in fact that isn't the reason. The real reason is, you weren't thinking about her at all.

This occurs only in the girlfriend and newlywed stage. Later, she won't give a damn what you're thinking. In fact, she will start to tell you what you're thinking. For instance, "You think you're so smart," or "You think you can do this better than me," or "You think we shouldn't go see my mother, don't you?" And now you're in shit for thinking what she thinks you're thinking.

There are men who will do anything to keep harmony in their house. Those men are always exhausted.

Chapter 41

I woke up on the floor in the corner. I guess I passed out there while struggling to work up the nerve to return Robin's call. I could tell the sun was up pretty high even though the curtains were still pulled. I was alone in the room.

I thought the hangover wasn't too bad until I got to my feet and stumbled and realized I was still drunk. There was a box of Ritz crackers toppled over on the coffee table and half a devoured block of cheddar. They must have kept drinking long after I passed out. There were clothes everywhere. Botch's socks. Amelia's black bra. Someone's panties. Both of the girl's pairs of jeans. I guess I missed one hell of party and I felt the sting of humiliation, as though they were merely biding their time, hoping I'd pass out so they could openly screw in front of me with the same disregard as bathing in front of a cat.

I had an erection again but for a different reason. I needed a bathroom. I crept upstairs. I passed an open door. There was Amelia and Lucy, out cold on Botch's bed. Lucy was lying face down, wearing nothing but white thong panties. Amelia was on her back completely naked, breasts rather deflated and hanging to each side of her rib cage, her pubic hair a mere patch like Hitler's mustache.

I pushed my way into a filthy bathroom. Thank God I didn't have to shit. Yet. If I tried to piss in the toilet with this erection I'd just piss everywhere. Not that it would make much difference. I pissed in the sink. Then I stupidly washed my hands. Botch's towels were hard. I could bend them and they would hold the shape. I wiped my hands on my shirt.

My keys were in my pocket. It was time to get out of there. I crept back downstairs. Then I smelled coffee. How a person in a bedroom with the door closed on the opposite end of a house can smell coffee the moment it starts to brew is, from a physics perspective, beyond me. But clearly Botch was in the kitchen. I couldn't duck out now. Yet the smack of shame was so fresh I still didn't want to talk to anyone.

I had no choice. I crept silently through the living room and peeked into the kitchen. Botch was sitting at the table in his underwear, hunched over a cup. His hair was standing up, his eyes red as the undead's. He looked up.

"The funny thing is, after all these years, I'm still a little afraid of sleep," he said, his voice raspy as sand.

"Is it the fear of not waking?" I asked.

"Waking is more like it," he said. He grabbed me a mug, poured a coffee. "There's no milk," he said and set it across from him. "No sugar either."

I sat down and for a fraction of a second I felt like projectile vomiting. Thankfully that passed.

"I know a guy who owes me money," he said.

"Who?"

"This director. Actually, a screenwriter. He's the one who ripped off *Botch* and made that movie."

"*How to Kill Your Neighbor's Dog*?"

"Yeah."

"I gotta be honest, I saw the movie and read your book and I really don't see a connection," I said.

"There's a clear connection, midget-fucker. He took all my characters from *Botch* and simply moved them back fifteen years. Confront him with that bit of news and he'll shit his girlie pants. He knows. And he knows I know he knows. He phoned me for years. We've met God knows how many times. We've discussed it. He's a thief and he owes me. I can tell you, that guy right there is good for five or six grand."

We stopped talking and sipped our coffees for awhile. Botch lit a smoke then held the pack out to me. I shook my head, then instantly changed my mind. "Yeah, give me one."

We smoked. Botch got up to get more coffee, but then he stopped suddenly and leaned over the sink as though he was about to retch. He pinched his eyes shut.

"I am so unhappy, Lord," I heard him whisper.

"Then straighten up," I said. "Stop drinking, stop gamb—"

"Is your name 'Lord'?" he snapped.

Fine. Done. I had more than enough insult and humiliation to last me several long years now. And I still had one ugly scene waiting for me at home. I pushed away from the table. "I'm going."

"Hey Botchelko," he said. "I'm only concerned with three people, okay? Me, myself and I." Then he looked out the back window a moment and added as an afterthought. "Two of them I don't even like."

Chapter 42

Robin's car wasn't in the garage when I pulled in. At first I thought she was at work. But it was Sunday. I called her name when I stepped in the house just in case. "Robin? You home?" I wandered down the hall, pushed open our bedroom door. The bed was made. I pushed open Maddy's bedroom door. The bed was not made.

At first I was relieved. Then instantly I was angry. This meant stalling the inevitable. Which I guess was the point. But I desperately wanted it over with. I hate confrontations as much as the next person. In fact, I think some of the stupidest self-revelatory statements I've heard people make are, "I hate confrontations," "I hate hospitals," and "I hate funerals." Show me the fuckers who like those things and I'll show you a boxer, a doctor, and an undertaker.

Our cell phones still didn't work. I dialed Maddy's number though. No answer. I just couldn't bring myself to call Robin's sister. But if I didn't, hell payment would increase exponentially. I had to at least go through the motions of looking concerned. So I made a deal with God. If she answers, I hang up. If the machine answers, I leave a message.

I dialed. The machine. "Hi, this is Cheryl and Tom. Leave a message after the beep and we'll call you right back." Don't we all know about the fucking beep by now?

"Cheryl, hi. This is William. I'm just looking for Robin. Thought I'd give you a try . . ."

"Will?" Cheryl picked up. And I blurted out, "Shit!"

"What? What are you saying 'shit' about?" she asked. "What's wrong?"

"Nothing, nothing," I said. "I dropped something."

"What did you drop?"

"It was nothing."

"What was it?"

"Nothing. Really."

"Was it a cupcake?"

"Yes," I sighed. "Yes Cheryl, it was a cupcake."

"Robin's not here," she said.

"All right, well—thanks . . ."

"Why don't you try her cell?"

"Our cells aren't working right now."

"Why not? They cut them off or something? You broke?"

I looked out back. I wished I had a spa. A pool would be nice too. There's room out there for one. Now that would be a lovely way to deal with a hangover, floating in a pool with a tall, cool drink. Then I spotted my neighbor in his bedroom through his new French doors. He was in his underwear. Fuck the pool. What I needed was a tall fence.

"You still there?"

"Yeah, listen, if Robin should call or drop by or—"

"She won't drop by."

"Just, either way, tell her I called."

"You guys broke?"

"Okay Cheryl? Can you do that for me? Okay? Thanks."

"You get fired? What was your job again, a UPS driver or something?"

"Bye now," and I hung up.

The phone instantly rang and I snapped it back up, thinking it was Robin.

"I think we got cut off," said Cheryl.

I hung up again.

I went and soaked in the tub. I took a big mug of tea with honey and lemon in there with me. It took ten minutes to find the honey. Because it was so big. A jug of honey. Who needs a jug of honey?

Robin was clearly shopping at Smart and Final again. The lemon was easy. We had a little tree in the backyard. But squeezing the thing made me dizzy, the peels on it thick as an elephant's ear lobe. I lay back in the tub while the hot water poured. I tried to shut my eyes but weird cataclysmic images flashed across the backs of my eyelids, things that looked like roiling clouds and shadows and faces even, then billowing pools of what looked like blood. On top of it all, and I don't why, I was so horny my penis itched. Hangovers sometimes did that to me.

Then I heard the door. I sat up with a splash. I could hear the heels stomping down the hall. That meant it was Robin. Robin never even tried to walk delicately. She stopped in the doorway, stared down at me, a Swain's bag in one hand and a RiteAid in the other. She didn't say a word and neither did I. Then she just walked away. I could hear her in the bedroom. She was getting changed I guess. I didn't want to get out but I had to. It was time to face it. I pulled the plug. Only to look up and find Robin standing in front of me completely naked. She had a tube of Astroglide in her hand and she squeezed a blob on her fingers and rubbed it in her vagina.

"What are you doing?" I asked, grimacing. It wasn't an erotic thing to watch.

"Look out," she said and she stepped into the tub.

"What are you doing?" I asked again. The water was sucking loudly down the drain and I was starting to get cold when Robin straddled me. She started rubbing her Astroglided vagina up and down the shaft of my penis.

"What are you doing, Robin?" I asked again and was shocked to realize I was instantly hard. She poked it inside her and she gripped the sides of the tub and she started mechanically riding me up and down while still staring into my eyes as stern as a schoolmarm.

"What's going on?" I tried to say but I came so quickly I grunted and as the last of the water disappeared down the drain in one loud long slurp, I heard Maddy scream, "Oh my fucking God!"

She was standing in the hallway, both hands clasped to her mouth like she'd just stumbled on a headless body. She screamed again and she bolted down the hall and we heard her bedroom door slam.

But Robin didn't react. She just remained straddled across me, arms folded across her chest, and she continued to stare at me.

I cleared my throat. "What's up?" I asked again. Robin stood. She climbed out of the tub.

"That was a test," she said. "Clearly you didn't have sex with anybody last night because if you did, you'd never get it up. You wouldn't get it up for a week."

"I do not need to hear this!" Maddy screeched from her room and suddenly her music came booming on. Robin reached for a towel and I looked her over. I had only an hour earlier seen two slim women naked. Robin was no longer slim. Her legs were heavy, her thighs broad, her buttocks dimpled with cellulite. She never bothered to trim her pubic hair and it spread across her crotch and even poked out around her bathing suit bottom when we were at the beach. She was getting a belly too. But her breasts were still big and full. Funny, I'd been with a large busted woman for so long now, the small ones were starting to intrigue me.

Then Robin set her foot on the tub rim and a blob of semen dripped out of her vagina and plopped to the floor and I suppressed a gag.

"You two are sickening!" Maddy shouted down the hall and I found I had to agree.

"Where were you?" asked Robin.

"With Botch," I said and swallowed hard to keep from regurgitating my tea.

"I know that. Why didn't you call?"

I just shook my head. "It was a long weird night. He's a difficult man. You know that. We got so drunk and I didn't want to worry you and then it got late . . ."

"Were there women?" she asked.

"No."

"I'm no longer asking if you slept with anyone. I'm asking if there were any women present."

"No," I said again.

She stared at me. I hated when she did this. If I looked away, she would demand to know why I couldn't look her in the eyes. If I looked her in the eyes, she'd know I was making a point of not looking away.

"I don't believe you," she said and walked out and Maddy poked her head out the door and shouted, "You guys are too old to be doing that!" and then added, "And learn to close a door!" and with that she slammed hers once again.

Chapter 43

In Botch's short story collection, *Masturbating in the Dark*, subtitled: *And Other Maritime Blunders*, he writes about a guy who comes home late at night and his girlfriend has sex with him as a test. She knows if he just had sex with another he wouldn't be able to perform. I have that book. Which meant Robin was reading Botch's stuff. What Robin wasn't allowing for was the fact that several times I've been unable to perform—or, let's say, the curtain dropped long before the scheduled conclusion of the show. On those occasions, I hadn't had sex in weeks. She, or I suppose I should say "we" got lucky this time because the hangover had made me randy as a teenager. I could have fucked a potted plant.

Robin stayed angry all day but she thought she could hide it with efficiency. She cleaned, she vacuumed, she had a one-sided chat with Maddy. I tried to ignore her and read the Sunday *LA Times* but for such a giant mass of ink and pulp it was a hell of a struggle to find even one story worth reading. Why was it on the days I had to work, every single story in the paper was interesting, but on Sundays the only good read in the entire paper was Dilbert? Robin once liked the Opinion section but only if there were letters and editorials criticizing Bush. And those she read aloud. Otherwise, if you were looking for an anti-Bush story back in the day, the *LA Times* was not the place to find one.

I went to bed at nine that night, hungry for sleep and hungrier still for the return of normalcy in the morning. But my body kept twitching and jerking every time I started to drift off and my eyes couldn't adjust to the dark and I kept thinking people were standing over me or dogs were in the room. I finally got up to take a Sominex and when I crawled back in bed Robin was there too.

We had a California king. It was a half acre of bed and it was wonderful. She was sitting up reading but the light wouldn't bother me, not now with the promise of a sleep-inducing pill slowly dissolving in my innards.

And then she said, "He's coming to dinner."

"Who?" I asked.

"Botch."

"No way," I said. "I'm not inviting him."

"You don't have to. I already did."

My chest instantly tighten. "When?" I asked.

"An hour ago. I phoned him and he said yes."

I sat up. "Why did you go and do that without talking to me first?"

"I wanna meet this Svengali of yours. I want to see what his hold is on you."

"The hold is a $70,000 debt and an aggressive debt collector," I answered.

"No. It's not just that. You've got a thing for him." That's when I noticed the book she had in her hands was *Botch.*

"What's this sudden interest?" I asked.

"That's what I'm trying to figure out," she answered.

I laid back down, my back to her. I was wide awake now.

"Don't expect me to cook," I said and she said, "Who asked you?"

Chapter 44

Robin was preparing pork and black bean chili. I passed through the kitchen and she had her Mary Chapin Carpenter CD playing and she was cutting up chunks of gorgeous looking pork and the black beans were soaking in a mixing bowl. I used to make turkey chili, which was delicious. With the fake sour cream and the rice cheddar and then a generous helping of Joe's Stuff which I got in New Orleans during the first and last vacation we ever took with Cheryl and Tom. But where'd Robin find this recipe?

Her intention, clearly, was to show off. Or at the very least, show me up. But she was courting disaster. This was not Robin's forte. I figured we could always order Thai when it turned out inedible.

I went outside and raked leaves. Then I told Robin I was going for a walk. She said, "Sure," in that upbeat way she puts on when she's trying to cover up feeling anything but upbeat. She was wearing my mother's old apron too which only served to reinforce the certainty that we were going to be sitting down to an indigestible meal.

I never take walks but she didn't give that a thought. I bought a pack of smokes at the corner store. Then I sat at The Green Hut picnic tables and smoked and watched the college kids stroll by. The girls were so miserably young. Maddy could blend right in. If she ever got to college. The Armenian girls looked like models—slim, fashionable. Though a fashion very particular to them. Then the big Mexican boys lumbering off to class, looking at their feet, hating every step toward those desks.

I loved college. But I felt as far away from those days now as the moon. And those kids walking by, those fine creatures, they merely reinforced that by glancing my way but looking right through me. A middle-aged man is the campus stealth bomber, not registering on any radar.

Chapter 45

The door rang early. I was ready. I got there before Robin. I heard Maddy shouting, "Who is it?" before I even pulled it open. Only to find three teenage girls standing on the steps.

"Maddy here?" the short one asked.

All three wore too much makeup, eyelids black and blue, lips spit-glossy as though freshly licked. One wore a tiny pleated skirt. Two wore heels.

"Who is it?" Robin called out.

All three wore pink nail polish. One had a Peanuts bandage on her finger. The tallest was flat chested but her nipples were enormous and bulged through her top. Maddy looked like Chesty Morgan compared to these three. And all of them had belly button rings.

"Maddy here?" she asked again.

If I spoke, my voice would crack. If I stepped back, I'd trip. If I blinked, my eye would twitch. If I tried to smile, if I tried to be funny, I'd be terribly, terribly sorry forever. Maddy finally rescued me.

"Jesus Dad," she said. "Come on you guys," and she waved them in. They squeezed past me.

"What's wrong with your dad?" the little one asked.

"He's an idiot," Maddy answered.

Amazing. I had instantly reverted into a fourteen-year-old boy. I had just time-traveled back to my teenage self. My armpits were soaked. My mouth was Velcro. My hands were trembling. Teenage girls. Dean

Koontz should write that book. They are more terrifying than the cruelest bully. They destroy with a sneer or a cackle or an eye roll.

It was crushing to discover with such certainty right there at my own front door that I would never grow up.

I was about to close the door when I heard, "Am I late?" And there he was, wearing a gray blazer, a bag in his arms. "I lost my watch again," he said.

I looked up and down the street. "Did you drive?" I asked.

"Choppered in."

"I thought you lost your license."

"I did."

"Which car is yours?"

He looked around, then he pointed. "Hyundai."

"Practical car," I said.

"Neighbor's car," he said.

He stepped inside.

"You have an odd relationship with that neighbor of yours," I said.

"She's lonely, cares for her dad all day. I throw her a boink now and again and she's grateful." He started taking off his shoes.

"Are you Japanese?" I asked. "Keep the shoes on."

"Sorry," he said. "Canadian." Then he reached into his bag and showed me a bottle of Penfolds. "I'm not sure what you guys drink. So I brought one bottle of red. But in case you prefer white, I brought a second bottle of red. That way I get more."

"Hey listen," I said and I dropped my voice. "Gentleman's agreement, all right?"

He frowned at me like I was speaking in tongues. "Sorry?"

"I said—" but it was too late. Robin appeared wiping her hands in a tea towel.

"You must be Alfred Botchelko," she said.

"The long-lost cousin," he said and held out his hand and she took it and said, "Robin," and he said, "I've heard a lot about you," and she said, "All good I hope," which everybody says and then laughs which Robin did but then Botch said, "Actually, no," and he didn't so much as crack a smile. Robin looked a bit stunned.

I was fucked.

"You have a daughter too, don't you?" he asked.

"She's in her room with friends," I said and Robin added, "Can't you hear the music?"

"I thought maybe you guys liked that stuff," he said.

"Do you know any middle-aged white people who like rap music?" Robin asked.

"I don't know any middle-aged white people," he answered.

Robin led us to the dining room. "Well I don't know about you two, but I'm starting with a martini."

"You are?" I said.

"You bet I am," she said.

"But is that such a good idea?"

"We're home. What's going to happen?" She turned to Botch. "What can I get you, Alfred?"

"Call me Botch. Martini sounds good."

"Gin?"

"Lovely."

"And you, William?"

"A carbonated enema please," I said. "Extra fizz."

Robin walked away.

"Are you kids fighting?" he asked.

I heard the bonk of the shaker. Then the ice maker clattering out wedges. I was waiting till she started shaking the drinks.

"Don't get my wife drunk," I warned him.

"Why?" he asked.

Robin started shaking the shaker. And I immediately grabbed Botch's arm and whispered, "Not a word about the other night."

"What other night?"

"With the girls," I said. "Not a word." Botch didn't react. "Okay?" He said nothing. "Botch?" Robin stopped shaking. She called out. "Don't you want anything, William?" I was staring at Botch. He was staring back. He was going to make trouble. That fucker.

I grabbed a bottle of red and went into the kitchen. I found the corkscrew, the good one, not that Waiter's Friend piece of crap that Robin had from her waitressing days which she always insisted on using. I worked on the cork while Robin filled the martini glasses.

"He's a belligerent drunk," I whispered.

"What's that mean?" she said.

"I'm just saying, don't give him too many drinks."

"Why?"

"I'm warning you."

"Will he flirt with Maddy? Beat you up?" Then she grinned. "Make a pass at me?" And with that she walked out, balancing two overflowing martinis, grinning back at me.

That confirmed it. There was no keeping a lid on this. I snatched up a glass and the bottle and hurried back out.

They were already sipping. Both their eyebrows popped up the moment their lips touched the gin.

"Perfect," said Botch.

"Dry as the Serengeti," said Robin.

"Just walk the vermouth by," he said and she added, "Face Italy when you shake it," and with that they clinked glasses. Then they saw me with my red wine and rather grudgingly clinked my glass too.

"What's for dinner?" Botch asked.

"You hungry?" asked Robin.

"It's pork and black bean chili," I said. "But if it doesn't turn out, we can always order something."

Robin set her martini glass down and stared at me.

"What is wrong with you?" she said.

"I'm just saying. Just in case. There's a Thai place down the street."

"Did you make it?" Botch asked her.

"Yes," she said and I added, "She's never made it before."

"I'm sure it'll be great," said Botch and she said, "Thank you, Botch," and they clinked glasses once more and they sipped in unison and their eyebrows popped up in unison as well.

"Damn," said Botch.

"Have you tried the chili yet?" I asked her.

"I don't have to stick my hand in a fire to know it's hot," Robin said and Botch said, "That's very clever," and I said, "She didn't make it up."

"Yes, but she knew when to use it," he said and again she said, "Thank you, Botch," and again they clinked those silly fucking glasses with a little tink and I got up from the table and went into the kitchen. I got a spoon. I lifted the glass lid off the cauldron. It was a very dark chili. I scooped some up, made sure I got a chunk of pork. I blew on it. Glanced back to see if anyone was coming in. Then stuck it in my mouth.

It was hot as Lucifer's turd.

I had to suppress a scream. I ran to the sink, stupidly trying to chew it a couple times, then spat it out. I frantically scooped tap water into my mouth. My eyes were watering. If I had stuck my tongue in a deep fryer it wouldn't have hurt as much. I grabbed the tea towel hanging from the fridge handle and bit into it. My tongue felt prickly and skinless and raw. I grabbed an ice cube and stuck it in my mouth. I heard Robin and Botch burst out laughing.

Suddenly, Robin rushed back into the kitchen with two empty glasses and immediately started measuring out shots of gin and dumping them in the shaker.

"You're finished those already?" I asked.

"Well they go down like martinis," she said. Then she stopped and doubled over with laughter and said, "I meant, like water."

Great. Drunk already.

"What's in your mouth?" she asked. "Did you try the chili?"

"No," I said and she said, "Yes you did," and she pointed. "There's a piece in the sink!"

I grabbed my glass and headed for the door.

"You burnt yourself, didn't you?" she said and as I walked out I heard her say, "That'll teach ya."

"Let's step outside for a smoke," I said to Botch.

"I got a second martini coming," he said.

"But I'm dying for a smoke," I said.

"Then go have one," he said.

"She doesn't know I smoke," I whispered.

He pushed back from the table with a sigh. "Acrimonious matrimony," he said.

We headed to the back door. "Honey, I'm joining Botch outside while he smokes."

"You want to have the drinks outside?" she called out.

"We'll only be a second," I said and she said, "Yeah, yeah. I get it."

We stepped out back. We walked over to the lemon tree. Botch slipped me a cigarette and got one for himself. He kept his lighter in the pack with the smokes and it took some effort to pluck it out. I turned my back to the house to light up.

"I need to know you're not going to bring up the other night," I said.

"Why?" he said.

"Because . . ." I had to take a breath. Why did he fucking think? "It'll end my marriage," I said.

"If you're marriage is on that kind of thin ice, there probably isn't much I can do to save it."

"I just don't need the shit, okay?"

"Psst!" I heard. We glanced back to the house. Someone was hanging out the bathroom window.

"Who is that?" I asked.

"Risa." It was a girl's voice.

"What can I do for you, Risa?" I asked.

"Can I bum a smoke?" she asked.

Botch pulled out a smoke and started over to her.

"No of course you can't," I said. "Now get out of here."

"Grumpy," she said.

"Go back inside," I said.

"I'm pinching a loaf," she said.

"Fine. Close the window and do your pinching."

I suddenly didn't feel like a fourteen-year-old boy anymore, the disgusting little thing. Why couldn't she shit at home? She closed the window. Then she popped it open again.

"It's going to stink in here," she said. Then closed it again.

"As I was saying before I was so rudely interrupted—" only to be interrupted by Robin leaning out. "Martini's getting warm," she said. I hid the cigarette behind my back.

"Can't have that," said Botch and he marched right back inside. Robin hesitated there at the door to eye me down, then she went back inside too.

Chapter 46

"I like your earrings," Botch said.

"Why thank you," said Robin. She reached up to feel them. They were blue and silver with a row of tiny chains dangling down. I hadn't noticed them.

"He never notices things like that," she said.

"I noticed," I said.

"Are you married, Botch?" she asked.

"Technically," he said.

"Same here," she said.

"What's that supposed to mean?" I said. And Robin burst out laughing and dropped her head to the table, then sat up again instantly, her hair in her eyes.

"Just joking," she said.

The two were halfway through their second martini. Things were getting sloppy.

"Well I don't like jokes like that," I said.

"Well I wouldn't make jokes like that if you didn't say some of things you say."

"What things?" asked Botch.

"He thinks I'm fat," said Robin.

"I do not," I said. Now that pissed me off.

"Now that pisses me off." I said.

"I don't think you're fat."

"Why thank you Botch."

"You're the perfect proportions for a woman," he said. "Very curvy."

"You think so?"

"Absolutely."

"He thinks my ass is too big."

"I did not say that. Maddy said that."

"But you didn't disagree with her."

"Yes I did."

"Well you didn't do it fast enough."

"Men like women with a bit of shape to them," said Botch.

"See?" she said to me.

This was getting ridiculous. She was drunk. And I was getting the creepy feeling the two were openly flirting. It was hard to tell though. I didn't know much about flirting. And I'd never seen Robin do it before. The girly act and all the laughing, all his compliments, that had to be what was going on.

Robin got up and came back with bowls. I caught her glancing back at Botch to see if he was checking out her ass. And the prick was. Funny how your wife's ass looks better when another man's admiring it. She was probably wearing one of her body slimmers. Wonder what Botch would think catching a sight of her trying to wriggle out of that mummy suit. Not too erotic—even in the dark.

Robin shook pre-cut salad into a bowl right in front of us. Half of it landed on the table. Yep, drunk and getting drunker. She went to the kitchen, reappeared with two huge wine glasses.

"Don't I get one?" I asked.

"You've got one," she said.

"Not a big one," I said.

"There's only two big ones," she said.

I caught Botch grinning at me. He held out his tankard. I poured some red wine in it. He winked.

"Did you just wink at him?" Robin said. "I think you're supposed to wink at the girl at the party." She sat down and started spooning out chili. Then she stopped. She set the bowl down. She looked right at me and narrowed her eyes. "Just what are you two up to?" she asked.

"Nothing," I said.

"Botch won't lie to me," she said and she turned to him and asked, "What happened that night when he was out until morning?"

"You really wanna know?" he asked.

"Of course," she said.

My face instantly flushed red. I thought I was going to choke. That son of bitch was pure evil.

"Mom, can I have twenty bucks?" asked Maddy. She was standing behind Robin with her three friends flanking her. She was dressed the same as them now but she looked so much older. She could probably have a drink in Jax and no one would card her.

"Mr. Botchelko was just about to tell us what happened when your father was out all night," Robin told her.

"Dad was out all night?" she repeated. She glanced excitedly back at her friends. They grinned at her.

"If you can stay out all night, I can stay out all night," I said.

"Real mature, Dad," she said.

I dug in my pocket. "Here, here," and I pulled out my last twenty. I hated giving it to her. That meant asking Robin for money tomorrow. But this was an emergency. "Take it. Go."

Maddy took it. But then she and her friends kept standing there.

"Go," I said.

"Fine," she said and she turned and her troop turned with her in unison and they all marched out. She was clearly their leader. She never struck me as the leader type. I couldn't lead a pack of lemmings to their death.

"Be back before ten!" I shouted but heard only the door slam.

"You were saying, Botch?" said Robin.

"I was saying," said Botch but then he paused and held a finger up to Robin. "I just remembered something I need to ask your husband." He turned to me. "I need to collect that money from that director. You know anybody who can take care of that for me?"

"I'll do it," I said.

"Great," he said. Then he turned back to Robin. "Here's what happened. I got into a little trouble that night, took a guy on. It got ugly. Your husband drove me home. But then the cops came banging on my door and we had to hide in the dark till they went away. We couldn't move. That's why he couldn't call you. We slept on the floor. I know he was probably worried about telling you the truth. But it was my fault entirely and he was just looking out for me. I won't put him that situation again."

Robin stared at Botch. Then she turned and stared at me. She couldn't decide if this was the truth or not. I stared right back. Then she nodded. Slowly. She finished spooning out the chili. She handed me a bowl.

"Did you know Maddy's friends smoke?" I said.

"Risa. I know," she said. "She thinks it covers up the stink of her shits."

"Little pig," I said.

Chapter 47

I drove past Kalesniko's place twice. He lived right in Glendale. Which would make the trip home easier once he rejected me for demanding money when there's no contract and the source material in question is, at best, questionable. His place was off Royal, the nicest street in town in my opinion—wide, with big classy houses and tall thin palm trees. The house was a long rancher on a corner lot at the top of little box canyon. I drove down the alley, thinking it was a street, realized it was a dead end and backed out. His garage door was open and there was a black half-ton Ford pickup inside. That confused me. A pickup truck didn't seem to be the vehicle of choice for someone in the movie business.

I parked just around the corner. I had to work up the nerve to ring the bell. My head was a bit fuzzy. I didn't think I'd had that much wine. Robin was openly drunk and slurring by the end of the night, laughing too hard and too often and touching Botch's arm and wrist and hand and even his goddamn finger every chance she got.

It was nauseating.

Botch, on the other hand, was on his best behavior. In other words, he was downright boring. But I noticed he was smiling a lot, listening and laughing over everything Robin said, every "story" that I've heard between two and maybe three–and-a-half million times. Like the one about being the first paper girl on her block so she could earn enough money to buy a ten-speed and be the fastest girl on her block as well.

Only to buy it and be soundly beaten by a kid on a one-speed with a banana seat and monkey bars two years her junior. Or how she used to pretend as a girl she had tragic diseases and migraines and even hangovers, though she didn't know what a hangover was (yet). Or the time her mom caught her playing doctor with a boy and her mom chased the boy all the way home and she didn't have the nerve to tell her she bullied the kid into pulling his pants down. Or the time her dad caught her doing her daily ritual of three pirouettes on the porch before she opened the front door and her father told her the neighbors were going to think she was nuts.

I have to admit, she did throw one new story in there. I pretended I recognized it but I didn't. Somewhere around the time I was pouring my second cup of decaf and they were pulling the cork on a third bottle of red, Robin told Botch she once had a boyfriend in college who was going to be a writer. Robin and I met in college. In the registration line. I was her only boyfriend. Who the hell was this guy?

Botch left around midnight and she hugged him tight at the door and kissed both his cheeks because he'd mentioned earlier that in England they kiss both cheeks. I pointed out that in America we kiss all four. No one laughed. Then Robin tried to clean up dinner but broke one of her giant wine goblets so I told her to go to bed and I'd take care of it. Instead, I had a quick smoke out back. Then I sat up in bed and listened to Robin snore like a phlegmatic rhino. I heard Maddy come home around one. I knew I wasn't going to say anything.

There were a lot of dogs in Kalesniko's neighborhood. Maybe that's why he wrote that movie. I'd want to kill them too. Every single house had at least two dogs and the house at the end of the alley had four. I thought you needed a kennel license for four. I rang the front bell. I waited. I rang it again. Nothing. Would someone leave their garage door wide open if they weren't home? Maybe if they were coming right back. I went around to the side door, the one on the alley. That really set the dogs off. I rang the side door now, a different tone. Still nothing. Then I heard a window slide open above me and someone call out, "Hello?"

I stepped back into the alley. There was a man hanging out the window of the second story above the garage. He had a shaved head, glasses. He looked pissed off.

"Can I help you?" he said but he didn't mean it. People never do. They mean, why are you here and when are you leaving?

"I'm looking for Mike Kalesniko," I said.

"Michael," he corrected. "What's this about?"

"Are you him?" I asked.

"Answer my question," he said.

Jerk.

"I represent someone named Alfred Botchelko."

"Represent him in what capacity?"

A boney woman with bad posture was coming down the alley being pulled by two dogs.

"May I come in?" I asked.

"No," he said.

The woman nodded. I nodded back. One dog tried to sniff my ass crack but she pulled him away.

"He's asked me to come and speak to you on his behalf regarding a debt," I said.

"A debt?" he repeated and a corner of his mouth lifted in a grin. "And who owes who money . . . according to Botch?"

"May I come in?" I asked again.

"Didn't you hear me the first time?" he said.

"Yeah."

"Good. Now we're communicating."

I could hear another dog growling. There was a tall hedge behind me. It was coming from there. The hedge was impenetrable though.

"Botch thinks I ripped him off with my movie, doesn't he?" he said.

"That's right," I said.

"Well if he can prove it, I'm all ears."

I couldn't prove fuck all. This was an exercise in futility. I dug out a smoke, lit up.

"Why are there so many dogs in this neighborhood?" I asked. "You guys all drug lords or something?

He didn't answer. I waited to be dismissed. But instead, Kalesniko pointed to a back gate.

"Come in through there," he said.

The place was bigger than I thought. You couldn't tell from the front. Dozens of huge trees. An old playhouse. Now that was from the movie. The neighbor girl keeps coming over because they have a playhouse. Then Branagh spies on her to learn how a kid talks for one of his plays. Sure enough, Kalesniko's office loomed above the playhouse. Obviously the scene came from his own life. Botch was really stretching it here.

I stepped through a squeaky iron gate. There was a kidney shaped pool, a spa, cedar decks on three different levels, green Italian patio furniture. A spiral staircase lead up to Kalesniko's office. He waved me up.

I gripped the rail as I climbed. Spiral staircases are oddly disconcerting. Especially when a bit hung over. I went to put out my smoke at the door but he told me not to bother. We sat across from each other on his sofas.

"Could I have one of those?" he asked. I gave him one. He lit up. "Did Botch tell you he hates my guts?"

"He didn't use language quite that strong."

"How much does he claim I owe him?"

"He wasn't specific."

"What's your name?" he asked.

"William Botchelko," I said. I waited for him to frown or his eyes to pop or something, but he didn't react. "We're not related. But—ready for this? My real first name is Alfred."

Kalesniko sat back and blew one perfect smoke ring. Just like Botch. Then he grinned. "Let me guess. At some point you used your real name, I don't know when, maybe a bank or a loan or on the Internet or something. And a debt collector suddenly appeared?"

"Exactly."

“So then go to a lawyer. Or the cops. Why come to me?”

“He’s not that kind of debt collector.”

“What kind is he?”

“The kind that can create an unfortunate chain of events that leaves you unemployed, puts your marriage on the rocks, and reignites old smoking habits.”

“Reignites,” he repeated. “I like that.”

“So I’m really helping myself here,” I said. “Not him. If you’re wondering.”

“I’m wondering why he thinks I owe him anything.”

I shrugged. This was foolish. I was here because I was afraid Botch would fink me out to my wife. Full stop.

“Have you seen my movie?” he asked. “It’s on cable a lot.”

“I rented it.”

“And?”

“I liked it.”

“And—which story of Botch’s am I meant to have ripped off?”

“Well . . .” I shrugged. I glanced around the office. There were three-by-five cards up on the walls, some so old they were yellowing. A widescreen laptop stood on the desk. It looked expensive. There was a little kitchen in back. The carpeting was blue and disgusting though. A pump action BB gun leaned against the wall just under the window to the alley.

“Shoot dogs?” I asked.

“Coyotes.” He pointed to the backyard. “Had a coyote fight back there the other night that scared the blazing shit out me. Sounded like werewolves eating babies. They were nice enough to take a short break to howl along with a passing ambulance though, then went right back to biting chunks out of each other.” He helped himself to another cigarette from my pack. He didn’t light it though, just set it aside. “I shoot deer in the ass too. I used to enjoy having them in the backyard, but do you have any idea how much a deer eats? It’s like owning a herd of ponies. They destroyed everything. But they’re smarter than you think. When they hear me pumping that gun, they bolt. So now I pump it in the bathroom with the door closed."

"The gun, you mean?"

"Don't be clever," he said. "Why'd he send you?" He was getting impatient.

"I think the issue is—I think it's less about content and more about . . . subtleties." I shrugged again. "Characters. Attitude. Things like that."

"Why you is what I'm asking. He's either trying a desperate—and doomed—attempt to squeeze more money out of me. Or he wants you out of his hair for some reason."

"The doomed one's my guess." Then I stopped. "Did you say more money?"

He nodded. He butted out his smoke. Then he lit up the fresh one.

"What did you give him money for?"

"I optioned *Botch*."

"You optioned *Botch*?"

"Five grand," he said. "It starts shooting in Ontario in July. Donald Sutherland's starring."

Now that pissed me off. "You gave him money?"

"Yes."

"For a book?"

"His best book."

"He's been in contact with you?"

"Last month."

"You have a contract?"

"Drawn up by lawyers."

"And the film's going into production?"

"Which means he will also get a production bonus. Eventually."

Why was Botch embarrassing me like this? Sending me on a fool's errand. There was no money in this for either him or me.

"Who's playing Natalie?" I asked.

"We haven't cast that role yet."

"I like Hope Davis. Or Frances McDormand."

"We're thinking Jennifer Tilly. Or Carrie-Anne Moss." He saw me frown. "Canadian. Tax reasons."

Then he stood. So I stood too. I held out a hand and he shook it.

“Good luck with it,” I said.

“Thank you.” He walked me to the door.

“Sorry to waste your time,” I said.

“No problem.”

He remained there as I navigated my way down the staircase. When I stepped out into the alley, he was leaning out the window again.

“You married?” he asked me.

“Yes,” I said. “You?”

“Not anymore. He ever meet your wife?”

“Yeah. Just last night.”

“They get along?”

“They got along well.”

“Real well?” he asked.

He didn’t say anything else. He was waiting for me to add it up. And slowly I started to do the calculations. Kalesniko graciously did the total for me.

“He tried to fuck my ex too,” he said.

Chapter 48

That green Hyundai was parked out front. So I didn't park in the garage. I parked a block away. Greg drove past as I was creeping up the street, frowning at me. Greg could just kiss my ass. I slipped up on the front door. Tried it. Locked. I silently slipped my key in. I eased the door open and stepped inside.

Nothing amiss. No extra shoes. No dirty champagne glasses. No underwear thrown about like a clothing bomb had exploded. Robin was too neat for that anyway. She'd have to stop in the middle of sex to pick them up and fold them. So I merely stood perfectly still and listened. And then I heard it. Thumping. Only to realize my heart was beating against my rib cage. So I closed the door, shut away the outside sounds. Then I remained motionless and listened again. This time I really heard it.

Sex.

Panting. Gasping. Her voice high. His a low uncommitted grunt. I couldn't move. Not out of fear, not out of uncertainty. Just a terrible aching sadness. The sound of my wife in ecstasy. With another man. Down the hall. My home. My bed. It could be the floor of the bathroom, didn't matter. She was so hungry for this man she couldn't wait twenty-four hours to have sex with him. She threw all caution to the wind to fuck him.

And it was me who invited the devil across our doorstep.

They were building to a climax. Suddenly I wanted to see those two coming together. I wanted to see the veins sticking out on her neck and the sweat dripping off his fat face. I was determined to burn that image into my memory forever so I wouldn't have a second of regret in divorce court. I marched down the hall. The sounds were coming from our bedroom. I stopped just before the open door. They were getting louder and louder, the bed squeaking, the head board tapping against the wall.

"Oh," she was saying, "Oh!" And he answered, "Oh! Oh!"

I would shame them. I would shame myself. I wanted to see his hairy ass thrusting at her flabby hips. I wanted to see it all. And I wanted them both to know I had seen it. I stepped into the room. Quickly. Before I lost my nerve.

There they were, under the good quilt, two pathetic middle-aged people humping each other like teenagers. I immediately darted across the room before they could see me standing there like the watery-eyed pathetic little cuckold I suddenly was. And I grabbed the cover and jerked it clean off.

It wasn't Botch.

Some dark-haired kid was screwing Robin. He was on top of her and he looked up at me with his eyes bulging in shock but he kept pumping away at her like he couldn't stop.

"What the fuck!" I said and Robin screamed, "Dad!"

The boy jumped off her and started stumbling back to the wall, a slick erection waving in front of him. "Easy! Easy man!"

I lunged at him, grabbed the back of his head, forced him down to the floor like a dog and he was screaming and for some reason Maddy was suddenly standing before me and she was pulling my arm and pleading, "Dad don't! Don't hurt him!"

Maddy was naked. I had not seen my daughter naked since she was eight years old. Then one day something changed. As though, overnight, we stepped from the Garden of Eden right into an apple orchard and she would scream if I so much as passed her room and caught her in her underwear, scream if I tried the bathroom door while she was on the toilet, scream if I walked past the washer while she was unloading her panties. She would even scream if I pulled a tampon box from the grocery bags. Now here she was and she had dark, thick pubic hair and breasts that stood gravity-defyingly high on her chest and I gawked at her and I heard my voice say, “You look just like your mother.”

“Dad!” she screeched. I let the kid go and Maddy scooped up his clothes and stuffed them into his arms and pushed him right out the door. Then she turned to face me.

She looked exactly like Robin.

Like when we first met.

Robin and I used to lie naked together all afternoon. There was a thin paint brush in a cup on my desk and we’d take turns tracing each other’s skin with the very tip, winding slow circles around nipples and belly buttons and eyes. For hours we walked our finger tips up and down one another’s length, sometimes talking, sometimes silent. I knew the tiny white scar on her lower back and the sprocket scar on her shin, I knew the creases on her ear lobes and the sun freckles on her chest and the way her nose got steamy and warm when she was aroused. I once stopped in the middle of love making and asked her to show me her clitoris. And she did. She pulled her labia lips apart and dug around and pointed. There it was, tiny and purple and it looked a bit sore so I kissed it.

“Do it again,” Robin said.

“Dad,” Maddy said.

We were so young once.

“Dad,” she said again.

“Get him out of here,” I said.

Chapter 49

We sat in the kitchen. Maddy made us coffee. I didn't know she drank coffee. I didn't know she knew how to make it. She was even acting a bit like her mother now, keeping busy, looking purposeful, bracing herself. I know I was supposed to be angry or shocked or appalled. But instead I was sad. So heavy with sadness I knew the chair couldn't possibly hold me for long. My limbs were concrete, the coffee cup a pound of brick. I couldn't lift my arm with or without it. Everything had changed between us so long ago. Tevye sang, "I don't remember growing older. When did they?" It all seemed so horribly inevitable suddenly, the final painful lurch of despicable change.

"Will you tell Mom?" she asked.

"I guess I should," I said.

"Mom won't care." Then Maddy sat next to me. Normally Maddy could barely sit next to me in the car. "All the kids are doing it, Dad. It's no big deal. So don't make a big deal—"

"Change your tone with me," I said and I thumped my finger on the table and it hurt. "If you want to act like an adult, then you start speaking to me like an adult. Understood?"

She nodded. We were silent.

"Are you and Mom getting a divorce?" she blurted out.

"No. Why?"

"That man who was here last night? He was here again today," she said.

“Where did they go?” I asked.

“I don’t know. She didn’t tell me. She didn’t even say goodbye. She grabbed her purse and left. She was so happy to see him.” Then she dared herself again. “Is that her boyfriend?” She was staring right at me and her eyes were worried and searching my face for reassurance.

“I don’t think so,” I said. “I hope not.”

Suddenly, Maddy laid her small hand on my back. Why was she doing this? I wished she wouldn’t. Any other time I would have welcomed it. But not now. I was overcome by the most powerful urge to sob and I tightened my chest to stop it.

“I need you to be good,” I mumbled but I don’t think it came out and she rubbed her tiny hand back and forth across my shoulder blades.

“Dad, don’t hate me,” she whispered.

“I’d never hate you,” I whispered back. “I just hate—everything else.”

Chapter 50

Robin loved trains.

She imagined the day when she would be interviewed by James Lipton and when he would ask the question, "What's your favorite sound?" she would answer, "A train whistle." She knew the audience would make that "aah" sound.

On holiday weekends, those rare nights where every sound carries, we can hear the train whistle from our place echoing its lonely plea all the way up the valley. When Robin hears that sound she instantly falls asleep with a little smile on her face. Then again, Robin can listen to me hack with double pneumonia and still fall asleep with a little smile.

Twice we've taken the train to San Diego with Maddy. It's not a bad ride and most of the trip is along the surf but it always feels hectic and frantic and a bit dirty somehow. The better trip is the overnight to Seattle. We've done it on our anniversary five times now. Maddy stays with Mom and Dad.

"Getting there is half the fun" is not only a trite cliché but also a flat-out lie. With the exception of Robin and trains. We get a compartment. Not the little one for two. We did that once and had to start in on the wine a little too early. It's a claustrophobic, shin-kicking hell. Even worse are the bathrooms. They're down the hall. And public. May as well pack the turd jackhammer now.

The big sleeper compartments, on the other hand, have their own clever little bathroom, entirely stainless steel, which means when you flick on the shower you drench everything in the place, including towels, toilet paper and shaving kit. Two tall chairs are bolted next to the window, a little table stands in between, the couch turns into a bed, and a second bunk pulls down from above. That one is always Robin's.

We try, at least once during the trip, to trudge down to the dining car. You have to share tables in the dining car. That's the problem. We hope against hope we'll meet someone interesting. By that I mean someone who can actually converse. But train travelers seem unable to.

Let me amend that.

Not just train travelers—it's an American affliction, that confusion between monologue and dialogue. "Time to play Oprah," Robin whispers just before we sit. As I understand it, questions are generally the way conversation starts. But then, as I also understand it, a question should then be volleyed back in turn. Apparently not on Amtrak. These people expect to be interviewed. Maybe they all dream they'll meet James Lipton one day too. We once made a point of not speaking to the people sharing our table. As a test. Just to see if they might actually start the conversation instead. Not a chance. They simply stared at us and dumbly waited for question number one. After that first futile attempt at the dining car, we generally take the rest of the meals in our compartment.

Robin is also impossibly horny on trains. If we catch the train at Union Station, we're usually already at it before the train's halfway up San Fernando Valley. We only pull the curtain if we've stopped at a station. Otherwise that's part of the kick for her, watching the passing scenery while straddling me, the movement of the train doing most of the work.

Listening to her in that little bathroom as she tries to balance on one foot and jam her diaphragm in, cursing the thing and her own vagina too, actually makes me hard. And I think Robin hopes, on every trip, the train whistle will blow precisely when she orgasms.

But trains were no longer Robin's passion.

Robin now loved the ponies.

"If you're going to bet by names or pretty colors, you might as well scrunch up your money and throw it in the trash," she said. "Isn't that right, Botch?"

"That's right," Botch said.

"Get the *Racing Form*. All the stats are there. It's so well researched. And you really have to think about your choices. Add everything up. That's why we don't bet every race."

Botch nodded. He was poking Thai food into his mouth. They brought the stuff home with them. I can eat Thai food. The soy is fish based. I can't eat Chinese food. That soy is wheat based. Robin and I were using chopsticks. Botch was using a fork. The wine was flowing again. But those two had already been drinking. I could tell. Robin was talking too loudly, saying too much, being too upbeat. She thought that's how she covered a buzz. Instead, that's precisely how she gave it away.

"The key stat's the Beyer number. Because that adds up the . . ." Then she stopped. She turned to Botch.

"Adjusts times, distances and track conditions," he said and kept eating.

"Right. So you can compare how horses ran at different tracks," she said and then she kept eating too.

No one asked me how it went with Kalesniko. It had been a fucking ruse all along. They just wanted me out of the house.

"I caught Maddy having sex with a boy today," I said.

Robin stopped eating.

"You're kidding," she said.

I just stared at her.

"Are you kidding?" she said again.

"Yeah, I'm kidding," I said and went back to eating.

"I don't think that's funny," she said.

I just shrugged.

"Why'd you say that?" she asked.

"Just to see your reaction."

"I know what you're thinking," she said.

"Really? You read minds now?" I asked. "You the Amazing Kreskin?"

"I'm not a neglectful mother, William. Maddy and I had this conversation a long time ago. Sitting on our bed in fact. And she promised if she was ever thinking about becoming sexually active she'd talk to me about it first."

"Maybe she's not sexually active," said Botch. "Maybe she just lies there." And he snorted.

We ignored him.

"She promised you that?" I said.

"A mother daughter pledge. Maddy would never break that pledge. She would die before she'd break it. It's that bond mothers and daughters have."

Robin topped off her glass. Only hers. When women reach for a bottle, they never think to top off anyone's but their own. I don't think it's entitlement so much as years of men topping off drinks for them. I caught Botch's eye. He was grinning at me.

"How much money you lose today?" I asked.

"Lose?" Robin said. She grabbed her purse, found her wallet, then counted out the bills on the coffee table. "I'm up $273," she said and she sneered at me and nodded at Botch. "Pays better than a day at work, that's for sure."

I reached for the bottle. As I poured Botch's I said, "Kalesniko tells me they're making a movie out of *Botch*." Then I set the bottle back down and kept eating. He didn't react right away. He shrugged like he didn't care. But Robin was looking at him. As though she'd been betrayed. As though she should have been told first.

"Five grand he paid you."

He shrugged again, took a slug of wine.

"Donald Sutherland's playing you."

"Can you fucking believe that!" he blurted and a noodle flipped out on his chin. "Donald fucking Sutherland! Can you believe that shit?"

"What's wrong with Donald Sutherland?" Robin asked. "I like Donald Sutherland."

"Do you know how old he is?" he said. "Guess how old he is."

"Seventy or something," I said.

"Almost eighty," he said.

"But he could play sixty," I said.

"Do you know how old I am?" he asked.

"You're fifty-four," I said.

"That's right," he said.

"But you could play eighty," I added.

"And an eighty-year-old is playing me. What a load of shit!" He drained his glass, then shook the empty bottle over it as though it was ketchup and more might be trapped inside. "Talk about adding insult to injury. An intellectual property thief. Fucking smug to boot. And then casting giant bony geriatrics to play me. Why didn't he just get George fucking Burns . . .?"

"Because he's dead," said Robin and Botch said, "I know he's fucking dead. That's the point. I don't think anyone reads my shit and thinks, poor old doddering fart. One foot in the grave. Gee, I know who'd be perfect. Let's cast Shecky Green."

"I'm not following you," I said.

"Is there no more wine in this fucking place?" he said.

"Not if you're going to ask like that," I said but Robin was already on her feet. "What are you doing?" I demanded as she ducked into the kitchen. "You wouldn't get me toilet paper if I spoke to you like that," but she was already gone. I could hear her rummaging around.

"What the fuck is going on between you two?" I demanded.

"Just sex," he said.

"You better be joking."

"Yeah, we go to the races, bet on horses, and manage to squeeze in some hot sex in their filthy shitters. Don't be a moron."

"I don't want you hanging around my wife," I said.

"Caught your daughter getting fucked today, did you? And now you're pissed off at me."

"I'm pissed off because I humiliated myself trying to coerce money for you."

"Bet you thought it was us in bed, didn't you?"

"What did you do with the money?" I asked.

"I'd love to have seen your face. Did you beat the kid up? For being normal? Were you more or were you less shocked to find out it wasn't us?"

"You are not to hang around my wife anymore."

"I like hanging around your wife."

"And I like hanging around you too, Botch," said Robin. She had another bottle and she was beaming, thrilled with what she'd just overheard. She bounced into her chair, corkscrew at the ready, bottle pinched between her knees.

"Let me do that," said Botch and he reached for it but I grabbed for it too. "Here, I'll do it," I said and I wrestled it away from him and snatched up the corkscrew but it was the one from Robin's stupid waitressing days. The next time she was out of the house, I was going to chuck this dog out.

"Twist it," said Botch.

"Gee, a corkscrew and you twist it," I said. "Master lessons from the master wino," and Robin snapped, "Stop being rude."

I set the bottle down. I pushed it toward the middle of the coffee table. Where it remained. Robin couldn't reach for it. For if she did, she had chosen a side. Botch couldn't reach for it either. He had already claimed too much today. She looked to him. And he met her eyes. My Robin. And this man.

A team.

And there the three of us sat in silence.

Chapter 51

After Robin read *The Rent Tent*, she told me I had to start respecting her menstruation. She said it was holy and a sacred time for a woman. Then she put the book on my side of the bed.

I live in a house with two women. By some hilarity of physiology, they both start menstruating on the same day. Funnier still, they start PMSing on the same day too. I live in the Red House. I sure as hell wasn't going to read a book about fifty of them stuffed in a tent.

After Robin read *The Bride Stripped Bare*, she started demanding oral sex. She said she wasn't going to subvert her needs for a man's anymore. Unless she was meeting the needs of another man, I have no idea what I was gaining and she was losing in the sack. Either way, it should be noted that we've been together almost twenty years. When we got our first apartment, Robin would shit with the door open. This was how Robin and her sister used to catch up. But I grew up with one brother. No sisters. We caught up by punching each other. So up until that moment, I'd never seen a woman take a dump. Or wipe herself.

That was the real eye opener.

The second revelation was something she called thrush. I wasn't acquainted with thrush. It sounded like a game bird to me. "I bagged a pheasant and four thrush!" But now I am well acquainted with thrush. According to Robin, women get thrush when they're either sexually active or under stress. It seems Robin's been very stressed over the years. The word "discharge" in this house does not refer to the end of a stint in Iraq.

And then there's the hair issue. Robin has thick, coarse pubic hair that spreads along the expanse of her hips. And it's long. When she's naked before the mirror, holding up one outfit after another, I can see it hanging down from her crotch like a small goat's beard. "That's the way woman are supposed to look," she says as though I'm creeping up behind her with shears. Yet she shaves her legs, shaves her armpits, religiously plucks the five dark hairs on her chin and the seven or so around her nipples. But when it comes to the social equality of body hair, that stops at the crotch. Arguably, men are supposed to have hair on their face too, yet I still shave every day. Actually, not since I started looking like Botchelko. But still, I once did.

On top of everything else, Robin is also quite vocal about refusing to douche because "women's bodies naturally clean themselves."

So let's do the math.

Ass wiping from between the legs instead of from behind, menstruation, thrush, and pubic hair as long as Rapunzel's.

Before Robin demanded more oral sex, I went down on her annually. After she demanded it . . . I went down on her annually.

Robin's bedside reading had suddenly changed again.

The book she held was called *Playing the Ponies*. There was a second book on her bedside table. *Betting the Races*. I had the feeling I was going to be very sorry for not burying my face in that pelt of hers more frequently. She paused occasionally to scribble something down, then back to the book. She didn't study this hard in college.

"Good story?" I asked.

"Very exciting," she said.

"Intriguing characters?"

She slapped it closed, rolled over, reached for the light, said, "I have to get up early tomorrow. I want to watch them hot-walk the ponies at Santa Anita," and she flicked it out and curled up.

"Tomorrow? What about work?"

"I'm taking some time off."

"How much time off?"

She didn't answer.

"How much time, Robin?"

"I quit."

I knew it. Somehow I knew it.

"But won't Buchanan bust you?"

"I gave him money."

"But what about Maddy? What about this house?"

"I can make more money at the track."

"You just got lucky, that's all."

"It's not luck. That's why I'm studying. It's knowledge."

We were quiet again. I pinched my eyes closed, clinging to images I could suddenly feel fading away like misty ghosts. Saturday breakfast at Foxy's, Robin and Maddy greedily pulling apart a steaming cinnamon bun and laughing, Maddy running to me after dance class, then stopping to show me one perfect pirouette with a smile, Robin petting Maddy's hair as she lay on the floor crying, Christmas gifts and wrapping lying all about, the excitement of the day finally just too much for her to bear. All those quiet and sweet things suddenly seemed like another life from another time and I instantly longed for the ordinary again like a man shipwrecked.

"Are you going with him?" I finally asked.

She didn't answer.

"Answer me, Robin."

"Yes," she said. "I'm going with Botch."

Chapter 52

"Listen to me cocksucker—"

"Who you calling cocksucker?"

"You, you piece of shit. You've got a wife. Leave mine alone."

"Well look who grows a set of balls. Now here's a question for you, are they your balls or are you pretending they're mine?"

"You're too clever by half, you fucking rummy . . ."

"Don't push me."

"Or what? You gonna take my other wife? You think I'm a fucking Mormon? You want my life so goddamn bad, I'm tempted to give you the fucking thing. See how much you like it."

"Hey, you've got mine. Fair trade."

Then Robin stepped into the kitchen just as I said, "I'm going to say this one more time . . ."

"Who you talking to?"

I looked up and almost dropped the phone. Robin was wearing the scarf her sister knitted. She got so many compliments about that scarf, she printed up cards with Cheryl's name and number on it and started handing them out. She was also wearing heels, the black ones, and a red skirt I'd never seen before that stopped well above the knee. On the rack, that get-up was a generation too young for her. For some reason, this morning she was carrying it off.

"It's our broker," I said.

"We have a broker?"

"Just some guy at Schwab. I'm getting rid of the MGM stock."

"I thought you got rid of all of that."

"There's still some left."

She shrugged and walked out of the room.

"Only a middle class pussy would have come up with a lame story like that," said Botch.

"You do not come around my house. If you pull up in this driveway . . ."

"I'm meeting her there."

"You listen to me, you fucking prick—"

"Oh my goodness!" Robin was back in the kitchen. "You cannot talk to our broker like that! Give me that phone."

"I can take care of it."

"Give me that phone, William," she demanded.

"I said I'll take care of it."

She grabbed the phone. Both hands. "Give me that." Damn she was strong. So I let go and simply turned the base off.

"Hello? Hello?" The phone was dead. She stood there, sizing me up. I was lying. She knew it now. She handed the phone back.

"If you want to end up in the poorhouse, you just keep me from going."

She grabbed her purse and marched out, fishing out the car keys as she went.

"I can earn money too!" I shouted after her.

"Then do it!" she shouted back. The door slammed. I heard the Toyota start.

"What's going on?" There was Maddy in a long tee-shirt. Her eyes were barely open, her hair in her face. She looked five years old again and for a moment I thought she would curl up in my arms. Instead, she dropped down in a kitchen chair.

"What's all the shouting about?" She sniffed Robin's coffee mug. She set it back down. "Did Mom go to the track?"

"Yes," I said.

"Is she going with that man?"

I didn't answer.

"What are you going to do, Dad?" she finally asked.

I still didn't answer. Maddy looked like she was going to cry. "That man is going to steal Mom. What are you going to do, Dad?"

"I don't know, Maddy. All right?" I said. "I don't know."

"We're a little concerned that we haven't heard from you in so long."

"That's the way it is," I said. "But I want you to know, I've stopped drinking."

"Don't know if that's a good or bad thing," he replied. "Just hold on a sec, Botch."

He put me on hold. "All You Need is Love" was playing. I found myself humming along. Then I started to worry that no one was coming back on.

"Botch. Andrew Rotman."

"Andy," I said.

"Andrew, actually," he corrected. "So Scott tells me you're writing again."

"I am. I'm working on a book."

"You know we're ready when you are."

"Great. Maybe we can talk about an advance."

"Botch . . . come on. We've advanced you twice. I mean, once bitten—"

"—twice clichéd," I said. Christ, I was even starting to sound like him.

"You write it, we'll publish it. That's all I can promise you. And that's a lot."

"Fine. I'll just call around. See if someone else would prefer my business."

"Good luck with that," he said. "I'm glad you stopped drinking. Because you clearly have alcohol amnesia."

Chapter 53

Just how hard could it possibly be to write a book? A book of poems? A short book of poems. A very short book of very short poems. His poems didn't even seem that complicated. They were just little scenes basically, little anecdotes written in a funny way across the page. For instance:

27
44

You lovely thing,
I tell her,
she has Don Quixote
by her bed
and a guitar in the corner
in tune
I gave it one strum while she
was in her filthy loo.
She has black eyes
big as eggs
and black hair
I can't stop touching
and a round, round bum

under a long frilly skirt
like a gypsy
and when she reads aloud
from her journal
I feel the pinch of intimidation.
"Every morning I'd say to myself
you must love him more,"
she tells me
explaining
why she left her boyfriend.
She's 27.
I'm 44.
She smokes like a convict
matches me drink for drink
or better.
I don't feel the pinch of intimidation
then
so much as the pause
of caution.
"You seem gay,"
she said when we first met.
"The way you use your
hands and say Darling."
"Well what do you suggest I do?"
I snap.
"Pinch every woman's ass in the place?"
Then I add,
"Darling's a theater affectation."
Which is true, but I've never
worked in the theater
so maybe she's loving a lie.
And then she sits on my lap
with arms draped easily around
my neck

and she kisses
"like she means it,"
I tell her.
"How else would I kiss you?"
she says
a bit dismissively I think.
I was saying
something unique and astute
but perhaps
I just read it somewhere.
Still,
the idea she's kissed other
men like that.
and she's 27
and I'm 44
She asks the cabbie how many
days a week he works and if
he likes his job
"Four kids," he shrugs
in reply.
She asks the waitress what's
her favorite fish on the menu.
"Blue-eyed travella," she says
so she orders it.
She watches a dark haired girl dancing
before the fire
"She's wonderful,
so full of life."
Then tells her just that
And the girl cries
and
she's 27
and
I'm 44

In the gallery upstairs
above the native stuff
which neither of us like
she points to a Picasso
and says it must be from his blue period
and how Schiele died young
after the pedophilia charge
and landscapes don't grab her emotionally
and owning an etching isn't really owning art
and then she squeezes my bum cheek
in passing.
He saw that.
"How old are you guys?"
he says, "If you don't mind me asking."
"I'm 27,"
I say.
"And she's 44,"
"I think you got that backwards.
Darling,"
she says between paintings.

Forty-four? That was an old poem. I didn't have any stories about dating young girls. I didn't have any stories about dating. He writes a lot about women. But I know only three intimately. Though the juries still out on my mother. There must be other topics. I flipped through the pages.

SUHARTO WIDOWS

I can see them from her
balcony
and sometimes they swoop
overhead at night
ululating like Suharto widows.

"What are those birds called?"
I ask.
Again.
Apparently.
And she says,
"You're obsessed with those
fucking birds."

My ex wife phones me
long distance.
It's her six month
anniversary.
Six months of what?
I ask.
Al-anon, she says.
"You stopped drinking?"
I ask. I had no idea
she had a problem.
she seemed to hold her liquor
well.
"Not alcoholics anonymous,"
she says.
"Al-anon.
For people whose
lives have been destroyed
by an alcoholic."
"I see," I answer.
Finally.
Then add,
"I guess this is a bad time
to say I could use a drink."

"Rainbow lorikeets sit on my
balcony rail every morning

making mischief,"
Kath tells me
"And those big ones. What
are they called?"
She lays back with her arms above
her head and
her breasts stand up
squeezably lovely.
"Cockatoos," I say
then suddenly shush her
when I hear the
Suharto Widows
in the Eucalyptus below.
I want them to be
called that now
the way I want the Fruits
in London pubs
to be called
Sticky Pockets
or something equally
absurd.
"Would you drop it with those
fucking birds," she says
and lights another Menthol.

We float on her brother's
Four Winns in Watson's Bay
and her little niece is
afraid of me.
We have only white
wine on the boat because
it doesn't stain and I
look about me
like I'm watching a movie

starring me and
it's not such a
bad movie.
Then Kath puts
her hand on the
small of my back and
I resurface
just for a moment.
Her brother backs the
boat into the Kirribilli
wharf, dark now and
we suddenly all hate to part.
I jump out first and
pull Kath up
and we wave
as they disappear
under the Harbour Bridge.
We walk home
past the PM's house
and the governor's too
and she says,
"I don't even know your
politics yet,"
but I shush her again
and point into the night
at two black and white
Suharto Widows
darting past overhead.
"You're going to drive me
nuts with those fucking birds,"
she says.

Kirribilli? Where's that? The place has cockatoos and something called rainbow lorikeets? Christ, I'd never lived anywhere else in the world. I don't have any exotic stories. I drove to Ensenada once. But Montezuma pretty much put the period on the end of that sentence. Either way, it's clearly a poem about birds. Hell, I could write about birds. We have birds all over Glendale. We once had a peregrine falcon in the garage. I shooed it out with a broom. Then found a headless chickadee behind the dryer a couple weeks later.

And I hear screech owls sometimes. Now that can make you lose the pinch of your pucker on a warm summer night. Suddenly, there's a scream like a witch having a Sterno colonic and it's coming from the oak in the backyard.

There's also those big ones. The horned owls. I saw one once. It looked like an Emperor Penguin had somehow climbed a tree. All the ravens and falcons were swooping it and screeching and cawing but the owl didn't seem to be the least bit interested. I know it was him I heard the next morning when I wheeled out the recycling. On TV, an owl's "hoo" sounds rather sweet, like a mildly inquisitive dove. This guy sounded like an old security guard with a twenty-year Marlboro habit.

Fine. I'll write about that.

So how do you start a poem exactly? At the start I guess. A title . . .

BIRDS

emperor penguins fly through
the air with headless birds
in their beaks and grumpy
great horned owls demand
to know who goes there.

How long should a poem be? Botch's were pretty long. I had to add something to this. Poetry was harder than it looked. It didn't help that I couldn't concentrate. The moment I paused to sip my coffee, my mind instantly went to Robin. At the track. With fucking Botch. Wait! A robin's a bird. And also my wife. There's never any robins in LA, but who cares. This could work as a nice double entendre thingy.

But it's the Robin who
rules the roost.

Not bad. Robin and roost. She's the big rooster and of course I'm the chicken. Fuck, I'm good at this.

Who answers the phone with
"Star fucking Ford,"
as I do all the cooking
and egg laying
and the baby chick's having
sex with her scrawny boyfriend
right in our nest
and I wished I was a Peregrine
Falcon so I could have bitten
his head off and then
flown out to the track and
swooped down and clawed the
eyes out of Botch
as that hawk and my Robin
put five on six to win.

Chapter 54

I poured myself another coffee and stepped out back. I felt rather grand lighting that cigarette. The long-buried artist was suddenly buzzing through my nerve strands. Maybe I would switch roles with him. He can have the wife. Take her. My life looks so great? This little house? Greg and his wife walking around in their gitch next door. Lawn cutting every Sunday, then scratching at itchy ankles for the rest of the afternoon. A cat that looks like a tiny swayback Shetland pony. A daughter who emits a low growl when you pass her bedroom door.

Have it. Take it all. And I'll have all those young girls. All those hard drinking nights. I'll go live overseas. In London or Sydney and I'll write poems about the size of women's nipples and how the girls light a cigarette and hand it to you with a kiss and the way they sing in a car along with Fleetwood Mac. Hey, you name it. I could write about riding a boat in a harbor too, or maybe something really different, maybe Africa and sleeping with Kenyan women. I've never even kissed a black girl. Though they have quite a bit of AIDS over there, as I understand it. But it doesn't have to be Kenya. It could be India, let's say. Though the poverty would get me down and it's so dirty and hot. Well screw it then, back to Sydney, Australia. Or Kirribilli, wherever that is. Probably the outback or something, doesn't matter, just return there as the conquering hero and I'd squeeze out even more poems but now from my perspective instead of the perspective of a tedious drunk with a gambling addiction and a pathetic propensity for trying to seduce other men's wives. I could do everything he did. I just did, for God sakes. I just wrote a poem and it worked on so many levels. Well, at least two levels. And I could go to bed with the fine weight of accomplishment permeating me and knowing, at last, true satisfaction. Maybe then my life would finally be an adventure.

The adventure I once dreamt it would be.

I used to lie awake back in college and imagine a future so wonderfully blinking bright. Robin used to sleep in my arms then. Once she even fell asleep lying atop me like a blanket and I loved it though it did get a little hard to breathe after a while. She didn't snore back then, though she would sleepwalk occasionally, and once she sat up in the dark and stared at me and said, "Jack?" like she couldn't believe it. When I ask her about it the next morning, she shrugged and said, "My dad's name's John but a lot of people call him Jack." Which, now that I think about it, doesn't make a bit of sense. What the hell would she be doing in bed with her dad?

Either way, the point is, I'd think about the future back then and the tears would slide down my temples with the sheer joy of what this life was going to be. Robin was studying economics and I was studying business and we were going to go out there and learn. Just learn. We always said that. We'd work for big companies and small, in New York for a year, in London for a year, then back to LA. Where we'd do something together. What exactly, we didn't know. That's why we were going to go out and learn first. We'd have a home on the beach and I imagined Robin in a long white skirt holding the hand of our little boy. The moment he spotted me he'd break into a run, his little legs hammering the sand, and I'd scoop him up and Robin would step up and kiss me full on the lips. Not hurried and dry as sandpaper, but a real kiss of tenderness. Then she'd take our boy inside. Maybe I should give him a name. Randy. No, not fucking Randy. I'll get that prick one day. Let's say William. My name. But we'll make it two names. And we'd always call him by both names. William Randall. No, not Randall. Why do I keep coming back to that fucker's name? No, William Anthony. And Robin and William Anthony would go inside and start dinner and I'd take that moment to stand on the sand and stare out at the setting sun. And thank the wonderful Gods for such simple, such heart-kissed blessings.

Instead, Robin became a teller at Wells Fargo. Then a junior loan officer at First Interstate. And I got a job managing a courier company called Quick Smart, which meant I was just a glorified dispatcher, then got the job as night manager at Kinko's. Then Robin was diagnosed with polycystic ovaries, which somehow explained the hairs on her chin and breasts, and she miscarried twice and then finally got pregnant with Maddy. And instead of stroking her swollen belly at night as we lay in bed together, I stroked her hair as she wept and mumbled, "I don't know why I can't stop crying."

I never stood on the beach and stared at the sunset. Instead I sat on the back steps and stared at the moon.

It was time to reinvent myself. I was about to re-launch. It felt glorious.

Then I went back inside and reread that shitty poem.

Chapter 55

When Nora bolted from her bowl, she left so many strands of julienne cut tuna in her wake it looked like we fed her on the floor. That of course meant someone had just pulled into the driveway. It was well past dark. And I had long since eaten. Stir fried veggies, mostly peppers because they were about to turn, but some brown mushrooms too, which I dumped into couscous and mixed up with a little olive oil and tahini.

Maddy poked at it with a fork. "Tastes like warm shit, Dad," and off she went to her room.

It did taste like warm shit, frankly.

I was smoking in the kitchen now. Waiting. I was not about to be found waiting in the living room.

I heard the door. They came breezing in, Robin saying, ". . . underestimating the trainer and not taking into account his past performance line . . ." The fucking horse expert now. No one called out my name. Botch dropped a pizza box on the dining room table. Finally, Robin came into the kitchen, backwards and laughing, and when she turned and saw me all she said was, "Are you smoking in the house?"

I took a drag.

"There's no smoking in the house," she said. "You know that."

It was down to the filter.

"Put that out."

If I put it out now, she'd look like she won. So instead, I reached for another and pressed the tip to the new smoke and puffed away. Then I butted out the old smoke.

"It's out," I said.

Robin stared at me. I stared back.

"You hungry?" Botch called from the dining room.

"I ate," I said.

Robin shouted down the hall. "Maddy, want pizza!"

Maddy appeared instantly. "Oh thank fuck," she said.

"Hey! The language!" said Robin.

"He says it," and Maddy pointed at Botch.

"He's not your father."

"Thank fuck for that," she said.

"Hey!"

But Maddy just took a slice and headed back down to her room.

"Where are your manners, young lady?"

"Somewhere around here," she said and pointed at her ass.

I was really starting to appreciate her rudeness suddenly.

"I'm not eating in this kitchen if you're smoking," Robin said and she marched out with two plates and cutlery.

So I got up. I grabbed the ashtray. I went into the dining room. I pulled out a chair. I sat across from them. And I puffed my cigarette. No one spoke. Robin served Botch a slice. Then she took one.

"Sure you won't have some?"

I didn't answer. I was staring at Botch. As he curled his slice up and slid it into his mouth. Robin did the same. Robin always ate pizza with a knife and fork. I've even seen her eat sandwiches with a knife and fork. She hated touching her food.

"Good day at the track?" I asked.

"Excellent day at the track," Botch said, mouth full, lips greasy. He didn't even think to reach for the napkin, he just kept staring at me and I held that gaze.

"Want to know how excellent?" Robin asked and I answered by saying, "Get out of my house."

Botch kept chewing.

"Get the fuck out of my house."

"William!"

"I heard you," Botch said. He wiped his face. He stood.

"And don't ever come back. Get out of our lives. Forever."

"That's enough! Don't listen to him Botch."

But Botch did exactly as he was told. Albeit slowly. And without a trace of intimidation.

"You don't have to go. William's just being rude. We'll have a glass of wine and we'll discuss this."

But Botch simply pulled open the door, paused to zip up his jacket, and out he went, pulling the door closed behind him.

"Did you hit him, Dad?" asked Maddy. She was standing in the archway, eyes shiny with excitement.

"Go to your room, Maddy," Robin said and she grabbed the pizza box and marched into the kitchen.

"Good for you, Dad. Punch that fat shit right in his fucking face."

"Maddy!" And Robin stormed back into the living room. "That's enough! Go to your room!"

Maddy glared at Robin. "He's a fat fuck, Mom."

"That's enough, I said!"

Maddy spun on her heels and marched down the hall. "He's a fucking prick!" she shouted back.

Finally, approval from my daughter. That only took a lifetime. Robin was getting a taste of being the odd man out at last.

Robin glared at me. Then she snapped out the light. "I'm going to bed." Off she went.

Cold war.

I'd outlast her. I locked the front door. Then I marched down the hall and right into the bedroom. Robin had her top off. She was wearing a green lacy bra. I'd never seen that bra before. The fat of her back was struggling to engulf the straps. I went into the en suite and stuck the Sonicare in my mouth and started buzzing away.

"You're going to apologize to him," she said.

I didn't answer.

"You're going to apologize to him."

"You tell her, Dad!" Maddy called out.

"He didn't say anything!" Robin said and she slammed the bedroom door. Then she stood with her hands on her hips and glared at me.

"You are going to apologize to him," she said again.

"Like fuck I am," I said.

"You tell her, Dad," came from under the door.

Robin jerked open the door. Maddy was crouching on all fours at the sill. She jumped to her feet and bolted to her bedroom.

"Go to bed young lady."

"I'm not tired."

"I said go to bed."

"Old people go to bed at nine-thirty. Not young people."

I heard Robin slam Maddy's bedroom door. But Maddy pulled it open again.

"You close that door!"

"I need the fresh air!"

"The fresh air's all smoke!"

"I love second-hand smoke!"

"You had better not be smoking, young lady!"

"Or what?"

"Or else."

"Or what else?"

"Don't push me."

Robin marched back into the bedroom.

"Put on a top, Mom! You're grossing everyone out!"

Robin slammed the door. I finished brushing my teeth. I pulled off my pants and shirt and crawled into bed.

"You're wearing your socks to bed?"

I laid back with my hands behind my head. Defiantly sock clad.

"I am screwed at the track without him," she said. "He knows what he's talking about."

"That's why he has a $70,000 gambling debt?"

"That was cards."

"I hope he knows horses better than cards."

"We are screwed, William. Don't you get it? How will we pay our bills? You don't have a job. I don't have a job. You want to be out on the street? You want Maddy frying grease burgers at the Green Hut . . .?"

"I'll fry burgers!"

". . . you want Maddy in some crappy school where she'll be having anal sex with sweaty Armenian men twice her age?"

"Sounds good to me!" Maddy shouted.

"You had better not be having anal sex, young lady!" Robin shouted at the door.

"Gee Mom, what's anal sex! I never had my sex talk!"

"We had your sex talk!"

"Oh yeah, you made it sound like sperm crawls across the floor and up your leg!"

Robin closed her eyes. She rubbed her temples. She took a deep breath, exhaled loudly. Robin took one yoga class about four years ago. The only thing she learned was "Uji breathing."

I still didn't say a word. I didn't have to. I had told him to leave. And he left. Without looking back. Or speaking. He was out of my house. Out of our lives. I was the man of this place. And Maddy was on my side.

I had won.

Then Robin snatched up her purse. She dumped the contents on my stomach. Twenties, tens, fives, singles. Money. Everywhere. I didn't touch it. I didn't move. I just stared at it.

"Seven-hundred and twenty-three dollars," she said. "I had to fill out a W-4."

I didn't say a thing.

"One day's work," she added.

I just lost.

Chapter 56

I knew he was home. The front light was on. The curtains were pulled. The green Hyundai was parked in the neighbor's driveway. And there was a black Lexus parked in his. Probably a woman.

I tried calling him on the phone first but Robin wouldn't have it.

"You're not calling. You're driving down," she said. Then she handed me money for gas.

Like she was my mother. So I only half-filled the tank. Then I bought cigarettes and coffee with the rest.

Like I was a teenager.

I parked on the street in front of his place. I'd been standing on his front steps for a good fifteen minutes now. I walked around back. I knocked on the back door. No one. If I turned around and drove home, it would just piss Robin off more. It was Saturday after all. The horses were running.

I went back to the front door. I pushed open the mail slot. "Botch!" And then I did what people in movies do and it infuriates me. I tried the handle. Unlocked. I pushed the door open a crack.

Now what? What if he thought I was a burglar? But Botch would never own a gun. A bat maybe. Never a gun.

"Botch?" My heart started thumping instantly. I'd make the worst burglar. How did they keep their bung holes tight every time they broke into a house? Mine was unpinching a bit already.

"Botch, you home?"

I stepped inside. I stood there. I listened. I was about to call out again when I thought I heard voices. Coming from upstairs. Was he still in bed with this woman? My terribly provincial manners almost propelled me back out the door. But then I realized, this would be a wonderful story for Robin. When I told her how I found Botch in bed with some woman, how I sat on the edge of the bed and apologized to him while the two lay naked in each other's arms. How the woman was gorgeous. Didn't matter what she really looked like. I'd describe Keira Knightly. Or better yet, maybe just to really bug her, I'd describe Robin Wright Penn. I could just see her face. Unblinking. Diamond-hard eyes. As I told her Botch graciously accepted the apology and would like to know when he and his gorgeous new girlfriend would be joining Robin at the track.

Lovely.

I thumped up the stairs. His bedroom door was open a crack and I pushed it wide with a big smile. But no one was there. Then I heard Botch's voice again. It was coming from the room just around the banister. That must be the guest room. Maybe he was on the phone.

I walked around the banister and stopped in the open doorway.

There sat Botch. Behind a desk. It was an office. I guess he needed an office. But with a laptop? I rather romantically imagined him writing at the kitchen table. Or that guest room above the garage. On notepads. Or an old Olivetti. It seemed so terribly pedestrian.

He locked eyes with me. There was fear in his eyes.

Now that was a response I liked.

I stepped into the room, fearless now.

"I just wanted to apol—" But I shut up instantly.

Because there were two men in the room with him.

One was a big guy in wide glasses, huge belly, well into his fifties or even sixties. The other guy was maybe in his late forties. Short. But with enormous shoulders and a barrel chest.

"Oh sorry, didn't see you," I said.

No one spoke.

"Am I interrupting?"

Still no one spoke.

"Why don't I just wait downstairs for you?" I said to Botch and I went to back out.

"No, no," said the short guy. "Come in, come in," and he grabbed my wrist. Hard. I stepped back inside. He let go of me. He grinned. And suddenly these two looked rather familiar. But I couldn't place from where.

"You a friend of Botch's?" he asked.

I looked to Botch. For the first time since I'd met him, he looked worried.

And at that moment I knew I was in, what they call, a situation.

"You guys friends of Abenathy?" I asked.

"Who's Abenathy?" the short one replied.

That sounded sincere.

"Look, I'm clearly interrupting something . . ."

"You're not interrupting anything. We're all friends here." He held out a hand. "Benny," he said. "My associate Ricardo."

Ricardo didn't shake my hand. He didn't even nod.

"This is the Botchelko you're looking for," Botch suddenly announced.

"What!?" I said.

"Yeah, no bullshit. Show him your driver's license, Alf."

That son of a bitch. He was going to have me rolled. Have my thumbs cut off like Eric Roberts in *Pope of Greenwich Village*. Good movie. That prick was throwing me on the bonfire. To save himself. Then steal my wife. And sleep in my bed. And drive my car. And play the ponies all day with Robin. And Maddy would run away from home and become a hooker.

"We know which Botchelko we're looking for."

"You guys think I'm joking?" And Botch got up from his desk and came over to me. He spun me around like he was going to dig out my wallet.

Instead, she shoved me right out the door and slammed it behind him and shouted, “Run!”

I ran.

I scrambled down the stairs. Botch couldn’t hold the door. He leapt over the banister, with startling agility I have to say, and he was on my heels.

“Back door! Back door! Back door!” he shouted.

I ran to the kitchen. The back door was locked. I didn’t know which way to twist the locks. It felt like one of those dreams where your legs go numb or the ground turns to sand and the bear chasing you runs faster than a pony.

I could hear their massive weight bashing down the stairs like two angry rhinos but Botch twisted the locks open and he shoved me out the door and pulled it closed behind him and there they were, fat red faces, as they slammed up against that door now.

“Back fence!” Botch pointed. And I ran toward an eight-foot-high wooden fence, apparently in San Pedro you could have them, but this meant we were trapped again when Botch ran up and simply kicked out two boards. He ducked through and I followed right behind him.

“Always have an escape route!” he shouted but instead of sprinting down the alley, he ran around the fence and right into his neighbor’s backyard. I followed him up the path as he booted lawn chairs aside and there was that massive Rottweiler lunging against his chain but we ran right past him, ran through a carport where a chinless woman in curlers was standing with a cordless phone saying, “I heard shouting, officer and . . . oh here they come now.” And she smiled and waved at Botch and Botch said, “Hi Angela,” and we ran down her driveway and found ourselves out in the street.

“Where’s your car!”

“There! Right there!” And I hit the remote lock and we scrambled inside and slammed the doors and we both hit the locks just as Benny landed right on the hood.

I saw Ricardo sprint for the Lexus.

I sat there. I stared at this man.

"Keys," said Botch. He said it calmly. As though he knew he must.

I dug in my pockets.

"They're in your hands."

Right. I jerked my hand back out and all my change came clattering out too. My hands were shaking as I picked through the keys, so many damn keys, why did we have to have so many fucking keys, what could they possibly open?

And then I dropped them.

"Calm, William. Calm," said Botch as Benny started kicking the windshield. I scooped them up. I found the ignition key. But then I couldn't get it in the ignition. The key had grown, had swollen somehow, it was too big.

Uji breathing. I'd do uji breathing, just like Robin. I stopped, took a deep breath . . . "No time for that," said Botch as the Lexus came smoking backwards out of his driveway. I tried again. The key slipped in. I cranked the ignition.

"Reverse," was all Botch said and I put it in reverse and booted it and Benny tumbled right off the hood and slapped onto the pavement.

I took off down the street. Backwards. For the entire block.

"You might want to turn around," suggested Botch.

I cranked it. Just like a cop. But that Lexus was on us already. I thought he was going to ram the door. Instead he tried to cut in front of me but I was already on the move. I had a six cylinder in this baby. A two-point-six, I think. I never bothered to ask at Jiffy Lube. But it was pretty peppy. Though I knew there was no outrunning that Lexus.

"We're fucked," I said.

"Just drive," he said. "They don't want to ruin that car."

"They Abenathy's men?"

"Nope."

"Another debt!" I shouted.

"This shocks you?" he said. And he lit a cigarette. The fucker actually lit a cigarette.

"Where do I go!?"

"One-ten," he said.

"But they'll just follow us. We'll never outrun them!"

"Watch," was all he said. And he grabbed the e-brake and yanked it on and the Lexus slammed into the back of us. The Honda felt like it bucked into the air and I hit the steering wheel with my chest.

Everything seemed bright white and creamy then, like time was slowing, and Botch had the steering wheel in his left hand and his left foot was over the console and on the pedals. He pulled forward maybe thirty feet, the Lexus still sitting there, then he threw the car in reverse, glancing over his left shoulder, cigarette dangling from his lips, and he stepped on the gas and rammed the Lexus again.

"That'll do it," he said.

"You wrecked my car!" I shouted.

"Cars can be repaired. One-ten. Let's go."

I took off again. So did the Lexus.

"But they're still chasing us!"

"Not for long. Air bags have popped. Grill's steaming."

I swept down the on-ramp. But the car was driving funny. Of course it was driving funny. It was fucked.

"Don't speed. Just drive."

I felt cold. I felt like I was freezing to death. My arms were copper hard. I could have pulled the steering wheel off with my hands. But I stayed in the slow lane. An even sixty. And I kept watching the rear view.

"They still there?"

"They're still there."

"Just wait."

And sure enough, the steam from the grill grew thicker. It began to envelope their car. And they dropped back and back and cars started to slip in between the gap. First one. Then another and another. Finally, I watched as they slowly, unhurriedly, took the Martin Luther King exit.

"They're giving up," I said.

Botch twisted around in his seat and watched till they were gone. Then he turned back to face the front.

"That settles it," he said.

"You're finally going to pay your debts?" I asked.

"No. I'm finally getting a gun."

Part III

"Like the gay guy said—when it comes to vaginas, I don't know what all the stink is about."

—Alfred Botchelko

Chapter 57

"Ohh! Look at the pretty one."

Maddy was on her feet, staring through the giant clubhouse windows with Botch's binoculars.

Botch and Robin ignored her. They were studying the *Racing Form* like med students cramming, brows pinched, fingers rubbing foreheads, pens circling and scribbling, Botch's reading glasses perched at the tip of his nose.

The *Racing Form* made no sense to me. I didn't understand the racetrack program either. I didn't understand the horse statistics or the jockey statistics. I didn't know what the announcer was saying. He could have been speaking Spanish. The tote board in the infield was complete nonsense. What was an exacta, a trifecta, a superfecta? I didn't understand the odds, the race payoffs, the race track map even. Win, place and show. That's all I knew.

Yet Robin, in a mere week, appeared to know it all.

"Dad, look at number five."

I took the binoculars.

"We should bet on number five."

Six thoroughbreds and jockeys in canary yellows and silky oranges and reds were being led around in the post parade before the race. I couldn't find number five.

"Beautiful horse," I said and handed the binoculars back.

Maddy peered out again.

"Oh look! He's jumping all over! He's rearing! He almost threw his rider! Oh man, Dad—we're betting five for sure!"

"Waste of time," said Robin without looking up.

Maddy sat back down. She grabbed one of her fries and covered it with so much salt it looked like a sugar-coated churro.

"Those other horses look bored to tears. That horse is ready to rock."

"That horse isn't ready to do anything," said Robin.

"It's more than ready, Mom. Five wants to run somewhere."

"Five's burning up all its energy too early. It'll be a dog by the five-sixteenths pole," she said.

"I give it four furlongs," said Botch.

Neither had looked up.

Maddy was quiet a moment. "Can I have a beer, Dad?" she asked.

"Of course not," Robin said.

"Why are we sitting in here?" said Maddy. "Why aren't we out in the grandstand? That's where the action is."

Botch merely pointed at the monitor mounted on our table and Robin said, "Simulcast," as though Botch was the body, she the voice. "We're handicapping some other races too."

Maddy watched her mother a moment. She tugged up her hip-hugging jeans. She pulled out her lip gloss and rubbed some on, smacking her lips with a "pop," exactly the way Robin did. Then she continued to stare at Robin and Botch.

"How long's a furlong?" she finally asked.

"Eighth of a mile," answered Robin.

"How many are in a mile?"

And Robin finally met her eyes. With a look of utter weariness.

"Don't want her in one of those shitty public schools, huh?" I mumbled.

Robin snapped me a look, turned back to Maddy. "Honey . . . it's an eighth of a mile."

"Yeah?"

"So there's eight furlongs in a mile."

"Well why didn't you just say that?"

"Because it's fourth grade arithmetic, dear," she said and she went back to work.

"She just called me retarded, Dad."

"No she didn't honey."

"She said I'm stupid as nine-year-old."

"Well—okay, she implied that . . ."

"Look," said Robin and she thumped her pen down. "You two wanted to come along. You wanted to know what goes on here. You wanted to see what we were up to. And now you're blathering away . . ."

Blather. A Botch word.

. . . when we're trying to concentrate. Maybe if you sat and watched, maybe if you just pinched your upper lip to your lower lip, Maddy, and watched, then maybe you'd learn something."

Maddy crossed her arms. She thumped back in her chair. Then the deep breathing started. Maddy used to do this even as an infant. Arms crossed, inhaling and exhaling, inhaling and exhaling, until Robin would eventually snap, "Oh would you just cry already!"

Maddy turned to me. "Give me twenty bucks, Dad. Twenty to win on five. Let's play it."

I didn't have twenty bucks.

"Give me twenty bucks, Mom."

"I'm not giving you twenty bucks to bet on one horse."

"But you said I could bet twenty bucks today."

"For the whole day. Not one race."

"What do you care what I do with my twenty?"

"Fine. Fine, here. Throw your money away."

And she tossed the twenty across the table. Maddy snatched it up and jumped to her feet.

"You should stick to straight bets," said Robin. "Just place. Or bet across the board." But she was saying it to Maddy's back. She was already gone.

"Why do you encourage her?" Robin snapped at me.

"How do I encourage her? I'm just sitting here."

"Exactly."

Robin scribbled more furiously now. Then she stopped and rubbed her eyes. She turned to Botch. "Sergio's Pride looks good in the fourth. She did well in her maiden."

"Win odds are all right. We'd collect as a show maybe. But not in the quinella. Let's stick to stake horses there."

"Maybe we should try stake horses in the exacta but take a shot on Sergio's Pride in the quinella?"

"Your call."

And they were back at it. I wasn't placing any bets. I didn't need to see Robin's crooked grin accompanied by the curious cock of the head every time I lost. There was that side of me that loved the idea of winning every race, whooping as my horse crossed the line and hugging and spinning Maddy in circles, that glorious long-shot ticket held aloft, until Robin's face was so red you could roast pistachios on her cheeks. But I knew the Gods. And the Gods preferred Robin. So I was going to sit here in defiance of them and those Gods and sip a beer instead and just take in the atmosphere and simply keep an eye on these two assholes.

And, of course, not be alone at the house in case unexpected "guests" stopped by.

I tipped my Heineken to my lips. The thing was a bit skunky. I guess only American beer was drunk here. But I was going to drink it in contempt of my guts. I looked around. The restaurant was cavernous but bright. It could easily hold a thousand people. The bar was a level higher than the restaurant and wound almost the entire length of the clubhouse. Every single stool faced the track. This looked like it should be a cheery place.

Instead it felt like one of the earlier rings of hell. Whichever one was pointless labor, this is what Dante would have had in mind. Everyone looked as though they were suffering with Sisyphean misery. Eyes worried, jaws tight, rubbing foreheads or necks or chins like distracting aches. Then that stare, both vacant and cold. So little blinking, so little breathing. Some of the older guys in suits, they seemed calm. Maybe because they had dolled-up girls on their arms. But the girls looked worn. And bored. Clearly the only ones, besides myself, who had nothing at stake in this place. They absently rubbed their men's shoulders and looked around, taking in nothing and everything. Just like me. The solitude of the ponies. Who in their right mind would think this was fun?

"Havin' fun?" Botch asked.

"A hoot," I said. And I sucked on a beer that tasted like what I imagined a rodent's refrigerated urine would taste like.

Maddy was back. "Twenty bucks on five to win," she said and held the ticket up. "I'm going to buy a new car with this money."

And Botch and Robin snorted simultaneously.

I knew that would do it.

I was pulling for Maddy. Praying those two would cross the line with her. Praying Maddy would do all my fighting for me, take that swing, and ruin their little parimutuel bound. Maybe she didn't respect me. I got the eye roll, the "whatever," the head shake and sigh. But Robin, she got the glare. Robin got the look of disgust. Of unmitigated hatred. I was at least smart enough to keep my mouth shut, not feel compelled to give advice or play the dad on the rare occasion when Maddy opened up with a story about friends or about school. But Robin couldn't help it. Robin wanted to be a part of her life. Robin could not step back, could not give her that space. She just had to be mother, had to comment on clothes—the single biggest mistake—had to try to talk like a friend, like sleepover bunkmates, the way they used to talk when Maddy was eleven and she once told Cheryl, "Mom's my best friend." And Robin went to the kitchen and cried with happiness. Those days were gone, baby. This was a different Maddy now.

And Robin had just initiated the launch sequence.

Maddy turned to me. She needed a partner. We'd be a team of necessity.

And I was thrilled.

"Can I have a sip of your beer, Dad?" she asked.

I handed it to her.

"What the hell are you doing, William?" gasped Robin.

"Giving alcohol to a minor," I said and Maddy slugged from that beer disturbingly like an old pro and she wiped her mouth and handed it back and said, "That thing tastes like a skunk's bunghole, Dad."

"I know," I said.

Robin couldn't concentrate now. We had her. Those diamond eyes again as they flitted about from *Racing Form* to track program, snapping up the sports section's race recommendations and shaking the pages.

Maddy was calculating. She was no longer locked on to her mother. She knew how to get to that woman. She was much better than me at this.

Instead, she locked on to Botch.

"You have no respect for women," she said.

"Women he respects," said Robin. "Teenage girls, on the other hand . . ."

Maddy ignored her.

"Your writing is misogynistic," she said. "Do you know what misogynistic means?"

"Of course he knows what misogynistic means," said Robin.

"He knows what it means because he is one."

"No. He knows what it means because he's a writer."

I had to struggle to suppress a smile. This was beautiful. And Maddy knew a big word. I was so proud.

"You think women are cunts," said Maddy.

Somewhat less proud suddenly.

"The language!" shouted Robin, and heads turned to look.

"It's his language, Mom!" Maddy shouted back. "It's in his poems. It's in his stories. He uses the word and I'm just reading the books. It's literature, isn't it?

"Those books are too mature for you and I don't want you reading them anymore."

"Because a nine-year-old shouldn't be able to understand them?"

"I didn't call you a frickin' nine-year-old."

"'Frickin,' Mom—that sounds dangerously close to a swear."

"You know how I feel about the 'C' word and if I hear it come out of your mouth one more time—"

"Come's a 'C' word."

"—I will get a can of Comet from that kitchen right there and a steel brush—"

"Comet's a 'C' word, Mom."

"—and scrub your tongue until it's raw."

"Child abuse is a 'C' word, Mom."

The exacta, the quinella, the daily double, the lovely superfecta and the thrilling trifecta, all crumbling into little pieces, all dying before the far turn, the quarter-mile pole, a mere two furlongs of family fun. I kept my face straight. I let Maddy do her magic.

"Would you talk to her, William?"

"Maddy?" I said.

"Yes?" she said.

"Seen any good movies lately?"

"That's not what I meant, William."

"*Hostel 3D* was pretty cool," said Maddy.

"You're ganging up on me," said Robin.

"Actually, Maddy was addressing Botch," I pointed out.

"I want to go backpacking in Europe after I graduate," Maddy announced.

"I used to live in Europe," said Botch. And he reached for his scotch and took a sip.

Perfect.

He opened his mouth. He walked in. Maddy recalibrated her sniper rifle.

"You should ask Botch about Europe," said Robin.

Don't get pulled in, Maddy. Don't suddenly start asking questions about life in some dusty French town or smacking some terrified bull's nose with a newspaper in Pamplona or riding some poor struggling burro up a cliff side in Santorini.

Stay focused.

"Is that where you learned to hate women?" asked Maddy.

Good girl.

"I don't hate women," said Botch. "I love them in fact."

Maddy crossed her arms. I knew what she wanted to say. I think I even wanted her to say it. But not yet. Not now. The explosion might be nuclear.

"What women?" Maddy asked pointedly

"I've written countless love poems."

"About who?"

Botch took off his glasses. He set them on the table and looked up to the ceiling a moment. "I loved a woman in London. She was much older than me. She was older than my own mother, in fact. I loved my wife. She was a poet too. Once. We had a child together. And I loved a girl in Sydney. She was much younger than me. But she was dazzling. Very beautiful. She was an old soul—"

"But you didn't respect them . . ."

"—just like you."

Maddy shut up. She stared at Botch. As he slipped his glasses back on and went back to his form. Robin looked away from Botch. As though she had somehow been rejected. For beautiful foreign women, exotic women, instead of mere Star Ford Parts Department Robin Anne Botchelko nee Krasomil.

Don't bite Maddy, I thought. Don't bite.

"You think I have an old soul?" Maddy asked.

Shit!

"You do," said Botch.

Robin started scribbling furiously.

"What do you mean?" asked Maddy.

Goddamn it!

As Botch took off his glasses again, set his pen down again. And this time he held Maddy's gaze.

"You have sensitivity. A sensitivity and an awareness that only an old soul could have. You not only know, deep down, what people are thinking. But you know what they're feeling. Because you feel it too. You're funny, you're well spoken. Your intellect glows from your eyes like the moon. And with all that comes an energy that is a rare, rare thing. Not rare in a woman. Or a man. But rare in a human being. You're going to blaze across this sky like a comet, honey. And I can't wait to see all the things you're going to do."

And with that, Botch slipped his glasses back on, picked up his pen, turned to Robin and said, "We better get our bets down."

Chapter 58

There was a girl back in the dorms named Deanna. The moment she started to feel the buzz of her wine, she would turn to the other girls in the room and ask how frequently they masturbated. Deanna believed a woman's sexuality should be spoken about openly. The girls wouldn't give her the satisfaction though. They'd just shake their heads and turn away. Which would compel Deanna to encourage them to purchase a vibrator and use it daily, just like she did, and they would find they feel better about their sexuality, they'd be able to focus on their studies, and they'd feel stronger and healthier.

The virtues of a trembling dong were, apparently, endless.

Then one night after a big Halloween party, mostly just tequila shots in the shared kitchen, Jason and I found Deanna passed out on Jason's bed. She was dressed as a witch in a tiny green skirt. She was lying on her back, one knee up, and we could see the crotch of her white panties.

Jason turned to me. "Shall we take a peek at this magical instrument of hers?"

Assent would be assault. But would silence? Jason didn't wait for an answer. He simply lifted her skirt and pulled the band of her panties down. Deanna's labia lips poked out, one much larger than the other. That's not what got my attention. It was the fact that she didn't have hair one on her crotch. She'd plucked it smooth and bald as Maddy's when she was five.

That may be the style now. But that was not the style then.

Robin, it seems, was suddenly very stylish.

She was sporting a Brazilian. She hadn't meant for me to see it. We were climbing into bed and as she struggled out of what looked like a new pair of jeans, she managed to wriggle her panties down too—much smaller panties I might add and hot pink, and for a moment she didn't realize they were around her thighs. And there it was. A little landing strip smack in the middle of a great expanse of air field. She quickly tugged them back up and her eyes flashed to mine.

Women wear pretty underwear, they argue, to feel more feminine. This is a lie. They wear them to be seen. They get breast implants, not for their husbands or boyfriends, but for the attention of co-workers and friends and complete strangers. A woman does not get a Brazilian thinking she'll be mistaken for a local at Ipanema. She gets a Brazilian because she wants her pubic hair, her entire vaginal region in fact, to be more appealing to another's eyes.

More specifically, another man's eyes.

"Pretty gitch," was all I said.

Robin crawled into bed. She cracked open a black hard cover sketch book. She started to scribble in it. I had no idea if this was another horse racing exercise or not. I didn't ask. It had been a long day and I was exhausted.

But also very relieved to find no one hanging around when we got home.

Robin scrambled eggs for everyone. We ate them without complaint. Even Maddy. She lost her twenty in the first race. She didn't seem to mind. She met another girl in the grandstand. The two spent the next four hours talking about their cell phones. I think. That's what it looked like when I stepped out for a smoke.

Botch broke even. Just part of a day's work for him. But Robin was in the red $175. By the look on her face, you'd think she was in the red seventy grand instead of Botch.

"You're happy I lost," she said.

I didn't reply. I was going to wait. I didn't turn out the light either.

I didn't roll over and ignore her. I just sat up against the pillows, legs heavy with weariness, an ache between my shoulder blades. Maddy was in her room. I knew somehow she was still up but I couldn't hear her on the phone, couldn't hear any music.

I knew Botch was up too.

In my house.

On my sofa.

Right down that hall. Where Robin could slip out later and present her newly minted vagina to him.

"You're a cooler," Robin said. She'd said that on the way to the car too. But back then she said, "You two are coolers." She included Maddy. Botch was whistling "Blue Moon."

"Don't blame me and Maddy for you having a bad day at the track," I said.

"I didn't blame Maddy. I blamed you."

"Maddy did all the talking. I didn't place one bet. I barely said a word—"

"That's the point. You were the boat anchor. You wanted to drag me down. You wanted to rain on the parade. You wanted it to be a shitty day and it was a shitty day and I say congratulations."

"Thank you. My evil plan worked."

"I'm writing it all down. I'm getting it out of my system."

"What is that?" I finally asked.

"My journal." She scribbled furiously. "And you're not coming with us again." She said it as though she was reading it off the page.

Nora jumped up on the bed. She started clawing at my balls through the quilt. I realized, flittingly, that was the most female attention my balls had received in a long time.

"I'm thinking of shaving my nut sack," I said.

"Shave your back while your at it," Robin said.

"Did you do it yourself? Or hire a professional *pussy plucker*?"

"I'm trying to write," she said.

"So you're a writer now too?"

"Botch said I should try to keep a journal."

"And I'll try to keep a straight face."

She continued to scribble. As Nora worked my bag and squinted up into my face as though we two were sharing the most singularly wonderful experience. The experience being sharp claws. In my scrotum. Not so much erotic as expected.

I pushed her off. I climbed out of bed. Robin snatched up my pillow and shoved it at me.

"You might want that," she said.

Chapter 59

"What parts of your books are true?"

"Every chapter."

"And what are the lies?"

"Every word."

We were both in underwear and tee-shirts. Correction: we were both in my underwear and tee-shirts. And we both had throw pillows on our laps, ashtrays balanced atop.

Botch had no trouble with silences. He never felt inclined to fill a gap. I, on the other hand, was compelled to fill a vacuum. I wanted this to start. But for the moment I simply smoked and sipped the scotch and listened to the tinkle of the ice and I vowed to out wait him.

"*Tristitia post coitum,*" he said finally.

"What's that?" I asked.

"The sadness after fucking."

Who was he fucking? I let it go, flicked my smoke in the ashtray in what I thought was a casual manner, but I knocked the cherry off and it was left dangling from the tip and I had to suck madly at the thing to keep it lit.

"Another drink?" I asked.

"Still working on this one," he said.

I got up. I went to the kitchen. I groped around in the dark. I found the Glenfiddich sitting on the counter. I brought the bottle back, shoved the *Sunset* magazines aside and set it on the coffee table.

"Robin likes to say she has a superiority complex," I said.

"People who are self-proclaimed geniuses never recognize where they are lacking," he replied. "Therein lies the genius, I suppose." He pulled on his smoke, the cherry glowing the tip of his nose pink. "You don't see any good qualities in your wife?" he asked.

"I know what I like about her," I said. "I'd like to know what you like about her."

"You don't seem to like her at all."

"I've been married to her for over sixteen years . . ."

"And you think I'm trying to take that?"

"You're here on my couch."

"You brought me here."

"I saved you."

"You're the husband, William. Your place is in that bed down the hall. All I did today was step back and watch the three of you and your headlong rush to hang yourselves. Which, I hasten to add, you did rather effectively."

"Yes, you just sat there. Homeless. Drunk. Debt ridden. And fat."

"I keep hoping I'm merely in my ugly-duckling stage."

"Well take it from me. You just grew up to be an ugly duck."

That was a good one. And he knew it. But he needed to beat it.

"If brevity is the soul of wit, why don't you amuse the shit out of me and shut the fuck up?"

"You didn't just make that up."

"But I knew when to use it."

"I've eaten enough of your shit, Botch."

"Well that would explain your breath."

"I need all this ended."

"Need I remind you how all this started?"

"It was innocent."

"Nothing's innocent."

"It was a misunderstanding . . ."

"You wanted to switch places with me."

"Now you want to switch places with me!"

"Hey you wanted my life!"
"And now you're taking mine!"
And then we went silent.
Because there was Robin standing before us in the dark.
"Maddy's not in her room," she said.

Chapter 60

There was no way Maddy was kidnapped. Botch and I knew that. But think we could convince Robin? The tension that woman could create made me want to swim out to sea and never stop swimming. How is it so many men live in terror of their women? Has this been the case since the beginning of time? Is that why Henry VIII finally just put the file to the axe and started whacking? Even the king of England knew nothing short of a wooden stake in the heart would ever stop the onslaught.

Botch came up with the solution. Which annoyed me. He suggested we call Maddy's cell. But not from one of our phones, or she'd ID it and not answer. This from a man who didn't own a cell phone. So Robin found the addresses of Maddy's friends. Then Botch and I drove down to the Mobil station. It was a relief to get out of that house. I called Maddy from a payphone. She answered. I could hear music, voices, laughter.

She was at a party.

"Maddy, it's your father."

She hung up.

I called Robin.

"She's at a party."

"Did you talk to her?"

"She hung up on me."

"She's grounded. She is grounded until college. You better find her and bring her home and you better read her the riot act and then spank her until her ass bleeds. You encourage her, William . . .”

I hung up. I climbed into the car. We were driving Robin’s Toyota. The rear end of the Honda was still a mess. I didn’t want any cop’s attention. Not with three scotches in me.

Maddy was out there somewhere. And we had four addresses. I started the car. We headed down Glenoaks first.

“I’ve never done this before,” said Botch.

“Done what?” I asked.

“Drive around and look for my daughter. Seems like every parent should do this at some point.”

“You daughter was a good kid?”

Botch shrugged. “Nice neighborhood,” he said. “Feels like a place a man could live. Walk your kid to school. Coffees with the wife. TV at night. Wine with dinner.”

“You just described my life.”

“Your daughter’s having sex and drinking all night. Did I mention any of that in my little scenario?”

“Your little scenario was my life only four years ago.”

“Gosh, don’t they grow up fast.”

The first house was dark. We turned around, drove up to Mountain, made a left, then headed up Kenneth toward the library. This time we didn’t have to check the address. We spotted it instantly. And knew. Cars everywhere. Beamers. Humvees. Christ—how much money did these kids have?

We climbed out of the car and stood there. Kids were on the lawn, on the street, shouting that incessant “Whoooo!” they always feel compelled to yell no matter where or when, denoting, apparently, the incredibly amazing time they are having and the world really must share in this knowledge.

And then the music. Nothing but thumping. Nothing but bass shaking the ground.

“Where the hell are the cops?” I asked.

Botch lit a smoke. He leaned back against the car and folded his arms. But I was nervous. And with that started to well an anger. With myself. With cowardice. I knew Botch would march right in there and his heart rate wouldn't increase so much as one beat per minute. My heart was hammering inside my chest again. It made me angrier still.

"You want to call the cops?" Botch asked.

"Nope."

"What's the plan?"

"I'm going to go in there and bash some heads," I said.

Botch flicked away his smoke. "This should prove interesting," he said.

Chapter 61

A skinny kid tried to stop us at the door. Then thought better of it. He knew we were parents. We were looking for someone. And we meant business. I felt enormous pushing through that door. I felt like a threat.

The kitchen was squeezed tight with young bodies. Everyone of them looked like a child playing with a beer bottle. A fat kid with sideburns jumped in my way and arched back like he was attempting to limbo and screamed, "Yeahhh!" and I shoved him aside and he had the stunned look of a child who's clearly never been harmed by an adult.

Things were about to change.

I shouldered bodies aside. Without an excuse-me. Without one of my typical apologies. Without one of my sorry for livings. Without one of my please ignore little me, please don't mind me, please I'm really a nice guy and please don't look at me and I hope I'm not upsetting you do you want my money I'll just go away didn't mean to intrude hope I didn't track dirt in so happy you make more money than me so nice that you're smarter than me so thrilled that your tougher than me so delighted you have the attitude and the posture and the voice and the heart rate and hand shake and walk and thought and swallow and gaze and blink and bowels and fuck it! I had enough. Done. And these little shits didn't even say "Hey!"—not a protest, nothing. They got out of the way. I was a giant here. I was a father.

I was a man.

We pushed into the living room and I stopped to look around.

"Can I help you?" some kid in a fedora said, standing right in my path, ballsy little prick, I'll give him that. So I put my hand on his face and shoved him back. I spotted the stereo. I pointed. Botch pushed through and turned it off.

A pasty kid grabbed Botch's wrist.

"What do you think yer doin', dude?" but Botch simply grabbed the kid's index finger and bent it back and the kid dropped to his knees and knelt at Botch's feet wincing in agony.

"Be good," was all Botch said.

And there was silence.

We would make great cops. Great renegade cops. Tough partners with a rep marching straight into the middle of a crack den. No one would screw with us.

"Dad!"

Maddy sprang off the couch. She was sitting on a boy's lap. And not the kid she had been having sex with either. A different kid. Clearly my daughter, for lack of a better word, was a slut.

"Dad, what are you doing here?"

The boy got to his feet too. He was much older than Maddy. Probably a senior. And he was huge. He had a football jersey on. Big square jaw. Shoulders like a four-by-four beam squeezed under his shirt. This kid probably beat up his father. For fun. This kid was used to being hit. For fun. And this kid stepped up six inches from my face.

Normally, at this point in my life, after an accumulation of forty-two years of more or less pointless existence, I would have fallen back on all the things I had learned with the layers of time, promptly fired a wee turd into my drawers, squeaked something to Maddy, and quickly found the exit, already recreating the incident in my head to make myself out as the hero. But this was my daughter. And that was Botch. And everything was different now.

I actually welcomed this.

"Touch me," I said to him.

"What?" he said.

"Put a hand on me." Then I added. "Please."

He was confused. So was I. My voice was so calm. Almost soft.

Maddy tried to squeeze in between us. "Dad . . ." but I gently, yet forcibly, pushed her aside.

"I don't know what your problem is, dude—"

"Did you call me dude? Or sir?"

The hesitancy flicked across his eyes. The uncertainty. I knew this kid. I knew him now. Because I had been him. Once. Like a DNA memory awakening. He was backing down.

I did not want him to back down.

"Let's go home, Dad. I'll just go home."

This was too easy. This was not what I thought it would be and not what I wanted it to be. I did not want this kid to turtle. I did not want the act of reticence. Instead, I wanted to beat him into a pool of shame that he would never forget. That he would feel the burn of for the rest of his days every time the memory flitted across his frontal lobe, awakening a flash of it here, the camera pop of the blow, that warm mercurial taste of blood swimming in the mouth.

Most of all, I wanted to shame Maddy.

I wanted to shame my own child. I accused Robin of always wanting to be Maddy's friend. But that was me. That's what I did. That's why I let them argue, I stepped aside, I dismissed it as a mother-daughter thing. Because I wanted to be liked. Instead of respected.

And in the end, I was neither.

"I have a question for you," I said to the kid.

Someone snatched the beer out of his hand. He flashed a look around. They all seemed to know what was about to happen before I knew it. But that was good. I was focused. My back muscles were hard as timber.

"What?" whispered the kid. He was so sorry he stepped up now. Because he was a boy up against a man. A very different man from the one who got out of bed this morning.

"What's your question?" he asked again. Politely, granted.

So I said it. I said it to shame Maddy. I heard it clearly in my head first. Then I uttered the words. “Are you fucking my wife?”

Those weren’t quite the words I had heard.

I felt my chest seize as the words echoed in my head like a gong. I heard a snicker. Then a snort. Then some kid actually burst out laughing and another said, “Paul! All righttt!”

Paul, on the other hand, was simply confused. As I felt my shoulders start to droop, my body shrink, my spine retract into my tail bone. Not one moment, the Gods could not allow so much as one single moment to be mine. I was a fool, the world’s court jester, the chicken geek the populace could point at and snicker and go home knowing that at the very least, no matter how miserable their own lives, there was yet one more miserable.

Botch stepped up beside me. He brought his fist to his mouth to suppress a chortle. Then he said to the kid, “That’s what’s known as a Freudian slip.”

“Are you fucking my wife!” I roared at Botch.

He stepped back. His eyes flashed.

“Dad!” Maddy gasped.

“Why does my wife have a Brazilian? Huh? What the fuck is going on!”

That confused him. “How would I know what she’s doing with some South American guy?”

“A Brazilian’s a pussy shave, dude,” some kid said.

“What?” Botch said and his face screwed up in confusion.

“Dad—you’re embarrassing me!”

“Shut up you little twat!” I shouted at her and her eyes popped and her mouth dropped and I knew I had shouted those words, I could hear them too, I could hear all the words, but none of them seemed to be coming from me but from someone with a voice just like mine who was standing in the middle of a room full of teenagers and shouting non sequiturs as the real me merely floated in some far corner and watched with something like awe and something like amazement.

“You little bitch! You think you can treat me and your mother like assholes! Well I’ve fucking had it! You are going to respect me and you are going to respect my household or you are going to get the fuck out of it . . .!"

"William . . ." Botch said and he gripped my bicep.

And I swung.

I drove my fist into his face and there was a scream, I remember a scream, and I was on top of Botch as we flipped over the sofa, flattening a coffee table, my fingers trying to gouge out his eyes and then the flash, the pop, the giant fist appearing like staccato bursts from a strobe light but I felt nothing, not even the contact of my own knuckles as they hammered into his cheeks, teeth bared, and I squeezed his fat neck, squeezed it until little bones and veins bent and slipped away under my finger tips but now I couldn't breathe, as though I was somehow choking myself and I sensed that he was squeezing my neck in turn and his face was a face of hate and I fucking hated him too, hated him for ruining my life, hated him for writing and publishing and websites and fan sites and women wanting him, women fucking him, for no other reason than he put words on paper, words that meant nothing, denoted nothing, empty meaningless selfish cocksucker, hated him for living in London and living in Australia, hated him because Robin, because my wife, because the woman I met in a college registration lineup, the woman I held when she miscarried, the woman lying on her back swollen with my horrid daughter, my horrid child, Robin wanted this fucker too, she wanted him in her bed and between her legs, she wanted his smelly cock in her mouth and I was going to kill him, kill my evil other, destroy the demon, the incubus, the succubae and everything started to blur, his ugly pink mouth, his ugly pink eyes, and I started to feel almost good, almost serene, knowing all of this was coming to an end, all of this misery and confusion and nothing, nothing more would ever be expected of me.

And that's when we were dog-piled.

Chapter 62

"Powerade?"

Maddy shook her head.

"Pringle? I've got Doritos too."

"Nacho Cheese or Cool Ranch?"

"Both."

"Nacho Cheese."

I dug them out of a plastic bag behind the seat, jerked them open first, then handed them to her. She picked through them until she found the orangest one, held it up a moment with a grin for me to admire, then popped it in her mouth.

I lifted Botch's binoculars to my eyes. I focused on a one-story house with a flat roof set in the middle of a dusty cluster of Jacarandas. A sheet of warped plywood was nailed over one window. There was an old four-door Maverick in the dirt driveway.

"You got any Frappucinos?" asked Maddy.

"Frappucinos? What would I be doing with Frappucinos?"

"The mocha Starbuck's ones? Everyone drinks 'em, Dad."

"Well I'm not a 7-Eleven. I thought you liked Powerades."

"Only after a workout."

"When do you ever work out?"

"More than you do," she said.

That wasn't saying much.

"Can I see?" she asked.

I handed her the binoculars. She lifted them to her eyes. "Have you done this before?" she asked.

"Once," I said. "Or twice."

She handed the binoculars back and I pressed them to my eyes again. Forgetting momentarily. And I winced. Because my right eye was black. Actually, technically, it was purple and black. The left cheek was bruised. My lower lip was swollen. There was a lump on my forehead and a carpet burn on my chin.

Maddy and I were sitting in the Honda. On a dry lonely road in San Bernardino. There was a lumpy field of scrub brush to our left and one sad looking horse.

And across from us was the house of one Darlene Botchelko and her daughter, Alene. The wife and daughter of Alfred Botchelko. LA poet extraordinaire.

It was Maddy's idea.

Around three in the morning I awoke to find her crouching next to the sofa, her face only inches from mine.

"You awake?"

"What? What is it?"

I could hear Botch snoring on the other end of the sectional. Though no one matched Robin for snoring.

"I have an idea. Come on."

"Where we going?" I asked.

"My room. Come on."

We stretched out on her bed, laptop straddled across our thighs. She still slept in a girl's single bed and the room hadn't changed much. Maddy still wore pajamas. She still had stuffed animals on the bed, the panda from the San Diego Zoo because it was cute, the gorilla from the LA Zoo because we saw a gorilla throw a stick at a guy in the crowd and hit him right in the face and Maddy clapped and laughed. There were two cats and two dogs and two American Girl dolls. I almost had to take a second mortgage for those two things. But the Barbies were put away now. She used to have a hell of a collection of those. The Corvette. The make up room. No Ken doll. Ever. Even little girls know Ken's gay.

"I've been reading his books. Have you been reading them?"

"Well yes, Madison," I said. "How do you think all this started?"

"Don't condescend, Dad. I'm helping us here. You don't want help? You want that fat prick-licker out there to destroy our lives and run off with Mom to, like, Turkey or Bulgaria or something?"

"I don't think they have racetracks in Turkey or Bulgaria."

"Well how would I know? I've never been further than Temecula."

"Not true."

"Whatever. Just look at these poems. Look at this one. It's all about his wife. And that one too. And here's one where he takes his daughter to the beach and tries to find shells for her and she cries when they don't find any and then he cries like a pussy too. And then one about changing her diapers and he likes doing it. Read that, Dad. He actually likes baby shit. How sick is that?"

"Because it's his own child's shit," I said.

"It's still sick." Then she paused. "Did you like my shit? Don't answer." She went back to the books. They were all dog-eared, some had Post-it notes sticking out. She was like a little attorney. "This man," she said, "is still in love with his wife. He's nuts about her. He's written more poems about his wife and kid than about anything else. Even booze and horses."

"So?"

"So? Do I have to do the math for you?"

"If you have to do the math for me, honey, I'm in big trouble."

"Do you want that dick sucker out of our lives or what?"

"Where the fuck do you get this language?" I asked.

"I think you just answered your own question," she said.

I sighed. My head was throbbing. But it was kind of nice to be snuggled up with Maddy on her bed again. We used to read Dr. Seuss together. And Clifford the Big Red Dog. And Curious George. I even read her all the *Anne of Green Gables*, starting when she was only six. And *Black Beauty* too. Then she started reading *Teen People*. Then

Cosmo. Going by the accelerated advancement of her choice of reading material, she'd soon be writing the advice column for *Penthouse*. Hell yeah I wanted that man out of my life.

"Then let's get him back together with his wife and daughter," Maddy said.

"How? We don't even know where to find his wife and daughter."

"I already found them." She clicked a key on her laptop. "San Bernardino. They're in the book. There's the address."

She spun to face me now, crossed her legs, actually setting one foot atop her thigh effortlessly, all youth bendable as Gumby.

"What do you think? You and me. We'll go see them. And we'll get them back together."

I looked at the address again. Cutter Road.

"We rock up," she explained. "They see us, father and daughter, see how much we care about each other. We'll put on an act for 'em. And it'll trigger something. We'll tell them, like, how lonely he is and how fucked up and how much he smells. Maybe not the smell. And they'll get all like weepy and then we bring them back here for the surprise sit-down and you'll cook something nice—and not gluten-free shit, Dad, please? Don't work against me here. Make something people can actually chew and swallow. And we'll pour lots of booze down their throats too. And then it's like 'oh, I love you and miss you,' and then the losers screw off out of our lives for good. Huh? What do you think?"

I was tired. I couldn't think. I shrugged. "I've heard worse," I said.

"Always the encouragement, Dad. Thanks. If my teachers were in this house fifteen minutes, I'd be carted off to child welfare . . ."

I put my hand on her knee. "We'll do it," I said. "It's a good idea. We'll do it."

She smiled. "Cool." Then she paused to look at my face, really peer into my eyes. It was such a kind, sweet look.

"You look like four kinds of shit, Dad," she said.

I felt like four kinds of shit.

Even my groin hurt. I think the bastard tried to knee me in the balls.

But thank God he looked like shit too. I did a number on him. When Maddy was rushing the two of us back to the car, I could see the blood flowing freely from his nose, could see the swelling already on his cheeks. He even paused to wiggle a tooth and spit before climbing in the car. I made a point of sitting up. Botch had to lie down in back. But I couldn't keep my eyes open. I moaned. Once I did, Botch moaned in reply. The entire drive home was one soft moan, answered by a deep grumbling moan in return.

When we pulled into the driveway, I still hadn't realized what I'd done. Neither had Botch. Until Robin charged out the front door, house coat flapping behind her, and she screamed, "You let Maddy drive!?"

Botch and I stood there and stared at Maddy like she had suddenly materialized from the shadows. It never crossed my mind. Or Botch's.

Maddy was so authoritative. She pulled the doors open. She pushed us inside. She took the keys. She got behind the wheel and adjusted the seat and the mirrors and put the car in gear like she'd been taking it grocery shopping every week for years. Botch and I were in such a daze, we just never clued in.

"She could have gotten killed!"

Robin pulled Maddy into her like she was a wee thing only recently rescued from a well. That lasted all of two seconds. Then she shoved her to the door.

"Get to bed! And stay in that bed! You are grounded! For the rest of the year! Forever!"

Maddy didn't argue. She didn't cry either. There was no fear or shame in that posture. Just sheer lovely defiance as she turned and marched into the house. That girl's balls were so much bigger than mine.

Then Robin stepped up and stuck a finger in my face and those very same tiny balls cinched up tight against my groin.

"You are a stupid, stupid man! A sorry excuse for a human being! She's just a little girl! Can you really be that stupid, William? Is it possible that you would let a child drive a car in the middle of the night? You were supposed to be rescuing her!"

Then she stepped back for a breath but her eyes were bulging still. She wanted to do the punching now, the kicking, the slapping. Anything. She looked us both up and down like she was choosing a good spot to land a blow.

"You two look terrible," was all she said. Then she turned and marched back into the house.

I slept on Maddy's floor that night. We didn't talk anymore. Somewhere around dawn, Maddy started to whimper in her sleep and her legs twitched. I reached up and touched her knee and said, "Maddy," and she stopped and spun away from me.

Maddy was up first.

"They're gone," she said. When I walked into the kitchen, Maddy was making coffee and toast. She was dressed in a white tee-shirt and jeans, her hair still wet. The house was empty. Botch's blanket was folded, the pillow on top.

"Wear something half decent, Dad."

I didn't know what half decent was. I wore jeans and sneakers and a collared shirt.

Maddy was waiting by the door with the keys.

"Listo?" she said.

"What?" I said.

"Ready?" she said.

Chapter 63

"I'm sorry if I embarrassed you in front of your friends, Maddy."

"Fuck them," she said. She was glued to the binoculars. "It'll give them something to talk about for the rest of the year. Believe it or not, it's going to make me cooler."

"It is?"

"Yeah, kinda." And I saw her smile. Then I saw the smile fade. Then she lowered the binoculars. She picked through the Doritos, pulled out one or two to examine, put them back.

"You called me a cunt," she whispered.

That's right. I did.

"Actually, technically, I called you a twat," I said.

"What's the difference?"

"Spelling?" I shrugged.

Maddy popped open the glove compartment and pulled out my pack of Marlboro Ultra Lights. She pushed the cigarette lighter in.

"What are you doing?"

She stuck a cigarette in her mouth and pressed the lighter to it and sucked away.

"What do you think you're doing?"

She rolled down the window and blew out the smoke, staring across the street at the house.

"I'm not your mother, Maddy. You're not going to provoke me.

Now put that out."

She flicked it instead.

"Botch said I had an old soul."

That's right. He did. As Maddy grabbed a second cigarette, stuck that in her mouth, lit it off hers and handed it to me. I took it. And I smoked it.

"He said I had a depth of intelligence and understanding that was rare in, not just a woman, but a human being."

I know he said that. I hated him for it.

"How come you don't say those things, Dad?"

"I . . ."

I didn't know why.

"Don't you think them?"

"Honey—yes I think them."

"When do you think them?"

"When?"

When did I think them? Did I ever think them?

"Always, honey. I feel that way about you always."

Then I touched her shoulder.

"Okay, Daddy. Okay."

She pulled away. There was no hug. Not that. Nothing like that.

"Why don't we go knock on their door?" she said and climbed out.

My little Maddy.

Once lost a pen.

It was nothing special, just an old green pen she found in a drawer, the ink like a green vein down its center. It was worth thirty-nine cents. But she clung to my legs and wept and I petted her hair and told her I'd buy her another. But she didn't want to hear it. She wanted her pen. There was no comforting her. So I said it. I said, "I'll find your pen." And I meant it. And there was such hope in her eyes. I couldn't let her down. Over a silly pen which suddenly wasn't silly at all, but was gold, was a ruby, was a gift of the Magi. Her pen. Hers. So we looked everywhere she'd already looked. We double-checked. Her drawers, her toy chest, under the bed and under the sofas. Then we checked the kitchen drawers and the bathroom drawers too. We checked the patio. We checked the front steps. Then, in the bottom of the hamper, wrapped in her little yellow sweater, I found it.

"Maddy! Look!" I said and I held it up and she squealed and ran into my arms and squeezed my neck so hard and I squeezed her back and Robin heard us, found us in the bathroom and she laughed too as I kissed Maddy's eyes and her forehead and her little neck.

Later that night, while crawling into bed, Robin asked me why Maddy was laughing when we were hugging but I was crying. I didn't explain. It would have sounded empty. Or silly. If I had told Robin that that day, in the eyes of my little girl, there was nothing I couldn't do. I could have lifted her into the sky and let her touch the clouds. I was her hero. Over a green Bic Pen. Has anyone ever made someone so joyous in all their lives?

My little Maddy.

"Let's go knock on the door," she said again and flicked her cigarette away.

Chapter 64

In the world of cynicism, careful-what-you-wish-for is true and a life lesson. But one we can do without. Who wishes for the dross that comes with the wish realized? Doesn't that mean the wish wasn't realized in the least? But simply sludge, simply more dirt and dust to tarnish something imagined as shiny and shimmering bright? When you wish to win the lottery, you don't wish for the lawsuits from ex-wives or the demands of distant relatives or your entire family turning on each other like coyotes. When you wish you could direct a movie, you don't wish for the critics attack or the direct-to-video release accompanied by the bewildering schadenfreude, all friendships now forever tainted. When you wish you could write a bestseller, you don't wish for the accusation that you stole the idea from a friend or the girlfriend you were about to leave miraculously getting pregnant. When you wish for a new car, you don't wish for the car accident.

I had wished my life was more exciting. I had wished, secretly, that my wife was more attractive. I had wished my daughter had ambition and zeal and wit.

How do you put the brakes on a runaway wish?

"Lanolin."

"That's a funny name for a dog," Maddy said. She was rubbing the hairy thing's neck but her nose was wrinkling.

"No, he needs lanolin," said Darlene. "It's why he smells."

Alene poured more coffee. From a percolator. I hadn't seen one of those since I was a child. We were sitting at an Arborite table on padded chrome chairs. I also hadn't seen these since I was a child. Alene hadn't spoken yet. Or not much. She said hello when she opened the door. I think it was hello. Then she showed us into the kitchen like she'd been expecting us. Or expected and accepted just about anything that landed up on her front door. She looked just like her mother.

And her mother wasn't much to look at.

"Built like a brick shithouse," my dad would have described her. Long gray hair in a ponytail, enormous glasses, enormous jowls and what, I'm pretty sure, were sideburns. She was dressed all in black.

"Why is he living with you? Is he in gambling trouble again?"

"He needs family," Maddy said. "He met Dad in a professional capacity and had dinner at our place one night. He talked about the two of you the entire time. We realized then just how much he longed for family again. So we invited him to spend the night. That was like two weeks ago. And we just don't have the heart to ask him to leave. It would kill him. He needs family around him."

Darlene looked at Alene. She looked back at us.

"He didn't send you here."

"No," I said. I felt I had better speak. I better look like a concerned father and husband at some point. Instead of a sub-humanoid former Kinko's manager. "It was our idea to come see you. He doesn't know we're here."

"He's written so many lovely poems about the two of you," said Maddy. "He misses you terribly."

A man suddenly stepped into the kitchen. He had a goatee and was wearing a white collared shirt with a name tag stitched on it that read "Ray." He was older than Alene but younger than Darlene.

"Davy," he said and the dog ran to him, tongue hanging out and tail wagging. Then he kissed Darlene on the cheek and kissed Alene on the cheek and he left with the smelly dog.

"That was Patrick," said Darlene. "He's a poet too."

"Is he your boyfriend?" asked Maddy.

"We haven't decided," Darlene said. "He may be Alene's boyfriend now."

Alene didn't respond. She just stood by the stove. She had her father's height. And she had his blue eyes too. So she at least had that over her mother.

"Botch once held me down and farted on my head," said Alene.

"He was only playing, dear," said Darlene.

"I still didn't like it," said Alene and she walked out of the room.

"She's a very sensitive girl," Darlene explained.

"Well, being farted on by your father can be disconcerting," I said. Which was stupid.

"How old is Alene?" asked Maddy.

"Twenty-four last Sunday. How old are you?"

"Fourteen," said Maddy. "But I already know how to drive."

That's right. We'll have to discuss that.

Alene reappeared.

"I did a painting of Botch."

She held it up. Botch was smiling in the picture. Like Bob Barker. I've seen him grin and seen him laugh. But I've never seen him smile like that. His eyes were green and one was three times bigger than the other and they looked a bit crossed and his hair was swept back like Elvis and the nose was enormous and the shadowing was some sort of crosshatching that made it look like the sun was shining from under his chin and behind his left ear simultaneously.

It was hideous.

It looked like something a ten-year-old might have worked on for an entire weekend and of course the parents gush and put it on the wall and tell the child she has talent and then they encourage her to quickly do another so they can replace the one on the wall presently drawing such cringe-inducing attention.

"Alene's very talented too," said Darlene.

"I can see that," I said.

"I'm going to give it to Botch for my birthday," said Alene, clearly confused on the concept of birthdays.

"Give it to him tonight," said Maddy. She saw her opportunity.

"Tonight?" said Alene and she took a small step back.

"Come for dinner. Dad's going to cook. He's a great cook. You can give it to him then."

Alene looked at her mother.

"A girl needs her father," Maddy said and she rushed up and wrapped her arms around my neck. Then she kissed my cheek. I tried to smile at them. Like this was natural. Even though Maddy was pouring it on thick as paving tar and beads of sweat were starting to bubble up on my forehead.

Darlene sighed. "What are you making?" she asked.

"Pork," I said.

No response.

"Or salmon."

Still no response.

"Or . . . steak?" I said.

"When do you decide?" asked Darlene.

"I like haliboo," said Alene.

Haliboo? What was haliboo? Did she mean caribou? Where the hell do you get caribou meat?

"She means halibut," said Darlene.

"I'm pronouncing it French," said Alene.

"You speak French?" asked Maddy.

"No," Alene said.

Silence.

"Haliboo it is," I said.

Chapter 65

"You think she's retarded?" asked Maddy.

We were watching the two walk around our backyard through the porch screen. Alene would stop and point, at a tree, at the ground. Darlene would nod. Then the two would wander another couple of steps, stop, and do it all over again.

"They seem to communicate telepathically," I said.

"No wonder Botch would rather have me for his daughter," Maddy said.

"Whatever gave you that idea?" I asked.

"Look at the girl. That's no old soul. That soul is oven fresh. In fact, it needed a little more time to bake. She's like an infant with tits."

Bake. That's right. I went inside to check on the halibut. I wasn't crazy about halibut. It's boring. So I prepared it with lemon slices—what else do you do with it? But then I sautéed up a pan of garlic and onions and thin slices of chili peppers and lots of butter and olive oil. I'd drizzle that over it before serving. I started work on the tomato salad with cilantro and chunks of goat cheese.

"How's the haliboo?" asked Maddy.

"Fine," I said. I glanced back at her. She was holding up the Botch painting while contemplatively puffing a cigarette.

"Yep. Definitely retarded," she said.

"Jesus Christ Maddy, would you put that damn cigarette out?"

"Make me."

"What did you say?"

"You heard me," she said and grinned.

Why that little cow. So I went for it. She hid it behind her back. I tried to reach around her but she moved it to the other hand. I grabbed her arm but she switched hands again and even managed to squeeze in a quick puff. I wrapped both arms around her waist but she blew smoke in my eyes and then dropped out of my grip like her skeletal structure had vanished. She bolted around the table, laughing.

"You frickin' brat," I said and Maddy stuck her tongue out in a disconcertingly flirtatious way and I heard Darlene say, "You two get along so well."

Darlene and Alene were standing in the kitchen.

And right behind them, unnoticed, stood Botch and Robin.

Chapter 66

Alene stared at her haliboo for at least twenty minutes. She poked at it twice. Every once in a while, Botch would reach out and touch her back or her shoulder and she would smile at him as though she just remembered he was there and he was in fact her father and showing her some kindness outside of warm flatulence on her cranium. Then the smile would vanish and she would go back to staring at her meal like it was about to swim away and she didn't want to miss it.

Everyone else seemed to enjoy the food. At least they said they did. Shockingly, it was Maddy who piped up first with, "This is great Dad." Then Botch agreed it was great and Darlene did too and took another mouthful. But Robin said nothing. She ate it all but didn't utter a word. And Alene continued her contemplative study of the effects of 350 degrees heat on marine life.

"Were you fighting again?" Darlene asked Botch. She pointed to his bruised face.

"A little bit," he said.

"Were you fighting him?" she asked and pointed at me.

"Everyone needs a hobby," he said.

"Are you enjoying your fish?" I asked Alene.

"I don't really like fish," Alene said.

I saw Maddy roll her eyes.

"I thought you said you like halibut," said Maddy—patiently, I'll give her that.

"I do," said Alene. "And grouper."

"Grouper?" asked Maddy. "You like grouper?"

"Very much."

"But those are fish," Maddy pointed out.

Alene thought about this. "But you don't see them in fish tanks," she said. Astutely. If you were Mork from Ork.

"You see them in public aquariums though," I said.

"Did you get these from a public aquarium?" she asked, in what I could read as apparent shock.

"No," I said.

"You don't eat animals from the zoo too, do you?" she asked—and this I would read as apparent indignation.

"I got it from Fish King," I said. Then added, "A seafood store."

Alene nodded. Then went right back to staring at her fish, certain now I had surreptitiously slipped her a serving of Zebra.

"So you seeing anyone?" Botch asked. But he didn't direct the question to anyone in particular.

"I'm seeing Patrick," Alene said proudly. "He's a poet."

"Patrick?" said Botch. He looked at Darlene. "Weren't you seeing a Patrick?"

"Now she's seeing that Patrick."

Robin looked away in thinly veiled disgust.

"Didn't you send me some of his stuff?"

"You weren't very kind about it," said Darlene.

"Hey, you want compliments?" said Botch. "Send it to your grandma."

"Patrick's grandmother died of a very rare disease," said Alene. And this I think I read as pride.

"Was it cancer of the talent cells?" asked Botch.

And apropos of absolutely nothing, Alene suddenly piped up with, "I painted your portrait." Then she hurried off excitedly. I have no idea where she thought she was going. We heard her scurry down the hall. She seemed to be in the bathroom. Then she sounded like she was in Maddy's bedroom. Maddy frowned at me. I shrugged.

"Alene!" Maddy called out.

Alene rushed back into the dining room, breathless. "Yes?"

Maddy held up her painting. And Alene's face fell. She slumped down into her chair. She mumbled, "Yours is much better than mine."

"This is *yours*," said Maddy.

And Alene's face lit up again. "It's better than I remember!" And she took it and jumped back to her feet, squeezing it to her body, then she said to Botch. "Ready?"

"Ready," said Botch.

She spun it around to show him. She was beaming. Darlene was smiling too. Botch, on the other hand, was not smiling. Or certainly not smiling like the clown killer in the painting.

Robin snatched up the bottle and poured herself more wine.

Maddy touched her arm.

"What do you think, Daddy?" Alene asked.

Botch didn't answer.

"Maybe you can put it on your book jackets," Alene offered.

Botch continued to stare at it. As though he was contemplating *Las Meninas*. Then he said, "I'll do better than that." He took the painting from her and walked over to my framed photo of Machu Picchu hanging near the bookshelves and he took that down and hung up Alene's monstrosity. He stood back to admire it.

"Now I can see it every day," he said.

Botch was either a better father than I thought. Or completely out of his mind. Either way, he was hands down the shittiest house guest on earth.

Robin looked at me. Actually, technically, she glared at me. Then she reached under the table and dug her fingernails into my thigh. It was my turn to touch her arm. Mostly to jerk her hand away.

"How's it look?" asked Botch.

"Beautiful," said Darlene and Alene actually clapped and squeezed herself in a hug.

“Coffee anyone?” said Robin and she didn’t wait for an answer, she went straight to the kitchen.

“You should help her, Dad,” said Maddy.

Jesus Christ, could I not make one fucking decision here? The marionette of Hillside Drive. I pushed away from the table, got up, went into the kitchen, passed Robin as she said—“Whose stupid idea was this dinner?”—and kept right on walking. I stepped out back. I lit a smoke. I stared over at Greg’s place. All his lights were on. I saw him walk through his living room and grab a handful of his wife’s ass. She was a former figure skater. She had a great ass. She smiled at him.

“Dad?” Maddy was hanging out the bathroom window. “How do you think it’s going?”

“Unmitigated disaster,” I said.

“No way. I think it’s going great.”

“Have you been sitting at the same table I’ve been sitting at?”

“So the chick doesn’t know a trout from a bear’s ass. Maybe Botch farted on her head so many times he gassed her brain. But I think they’re getting along great. He hung her stupid painting, didn’t he?”

“Yes Maddy, but he hung it in our living room.”

“Can I have a puff of that?” she asked.

I handed it up to her. She took a drag. “Holy shit. Is Greg screwing his wife over there?”

What?! I got up on tip toes. I couldn’t see anything.

“No, no. I’m wrong. Her pants are still on. But he’s feeling her tits.”

“Stop looking over there.” That’s it, fence law or no fence law, I was putting up the Wall of Jericho before Christmas. I did not need my daughter learning any more tricks.

“So what’s the plan?” asked Maddy.

“Plan? I have no plan. This was all your idea.”

“I say we get ’em drunker.”

“The only one drinking in there is your mother.”

“You should talk to her, Dad. She’s being weird. I think she’s having her period."

"How would you know?"

"Because I'm having mine. God, she's your wife. You don't know when she has her periods?"

"Stop talking to me about menstrual cycles please."

Maddy handed me back what was left of my cigarette. That girl wiped that thing out in two drags.

"Can you believe Botch was married to that woman?" she said.

"She was probably pretty in her day."

"That day's gone. Come on, let's get 'em drunk."

"Maddy . . ." But she ducked back inside.

I butted out the smoke. I stuffed it deep in the potting soil of the fichus where Robin wouldn't find it. I took a deep breath. The air was so fresh. It was getting cold. This was my favorite time of year, fall. Even though every October we have one last heat wave. And every time I am annoyed because I think this time we won't have the heat wave. And I've spent the better part of my life here. Well, maybe not better. But the greater. Well, maybe not great either. Still, it's my favorite time, with the sour stink of the bagged manure sprinkled on the lawns and the vaguely nauseating smell of the ivy plants, as though quarts of bleachy ejaculate had been spilled on them. Fall in California is what a porn set must smell like it.

I could hear a little dog barking inside someone's house. I heard a car alarm going off on the other side of the wash. Then I heard the sound. I held my breath. I heard it again. The train whistle. I could just barely make it out.

As Robin's laughter raked the stillness.

Chapter 67

Everyone had moved to the living room. The dining table was a mess of dirty dishes. With the exception of one perfectly clean plate with an entire piece of untouched halibut. I had made the meal. I had set the table. And now I was going to have to clean up the entire thing too. Was Robin even able to wipe her own ass these days?

"Botch was just telling the funniest story," Robin said.

She had a martini in front of her. No one had coffee. Darlene was sitting with her hands on her lap, face neutral, looking strangely serene. Actually, rethinking, no I couldn't imagine that woman being pretty back on any day. Alene was sitting next to her father. She was chewing worriedly at her cuticles. Maddy was sitting next to Robin, posture perfect, legs crossed and wearing a sweet smile. Maddy hadn't joined us or any adult in this living room for more than half a passing second in the last two years. This was the sort of daughter I had imagined. Maybe there was hope for the girl yet.

"I don't like this story," said Alene.

"I won't tell it then," said Botch.

Robin jumped in. "Botch was just saying that …"

"Mom," interrupted Maddy. "If Alene doesn't like the story . . ."

"There's nothing wrong with the story. I've heard the story."

"You've *heard* the story?" gasped Alene.

"Alene doesn't like the story Mom."

"Let's change the subject," I said.

"I'm telling it," said Robin and she took a slug from her martini first, spilling it on the way up and spilling more on the way back down. "When Alene was little, some guy once thought she was a boy. He kept going on and on about what a good looking boy Alene was and what a big boy she was and how she'll be a great baseball player one day and Botch just listened and nodded and didn't correct him and suddenly Alene yanked her pants down and pointed at her crotch and shouted, 'Look! No pee-pee!' And that's the story. That's it. It's just a cute little story . . ."

"I don't like that story," Alene said again. And then she said, looking down at her feet, "I bet no one ever thought you were a boy."

Robin didn't answer. Neither did Maddy. They exchanged a look.

"Who?" asked Maddy.

"You," Alene said but she still didn't look up or point or indicate anyone in the room. "You're so pretty. And confident. And you know when to talk and when not to talk and when you clear your throat you make a tiny little fist in front of your mouth first like you're stopping a goober that might come flying out."

Maddy hesitated. "Thank you," she said.

"No, I meant her," and Alene pointed at Robin.

"Oh," said Robin. She smiled and looked around the room. "Thank you Alene."

"And Maddy knows so much about fish," she added.

Maddy waited for more compliments. They didn't appear to be forthcoming.

"Thanks," said Maddy.

"And your feet are so small."

Maddy paused to admire her own feet.

"And your ears don't stick out."

Maddy reached up and touched her ears.

"And when you burp you don't make any noise. Then you blow it out of the side of your mouth like cigarette smoke so the stink doesn't get in anyone's face." And with that, Alene got up and went and stood in front of her painting. She didn't move. She just stood with her back to us.

Then she said, "No wonder Daddy would rather be here."

Darlene simply watched Robin.

Robin wouldn't meet her eyes.

Botch, on the other hand, was no longer here. He had the thousand-yard stare on his face. He was back in London, back in Sydney, at the track, God knows where.

And no one made a sound.

Until Maddy belched like a Roman emperor after gorging and died laughing.

Patrick picked Darlene and Alene up in a Triple A wrecker. Darlene gave him a long tonguey kiss as his hands groped frantically at her thick waist. His lips were still wet with spit when Alene stepped up and did the same. She seemed to be trying to jam her entire tongue in his mouth. Then the three climbed into the cab, Alene in the middle, and Patrick backed out, the wrecker beeping so loudly I saw the neighbor's curtains pull aside. And off they went. Not a wave. Not a nice-to-meet-you. And not a hope in hell of a thank-you.

When we went to bed, Botch was sitting up in the dark, a glass of neat scotch on his belly, staring at his painting.

Part IV

Yellow with brown streak.
The flag of the coward."

—Alfred Botchelko

Chapter 68

Maddy was at school. I think she was at school. And Robin and Botch were at the track. At least I think that's where they were. And I was in the bedroom slowly gathering up socks and trying to decide whether to do laundry or burn down the house. They both seemed like valid options. I sat down for a moment on Robin's side of the bed and wondered how to pull it off without it looking like arson. I suppose a kitchen fire was best. But someone might see the smoke and call the fire department long before the house was engulfed and it might look weird if the laptop and all the tax records were safely hidden in the car. Then I considered a dryer fire but then probably only the garage would burn down and the house would still be standing and besides, I wasn't even sure where Nora was right now. Lacking anything like valor, I knew I wouldn't rush into the flames to save her. So that meant the cat, the taxes and my laptop would be in the car.

And the big clock in the living room.

That thing was an easy two-and–a-half feet in diameter and, for some inexplicable reason, I loved it.

And my *Oxford Food Dictionary*. I'd have to rescue that too.

Nope, I just wasn't smart enough to manage it. How does one collect on insurance but not lose anything? Outside of being broadsided by a Bentley, I just couldn't come up with a solution. Then I spotted the sock I was looking for. And right next to it was Robin's new journal.

I picked it up.

The sock.

Then I picked up the journal.

My heart rate instantly doubled. I looked around, even though I knew I was alone. Do I open it? She left it there. If it was so important, wouldn't she have hidden it? That was twisted logic. But is it written somewhere that a journal is a sacred thing? It would seem to me it's merely implied.

I quickly made a deal with myself. If the first page said, "William, close this book and put it down right now," then that's precisely what I'd do. Then I'd go do laundry and make myself a tuna sandwich and then, maybe half an hour later, maybe forty minutes, I'd come back and read the thing anyway. I knew who I was. I knew my weaknesses. I knew my self-esteem was on par with the omega runt left to feed on the steamy turds of the alpha dogs.

I opened the journal.

I skipped the first page.

Robin had dreadful handwriting. Worse than mine. But after so many years, I learned to interpret it the way one would eventually decipher hieroglyphics if left in Tut's tomb long enough.

I started reading.

"*. . . my heart was no longer pumping blood, but mere dust, mere puffs of dry thin powder. I could feel their presence draining me, my soul deflating like a slow leak, as though punctured by their eyes and their very breath. And I could see Botch was vaporizing too. He was dissolving before me. They had taken so much from him. Those two people, empty vessels, expecting something super human from a mere man. I wanted to wrap him up in my arms. I wanted him to wrap me up in his. But he was so far across that table, he may as well have been across the seas. If I could just feel his kisses on my eye lids, on my face, on the back of my neck, I know I would sleep in sweet peace this night . . .*"

I slammed the book shut. I went to chuck it against the wall but thought twice. I got up and hunted down a cigarette. I came back into the bedroom, smoking, staring at that journal as though it was alive, the tome of demonic secrets.

So it was true. It was all true.

Robin loved Botch.

I sat down and opened it again, flipping pages madly, the eyes catching a line here, a line there.

"*. . . what is it I feel when I think of all those women from his past? Is this jealousy? Would I feel a greater sense of worth if he had written such things about . . . to be so loved that you move a man to long for you in song and in poetry . . . Maddy doesn't see me as a woman nor a mother, but as the authoritarian . . . William my second child instead of a husband and lover . . . I stood in the lot and breathed as though I could inhale the purple of the dusky sky and finally I asked God for one thing only. Strength. Lord, please give me strength . . . the exhaustion of being William's maid and nurse maid . . .*"

Ex-fucking-scuse me!

"*. . . I'll talk to him this weekend. Finally. It must be addressed. It must be said . . .*"

What must be said? My eyes couldn't seem to read the words fast enough.

"*. . . we're at the button . . .*"

Button? Does that say button? No, bottom.

"*. . . we're at the bottom. We're at the end now. It must be faced. The decision must be made . . .*"

Oh shit fucking Christ, here it comes, here it comes.

"*. . . we simply have to draw on the equity in the house . . .*"

Come again?

"*We're broke. I'm using the Visa at the track now. I've been in the hole every day for two weeks straight. I feel terrible about drawing on the card and dumping the money out for William, just to see the look on his face, just to finally get that validity. The validity only Botch has the depth, the strength, the soul to show. In his eyes, I flower into a woman . . .*"

I closed her journal.

I set it back precisely where I found it.

I laid the sock next to it too.

Then I grabbed the suitcase. The big blue Samsonite we won in the Christmas raffle. I opened it. I closed it. I knelt on the floor. I could see dust bunnies under the sink. I should vacuum.

The door bell rang.

"By this time next week you won't have your home, your cars, your furniture, or even a credit rating to save you. I've been more than patient, Mr. Botchelko. You know not to fuck with me. Kiss suburbia goodbye. Welcome to skid row."

Abenathy turned, climbed into his Taurus, and drove away.

I went into the kitchen. I made my tuna sandwich. With mayonnaise. Lots of mayonnaise. I squeezed the tuna juice into Nora's bowl and watched her lap greedily at it like a rummy with a fresh pint.

Then I picked up the phone, dialed 411, got the number of the Hollywood Palladium, and I asked to speak to the manager.

Chapter 69

Jimmy Ferraro cracked me beers. Harps and Bass. I drank them. He poured me a Knob Creek neat and I drank that too. He left me an entire carton of Marlboro Reds. I started smoking them.

This was a Hobson's Choice.

It was no choice at all.

"The line started at eight this morning," he said and clapped my back. "We're letting them in now."

I almost shaved last week. I even started clipping at the beard, then stopped. I don't know why. Even after everything, it felt too much like returning to the old me, like admitting defeat. I had Vanni booked for the haircut. I cancelled. I put the shaving foam back in the cabinet. I'm glad I did.

The posters went up the same day I called. They were small and cheap and printed single color black-on-red recycled cardboard stock. Which was perfect. Anything glossy would have smacked of the inauthentic.

There was a small ad in *LA Weekly* and the same ad in the *LA Times* Calendar section Wednesday, Thursday, and Friday. Jimmy kicked out a series of four jazz combos for Friday night. He knew I was worth it.

He knew a Botch reading was worth it.

I spent the week choosing poems. I went for the dramatic. For the funny. I avoided the sentimental. No short stories, no prose. I chose several about lost love. I was drawn to those. But I threw in a bunch about the track too. And anything about fighting and drinking and fucking. I put them in order of what I imagined to be crowd pleasers. I didn't know how many poems could be read in an hour and half so I went for overkill. Then I walked down to BJ's—not Kinko's—and made copies.

I knew what Botch's usual demands were but I didn't have to make them. Jimmy told me himself. A fridge on the stage full of beer. A table, a chair and a microphone. A big ashtray. Two lighters. A carton of Marlboros. And we'd split the gate. I thought twenty bucks a head was fair. Jimmy set the price at sixty.

If Robin or Botch saw the ads, I was going to say nothing. Give them nothing. Tell them nothing. My name was Alfred Botchelko and I was going to read poems by Alfred Botchelko. Arrest me. Yell at me. Fight me. Kick me out of my own house. Chase me with a knife. Anything.

Because there was a side of me now that felt I was growing into Botch. But not the Botch I knew. Not that fat, brooding, red-eyed slob. But the image of Botch. The one they expected. And the one I once expected to meet. I felt strong and tough and crusty on the surface, but with such depth and warmth and heartbreaking soul inside.

I planned to tell Maddy. Then somehow never got around to it. It didn't matter. No one in the house spotted the ads. Reporters started to call during the day. I have no idea how they got the number. I let the machine answer, then erased them. I turned the phone off at night when everyone was home. No one seemed to notice. I made dinner every night. Deep fried catfish with mustard and honey sauce. Steelhead trout with lemon and butter. Forty-clove roasted chicken stuffed with chopped onion. I stocked the house with wine from Trader Joes. I did the laundry. I vacuumed. I scrubbed the bathrooms. I even took the Accord to Jiffy Lube.

I was calm. I was disturbingly calm. I felt no fear. No jitters. No second thoughts. I had clarity.

I had become Botch.

And Botch had become me.

A shadow to Robin, a dog on a leash, a little china-woman shuffling in the wake of the dominant spouse. We spoke little at night. Maddy joined us for dinner. She didn't eat much and she spent the remainder of the evenings in her room. Botch and Robin talked about the track. Robin claimed to have won and won and won again. Robin was a liar.

Just like me.

And now the result of my plan was seated right out there. The reality was gathered just outside that door. There was shouting and whistling and foot stomping. And waiting there in the greenroom, pouring beer after beer down my throat and lighting one cigarette after another, I was starting to get a taste of what David Banner must feel.

Because Alfred Botchelko the poet was slipping away. And in his place, like a conjurer's sweet trick, like Mezmer's shimmering ghosts come to life on stage, I was reappearing—William Alfred Botchelko, unemployed former Kinko's manager.

I was scared shitless.

I had never felt such terror. Granted, I've never jumped from a plane. Or climbed El Capitan. Or led the police on a freeway chase. Or run with the bulls. Or wrestled a salt water crocodile or tried to out-swim a mako shark. I've never stared down the barrel of a gun. I've never been on a jet liner with the engines aflame. I've never rode a barrel over Niagara Falls or stormed a beach in Normandy or even tried to cross the 134 freeway on foot. None of that mattered.

This was the most terror I had ever felt in my entire life.

The beer wasn't helping. The Knob Creek wasn't helping. I was a fraud. A fool. A small, small man. What did I think I was doing? What had I ever achieved that made me think I could pull this off? I had almost never been alone my entire life. I had never traveled. Never faced adversity. No one I loved had died. I was healthy. I had a tonsillectomy when I was thirteen. That was it. I barely had to work in college. I barely had to work at work. I never once missed a mortgage payment, a car payment, a light bill even. Not because I was good and decent. But because I was terrified of what happens to someone who's not good and decent.

Jimmy leaned in. He said nothing. He didn't have to. With the door open came the boom of the crowd. They sounded like they had overrun the building, conquistadors looking to pillage and bugger. Jimmy had two big young men with him wearing black tee-shirts that read simply "Palladium."

"How many?" I asked.

"Seven or eight hundred," he said.

"Why?" I heard myself ask.

"Because you haven't done a public reading in almost fifteen years."

"But what do they expect?"

Jimmy laughed. Then stopped laughing. "A show," he said, as though it was obvious. Then he waited. I wasn't making this easy for him. So once more he asked, "Ready?"

The young men stepped into the room. They were the hangman's assistants. And Jimmy was Albert Pierrepoint, the chief executioner. They were going to cart me down Pall Mall where the crowds could spit and pelt me with fruit. Then they were going to take me to Tyburn Square and shout "Hat's off!" to the crowds stretching across Hyde Park and they were going to dangle me from the Triple Tree.

I was dead already.

Jimmy held the door open. I rose. I stepped out in the hall. I turned towards the noise. The guards flanked me. We started moving. I was being sucked towards the vortex of hell's wailing. I stumbled. But I wasn't drunk. My legs were going numb. My lips started tingling. How could I read a poem if my lips were numb?

There were more people waiting ahead. Staring at me. Every eye was on me. They were standing at the foot of a small flight of stairs. Leading to the stage. To the chamber. I stopped at the bottom step. There was stomping, clapping, whistling. The howling of the damned. And no one spoke to me. They only stared.

"Shall I introduce you?" asked Jimmy.

I needed more booze. More scotch. More cigarettes. More codeine or Pepcids or heroin or anything.

"Shall I introduce you?" he asked again.

I needed more courage. Some courage. Any courage. The tiniest littlest drop of courage in this ocean of sniveling fear.

"Mr. Botchelko?"

"No introduction," I said and I marched right up the stairs and strode out on that stage and was hit by a roar, a wall of noise that hammered into my chest and my head and eyes. I went straight for the table. But it seemed to be retreating with each step. Then I bumped it. I touched it with my hand. I sat down. I had to. And the roaring continued. It wouldn't stop. My stacks of pages were before me. I could see cigarettes. There was wine too. But I couldn't reach for them.

And then I became aware of the noise starting to fade and fade and fade away until . . .

Silence.

A throat cleared.

And still I sat.

"Let's hear a poem!" someone shouted. A couple "yeahs" agreed.

I couldn't. I couldn't speak. My arms lay dead in my lap. My chest was tight, my lungs concrete. I was going to pass out.

I looked up.

Faces. An entire wall of faces. Of eyes. Hundreds and hundreds of bodiless heads floating out there in the helium.

I had to get off this stage.

"Let's hear a poem!"

Fuck them. Fuck the consequences. I just needed enough strength to get up and walk off this stage and keep walking, down that hall, straight out the door, down Sunset and keep walking and walking right out into the desert where I could lie face down in the sand and dine on the sickening stew of my shame, of my pathetic life, for the rest of the long, long days . . .

"You want a poem? I'll give you a fucking poem," I heard.

I looked up.

And there, stepping over the bodies crowded on the steps, pushing his way past the shoulders and heads, came the real Alfred Botchelko.

The words came bursting out of me with relief and joy and exaltation.

"Ladies and Gentlemen," I said with sudden shocking authority. "Botch!"

And the crowd screamed as Botch bounded up on stage with teenage agility.

"Get off my stage you imposter," he said and I threw my arms around him and hugged the man like he was my long-lost brother and then he pointed at me as I made my way offstage and he said into the mic, "My brother, William Botchelko." And I heard what sounded like a gasp but they applauded louder still, those wonderful people who I no longer had to look at or entertain or do anything at all but watch and know I had delivered them Botch—me, I had pulled him out of the dark cave, Lazarus alive again and back on stage after fifteen long years, returned to the world with the rest of us and the crowds were cheering and cheering and I was cheering too.

Botch went to the fridge and pulled out a beer and that brought about another roar and someone shouted, "How bout a beer Botch!" and Botch said, "Get your own fucking beer." And they died over that. This was the man they came to hear.

He settled behind the table. He pulled out a smoke, stuck it in his mouth, and lit it just so, the cock of the head, the cup of the hand, the very tip of the flame to the very tip of the cigarette.

"I thought this was a non-smoking event!" someone shouted and got the laugh and even a wry grin from Botch.

"Hey, I'm the funny one here, dickhead," Botch said, which got an even bigger laugh.

Botch picked up a page from the stack I had copied. He frowned at it as he puffed on his smoke. Then he glanced up at the crowd as though he just realized they were there.

"Christ," he said. "Would you look at this bunch. They'd change fire laws if they knew where you people lived." Then he pointed at a guy in front. "Check out this one. Someone call Darwin, I think we've got good news." And they died over that and even the guy in front laughed and clapped.

"So this is my adoring public, huh?" He took a puff. "And you wonder why I stayed hidden for fifteen years."

It was abuse and they were loving it.

"Look at this one." He pointed into the crowd. "He's got tattoos going up his fuckin neck."

He was pointing at Max. He was pointing right at that idiot I punched in the face a millennium ago.

"It's called a fad, *Dude*," Botch said. "You don't see me with bell bottoms stapled to my ankles, do ya?"

He held up the poem again. "Does everyone here remember their first sexual experience?"

A few hands shot up.

"I didn't need a show of hands, this isn't the third grade. And I didn't mean with a man either buddy," and he pointed at someone else. "That's not called your first sexual experience. That's called—someone should keep a closer eye on Uncle Bob when his little nephew goes to take a pee-pee."

He held up the poem again. He paused. "By the way, this isn't about my first sexual experience." He took another slug of beer, squinted through another puff of the smoke. "This is about the time I was chased by a bear." Then he read the title: "Mother's Day Flowers."

> *"I dreamt we were raising a baby grizzly*
> *half the size of a Great Dane*
> *coarse mustard fur and razor back*
> *it ran and jumped on the couch*
> *skidding it across the floor*
> *"It's ruining everything,"*
> *I tell Darlene.*
> *"Get rid of it."*
> *They're more afraid of you than*

you are of
them
they say.
I say,
tell that to Grizzly Man.
Rico trees one for me
beige snout peering down through
the branches
"Let's bug him," I say
and pump the BB gun
"Hey bear, hey!"
He looks and I shoot him
in the nose
"Hey bear, hey!"
He looks and I shoot again.
And he roars
and drops down through the
cracking branches and I run
but Rico knows I want that bear
I must
why all the fuss otherwise?
so he chases it to me
and I lay underneath the Nova
till it's gone.
In the rental off
Lincoln we push the new
Beautyrest
up against the window
to feel the night breeze
But I awake
to feel the grizzly stepping
on the corners of the bed
the mattress depressing
under his great weight

and I fake sleep
play dead
that fools bears you know
until his fur and his pounds
drop across my back
crushing me
and the air from my lungs
and it growls in my ear
almost lovingly.
"Why didn't you ever save me!"
I shout at my mother
and shove away from the table
leaving her to sip her burgundy
and swat mosquitoes
thinking
what the hell was that about?"

They applauded. Botch got to his feet. "Yes, that's right. I was beaten by my stepfather. But hey," he shrugged. "He made me a writer."

Botch pulled out another beer.

"How about a cold one!" someone shouted.

So Botch started pulling beers out of the fridge and tossing them into the crowd like they knew he eventually would. This was all part of the act. And people jumped to their feet and scrambled for them, fought over them like Dodgers fans scrambling for a tick ball.

"Did you come here for poetry or beer?" Botch asked.

"Both!" someone shouted.

He chuckled to himself and shook his head. "My kind of people," he said and they laughed and applauded.

Botch read "Irascible Roses." He read "DeWitt's End." He read "Glen Again and Again" and "Swimming for 40 Minutes" and "I Look Like Anthony Hopkins."

He lit another smoke and paused as though he just had a thought.

"So I'm screwin' this girl the other night. And she's screaming, 'Fuck me! Fuck me!' Which, to be perfectly frank, I thought I was doing. So I asked her, 'What's with all the shouting?' And she says, 'I find it makes the experience more enjoyable.' And I thought to myself, For who? The neighbors?"

They died. And it was back to the poems. "Death Like a Heartbeat" and "27/44," "Slip of the Tongue" and "Whose Sorry Ass?" He read "Walter by Walter" and "Knees" and "Naked Knife Fighting" and "Christen a Boat With Beer."

He poured a glass of wine. Had another smoke. "While I'm thinking of it, would you people stop writing me? Have you noticed I don't write back? And please don't show up at my door either. I had this one guy, fucking idiot. Don't know what he thought we'd have in common. Recent college graduate. So I ask him, 'What's your degree in?' And he says, 'Animal Sexuality.' So I ask him, 'What in fuck are you going to do with a degree like that? Get a job as a fluffer at the zoo?'" He let the laughter die down, then added, ". . . as I cleaned the monkey cum off his neck."

Botch read for an hour and a half exactly. And that was it. He got up, said goodnight, and walked off the stage. The audience screamed and applauded, but he simply stood next to me backstage and lit a smoke. He winked at me. "Make 'em wait."

Finally, when the audience was just starting to fear he might never return, he did. To cheers and applause that sounded like relief. This time he didn't sit. He stood before them at the edge of the stage. He reached into his back pocket and pulled out a piece of paper. He unfolded it. He didn't speak. He waited until they fell silent.

Then he whispered, "Shh, I say, Shh."

"When are you coming back?"
Rachel asks.
They own me now and
don't want me here.
they suspect I'm not working.

"I'm living the life of a
monk," I say. "I don't know
a soul." She knows I'm lying.
"Do what you gotta do,"
Mark says
though he doesn't mean it.
"When you leave, half my
social life goes."
The other half is his wife.
"Enjoy and enjoy and more
enjoy," Milos writes.
Then stops writing.
No one wants to hear
how happy you are.
And my eyes are clear
as mirrors
when I wipe the steam
with a towel Kath used
and I sleep even with her
head on my chest or her
knees tucked behind me
or her leg draped possessively
across my pubic bone.
She sleep-talks without parting
her lips and I press my thumb
to them.
"Shh," I say, "shh."
She sleep-smokes too
pressing knuckles fine
to lips and blowing and
even, unbelievably,
tapping the ash.
"Tell me something funny,"
she says when she calls from

work transformed now in
business clothes
legs longer in heels
hair blacker
lips redder
and someone else
again in a camouflage
G-string pinched
between brown round
buttocks diamond tip
of pubic hair
just peeking from the top.
"You'll fool the Vietcong in those,"
I tell her.
And someone else again
in the red mini dress
lying on the lawn
as the green ferries
chug past behind her.
And then the girl I know
in her long red skirt
with the wide metal belt
that clatters to the ground
when she's dancing in
shoes she's owned since 12.
"You're a tactile little monkey,"
I tell her as we kiss and
puff menthols
Kath whispering profundities
in a voice small as pebbles.
She cries silently in my lap on
the white balcony chairs
and I want to cry too
but instead kiss salty cheeks

and say "Shh,"
I say, "shh."
I don't like that I'm leaving
either and I suddenly can't remember
a time when Kath wasn't mine.
I can't sleep with the ache
of my last night with her
and roll over to find her
silhouette staring down
above me.
She's still sleeping.
I push her back gently
on the pillows soft
and kiss her forehead
but not a sound
not this time
no sleep mumbling like
the kidnapped gagged
no sleep smoking
no profundities whispered
just Kath's
bewildered eyes staring
searchingly from the night.
One freighter's horn.
One Currawong's whoop.
And the gray dawn starts
its slow wash of the
filmy windows
I close her eyes with
my finger tips
brush thumb across
black eye lashes.
There's still time
much, much more time

to lie here together
till morning.
"Shh,"
I say.
"Shh."

Chapter 70

"You buy your wife a house, you put your kid in a good school, you pick her up at the end of every day and write poetry about them both. And then the woman won't speak to you because you didn't dedicate a book to her. Your parents complain they never see you when you're sitting directly across from them. And you didn't dedicate a book to them. Your friends are upset when you don't drop everything when they come to town. Yet when you're in their town, they drop nothing. You fly your girlfriend to London, to Madrid, to Canberra. But she's angry when you have to meet your publisher instead of attend her nephew's birthday party.

"And finally, William, finally you just don't do any more. And then no one's disappointed. Not your family. Not loved ones. Not wives or friends or girlfriends or publishers or agents. Because your final disappointment is no disappointment at all. You've simply lived down to their expectations. And thus . . . you're free."

One lamp was on. We had Crown Royal on the coffee table. Nora was asleep in Botch's lap. Robin had long since gone to bed. So had Maddy. They were both in the audience that night. I had no idea till I saw them in the green room later. I hugged and kissed them but only Maddy was excited. I snuck her a Miller Lite in a coffee mug. Robin never uttered a word all night. Even during the drive home, not a word.

I spotted Red at the foot of the stage and I pulled him in behind me. He offered up his special pen and special book for Botch to sign and he did so with a smile and handshake.

"To Red," he wrote. "First Wednesday of every month. Musso and Frank. Be there. Botch."

"You were amazing up there," I told him.

"Shocked?" he asked.

"Sorta."

"Don't give 'em the man, give 'em the legend," he said. "They still manage to take a piece of your soul regardless."

"Yet you showed up."

"Hey, I've still got a rep to protect. And you ain't me."

Botch picked up the shoe box at his feet. He shook it and grinned. There was $28,000 cash in there.

"I couldn't do it," I confessed. I felt I must. "I couldn't do what you did. I thought I could. I fooled myself. I guess by hanging around you, getting to know you, I convinced myself that you were—"

"—ordinary," he said.

"I wouldn't go that far."

"Not extraordinary then," he corrected. But he wasn't picking a fight. He was bemused. "People, they read something you've written. And you make them feel something, you move them. You've spoken to them, so they want more. They want your friendship. And often your love. They want that feeling all the time. They've confused what they've read with who you are. But they don't know you. They only think they do. They don't know that writing is lies. Words manipulate. And soon there's a woman in your bed, still hearing your poems echoing in her head but not your voice, not the words you speak. And then one day she suddenly hears your words all too clearly. Because there's no poetry to be found in, 'Hey, while you're up, can you get me a beer?' Turns out you're just a man. Just an ordinary human being. Just like them. You've let me down, they say. You've changed. And out the door they go."

He could have been describing Robin.

He could have been describing me.

And that's when Nora bolted off Botch's lap.

"Jesus Christ!" he said. "That fucking cat hooked my nut sack!"

I got up to look out the window. Botch fished around in his pants.

"My fuckin' prick's bleeding. What's wrong with that animal?"

"Someone's here," I said.

Botch jumped to his feet.

There was a car in the driveway.

"Recognize it?" he asked.

"Nope."

It was a Toyota FX. The headlights snapped off. It sat there a moment. Then the driver's door swung open. And out stepped Beatriz. Then the passenger door opened. And there stood Randy.

"You know these people?" asked Botch.

"I used to work with them," I said.

I opened the door before they rang. I put my finger to my lips and waved them inside.

"Sorry is so late," Beatriz said.

"Beatriz, Randy—Alfred Botchelko."

Botch shook their hands. Randy had no reaction. But Beatriz said, "You are heem. My ex-boyfren', he reads you alla time and makes up music to your poems and he spits."

"Ex-boyfriend?" I repeated.

"Donovan has beeg plans. I don't have beeg plans. He's not so happy anymore after you leff. And he doesn't like heem." And she indicated Randy with a nod of her head. "He says he goes. So I tell him yes, go. With blessings."

"*Vaya con Dios*," Botch said.

"*O sin Dios*," Beatriz amended and shrugged.

I asked them to sit down. They did. Randy still hadn't spoken. He kept looking at his feet as though his shoes were fascinating.

"Crown Royal?" I asked. Randy took one with a meek nod. Beatriz tried a little, gasped, and shook her head. "Thees ees for sailors," she said. Then she pointed at Botch and said, "Thees will keel you. If you muss drink, then drink good wine. And if you muss smoke, smoke the ceegars. They stink but they don keel you."

"Maybe I need a good woman to take care of me," Botch said and smiled at her.

"Oh, *es verdad*?" said Beatriz. "I trade a phony Botchelko for the real Botchelko? Life is too short. Si, Randy?"

Randy nodded.

"Life is too short, no Randy?"

"No it's—yes it's . . . okay, you phrased that funny."

"Randy tells me something tonight," she said. "Something I don' like to hear. And I tell him, for his soul, he muss come here. So don' sit there like a *pequenito* boy stealing Chiclets. You tell William what you come to tell heem."

Randy took a quick slug of his drink, took a deep breath, then blurted out, "I got you fired."

"I put that together already," I said.

"See Beatriz? See? I fucking told you," said Randy.

"Thees makes no difference," she said. "Tell what you did? Then tell how you will make thees up to heem."

Randy looked at his feet again. "I forwarded the website with your picture on it to Provo. Then I found the book on E-bay and sent that too. And the photocopier repair bills. I wasn't trying to get you fired Will. You gotta believe that. I was just trying to get promoted. I read that stupid book. *The Art of War*. That's not an excuse. I just fucked up."

Nora made her way back in the room. Beatriz stroked her tail. Then Nora jumped up in Botch's lap and settled in again.

"Is there no more, Randy?" asked Beatriz.

"Yes," he said. "Yes. I can get you your job back. I'll take complete responsibility, explain it away as a misunderstanding. I already spoke to Sue Banishee. Everything's going to be fine."

"And?" asked Beatriz.

"And . . ." said Randy, barely concealing the irritation. "And I know you've lost wages. I don't have much of a savings. But I can write you a check for three thousand."

I didn't answer. I had no reaction.

"How's your soul feel now?" I asked him.

He shrugged.

And that's precisely when Nora bolted off Botch's lap again.

"Jesus fucking Christ!" said Botch and he clutched his groin again. "I'm going to lose a testicle from that fucking monster!"

I jumped up to look out the window again. Another car was in the driveway.

"Oh shit," I said.

Botch jumped up too.

"Oh shit," he said.

It was the black Lexus.

The big black Lexus.

And three men climbed out.

"Do you have a weapon?" Botch asked.

"I have a complete set of Global knives," I said.

"We're not filleting a mackerel, for fuck sakes. I mean a shotgun or something."

"Do I look like a bird hunter to you?"

I couldn't make out their faces in the dark. But one was big. And one was wide. And one was small.

"I can't have them in this house. Not with Robin and Maddy here. I'm calling the cops," I said but Botch stopped me with the palm of his hand.

"Let's see what they want first."

"We know what they want."

"And now we've got what they want. So let's talk."

Randy and Beatriz stepped up next to us. "What ees going on?" asked Beatriz.

"You guys stay in here," I said. "Have your cell ready. If this should get ugly, call 911."

The men were coming up the walk. Botch and I moved for the door.

"Leave the door open," Botch said. And I said, "Always an escape route."

We stepped outside, thumped down the steps in unison, and

stopped there.

"Don't come any further," Botch said. He said it with authority. They stopped.

It was them all right. The two who chased us. But leading them, of all people, was Abenathy.

"What do you want?" I said. I wasn't feeling afraid. This time they were on my turf.

"Mr. Botchelko," said Abenathy in that irritatingly calm way of his. Then he pointedly turned to look at Botch. "*This* Mr. Botchelko," he amended. "We heard about your reading tonight. Me and these gentlemen. We've since become acquainted, you being our common problem. We understand you were quite a big hit. How many heads?"

"Nine hundred and thirty-three," I said.

"At $60 a pop, that comes to . . ."

"A little over fifty thousand," I said.

". . . fifty-six thousand and forty to be exact."

"Impressive," I said.

"Former CPA," he said. "Which means you have in your possession twenty-eight thousand and twenty dollars."

"And we'll be taking all of it," said the wide one. And with that he stepped forward. And suddenly there was Randy and Beatriz flanking us.

"Fuck with them, you fuck with all of us," Randy said. He was in a kickboxing stance. And Beatrice was holding one of my Global knives. Ironically, the filleting knife.

"Okay you guys, let's calm down," I said.

But Randy was circling the wide one. "Come on fat boy," he said. "Take a swing. Let's see what you got."

The big one started howling laughing. "Oh shit, Benny. You got a fish on the hook!"

"Come on fat boy! Let's go!" shouted Randy.

"Watch the insults!" Benny shouted back. They circled each other on the lawn, Benny with his fists up now.

Then I saw Greg pop his head up over the bushes, fumbling with his robe. "What's going on?" he said.

"Ah Greg, just go home!" I said. "It's nothing."

"I'll call the police," he said.

"We don't need the police," I said but Greg was gone.

"Come on, you fat fuck!" Randy shouted and bobbed and weaved. "I'll kick you right in that big melon!" Randy meant it, aggressive little bugger. Thank goodness I never took a poke at him.

The big one was bent over double, laughing. "Oh shit! I can't take it!"

"Guys! Guys! I've got the money right here!" said Botch.

And that stopped everyone.

Botch went back inside and came out with the shoe box. He sat down on the steps. "But only twenty-two thousand. This man's keeping six to get back on his feet." He pointed at me.

"I said we're taking it all," Benny said.

"Cops are on their way," said Botch. "You want the twenty-two or not?"

No one spoke.

"And ten grand every month till the debts are cleared," he added. "If that suits your needs."

Abenathy glanced to the others. Then he plunked down on the steps next to Botch. "Start counting," he said.

"We're taking the entire twenty-two then," Benny said to Abenathy.

"We have discussed this," Abenathy replied. "You will take half. Otherwise, I will make your life a living hell. Ask this man." And he indicated me.

"It's true," I said. "I don't know how he does it, but he'll bone your ass, destroy your life, and ruin your marriage. Trust me. I know."

The two goombahs exchanged a look.

"Cops are coming," reminded Botch.

"Start countin'," said Benny. "And watch it with the insults you little shit . . . and tell the chick to put away the knife."

Beatriz lowered the knife. Randy lowered his fists.

"Randy?" Beatriz said. "Something you want to say to thees man?"

"Jesus Beatriz you can drive me fuckin . . ." He took a breath, turned to Benny. "Sorry I called you fat," he said.

"Apology accepted," said Benny.

"No offense."

"I'll get over it."

"What's going on out here?"

Robin and Maddy were standing in the doorway, frowning and blinking away sleep.

And far in the distance, we could hear the police sirens.

"Maybe we better do this inside," suggested Botch.

We were all squeezed behind the sofa, the big one between the shelves, Botch and Abenathy under the dining table. The doorbell rang.

Flashlight beams slipped back and forth across the floor.

Botch was counting the money. Abenathy was recounting it. The phone rang. The machine picked it up.

"Mr. Botch—Botchi . . . Botchiko. Christ that's a mouthful. This is corporal Gutierrez of the Glendale Police Department. We received a disturbing the peace complaint. We are outside your front door at present. Would you please come to the front door and make yourself known? We would appreciate your cooperation in this matter."

No one moved.

Maddy suppressed a giggle. "This is fun," she said.

"I get the feeling you two have done this before," whispered Robin. She was squeezed against one side of me, Beatriz on the other. Beatriz was still holding the knife.

"Why'd you choose the filleting knife?" I asked her.

"Easy to go through the ribs," Beatriz said.

Botch glanced up and smiled at that. "I like your style," he said and winked.

"Thank you," she said.

Then she smiled and winked back.

And Robin shook her head

"I could use a drink," she said.

Chapter 71

The Pacific Surfliner only runs along the ocean until a little outside Santa Barbara. From there you don't get a glimpse of the Pacific again. But the hills are fine passing by and people still wave for some odd reason and I get a schadenfreudistic kick out of winding slowly past Folsom Prison.

Robin and I had a first-class compartment. We caught the train at Union Station instead of the little one in Glendale. It made it a bit more special, more romantic, harkening back to another time. One of no cell phones. No iPods.

And no Googling.

Botch had spent the rest of night squeezed into a dark corner with Beatriz. At one point I heard him say, "That's very astute. I like the metaphor, being caught between gears. You described my life."

Botch moved back into his house the next day. I took him home.

"You really should get started on another book," I told him.

He pulled open his hall closet. Stacks of pages tumbled out.

"Pick the ones you like," he said. "You send 'em off. I trust ya."

"You've been writing all this time?" I asked.

"I never stop writing, darling," he said.

Most of his furniture was missing. The big leather sofa. The Mission chair. His TV. His master suite was cleaned out entirely. The debt collectors obviously.

"Not the first time," he shrugged. "I'll get more."

He dug out an old Spanish cafetiere in his bottom kitchen cabinet. His Mr. Coffee was gone too. He made us two cups of mind-bendingly strong coffee. We stepped out back, unfolded two old lawn chairs. Angela next door popped her head over the fence once. Then she was gone.

"You ran a business," said Botch. "So treat me like a business."

I recommended we do a reading a week. The West Coast first—San Francisco, Portland, Seattle and Vancouver. Then probably two in New York, up to Boston, then one in Toronto and home to squeeze in one more in LA. Once the new book was published, I suggested we take a shot at Europe.

"I'm exhausted already," he said. "But hey, gotta do what you gotta do."

We sat in the sun and watched the seagulls circling overheard.

"You have many friends?" he asked.

I'd never thought about it. It seemed like a rather shocking realization suddenly. "No. I don't have any friends," I said.

"Me neither," said Botch.

Then he held up his coffee.

I held up mine.

And we drank.

That night over dinner—pizza from GoodFast because I just couldn't be bothered to cook—Maddy announced she was going to be either a writer or an actress.

"Why can't you do both?" I asked. "Then you can write your own roles."

"Good idea," she said and smiled. She was going to try out for the school play. *Guys and Dolls*. She wanted the part of Sergeant Sarah Brown.

"Isn't that one of the leads?" asked Robin.

"I guess."

"But isn't there singing?"

"I can sing. Don't you think I can sing?"

"I never said that. I just never hear you sing."

"She sings to her Walkman," I said.

"My what?" Maddy asked.

"Your iPod thingy," I said.

"See?" she said to Robin. "Dad knows I can sing."

Robin got up and grabbed her martini shaker.

I took Randy's $3,000 check. He owed me. But I didn't take the job. I had a job.

I was Botch's manager.

Robin put in an application at Wells Fargo. They called her the next day. She was going to start work after we got back.

"A bank teller," she said. "Me and a bunch of Armo teenagers."

"You'll rise quickly," I said.

"To loans officer," she said. "Someone pinch me."

Botch stopped by with Beatriz on their way to San Francisco. They were going to drive in her little Toyota to all the readings. Apparently Beatriz didn't like to fly. Though I think it had more to do with her immigration status.

"We may stop by the set of *Botch* too," Botch said. Which made him smirk. "Beatriz is into that kind of stuff."

"Meet Donald Sutherland," she said. "Hees so sexy. And he don' spit ever."

"Where does she get this spitting thing?" Botch asked me.

"Clearly she's never read your work," I said.

"And isn't that wonderful?" he replied.

I handed Botch a gift. A prepaid Motorola from Target. He looked it over.

"They work like normal phones, don't they?"

"Exactly the same. Now we can keep in touch."

He shrugged and slipped it in his pocket.

We talked on the front steps. Robin wouldn't invite them inside. In fact, she all but barred the door.

When they left, walking back across the street to her car, Botch slipped his arm around Beatriz's waist and kissed her on the top of her head. She turned and kissed his cheek.

Robin spun around and marched back inside.

"She's fat," was all she said.

I stayed on the steps to wave them off. Botch rolled down the window of the car.

"See you in San Francisco," he shouted. Then he lit a cigar, smiled, and gave me what looked like a backwards peace sign. Which I think means "fuck off" in England. Beatriz beeped the horn. And off they went.

Robin called Maddy from the train. It was her first time home alone. I felt okay about it. I trusted her. She was a new girl and I said so to Robin.

"What was that noise?" Robin asked Maddy.

"The cat," Maddy said.

"Why are you shushing Nora?"

"Because she's meowing."

"Why is she meowing?"

"Maybe she's hungry."

"Aren't you feeding her?"

"I feed her."

"Do you have friends over?"

"I don't have friends over."

"I think you have friends over."

"There's no friends here, Ma."

"You know what we said, Madison."

"I'm all alone, Mother."

"You're having a party, aren't you?"

"Gotta go. Lots of love."

And she hung up.

"That little . . .!" Robin slammed the phone shut. "Oh yeah, she's a new girl all right."

I'd ordered a bottle of champagne. It was waiting for us in the compartment when we entered. Robin drank most of it by the time we left the Santa Barbara station. Then she pulled the blinds down on the window. Which I found odd. Then she came over and grabbed my head with both hands and kissed me. It was a real kiss and a bit aggressive.

"Let me put my diaphragm in," she said and she ducked into the bathroom.

I went to pour the last of the champagne. There was none left. I heard Robin start cursing in the bathroom. The train was moving. She was having trouble. And I started to laugh. I couldn't help it. Then just as I pulled my pants down to my ankles, Robin suddenly jerked the door open. She was still dressed.

"Let's go to the bar car," she said. And she walked out, leaving me standing there in my boxers. I tugged my pants back up. I reached for the door.

But just before walking out, just before following in her doomed wake, I paused in the doorway and smiled to myself and said aloud,

"I win."

«««»»»

CPSIA information can be obtained at www.ICGtesting.com
Printed in the USA
LVOW090308121111

254671LV00002B/41/P

9 781609 114565